'My lord?'

Antonia glanced at [...]

'Miss Hadley, while I am gratified that your father holds me in such esteem, I hope you will forgive me if I tell you that it is *your* feelings I am concerned with, rather than his.'

'Mine?'

'Yes. Because I have the distinct impression that you do not like me…'

Originally hailing from Pembrokeshire, **Gail Whitiker** now lives on beautiful Vancouver Island on the west coast of Canada. When she isn't indulging her love of writing, you'll find her enjoying brisk walks along the Island's many fine beaches, or trying to catch up on her second love, reading. She wrote her first novel when she was in her teens, and still blesses her English teacher for not telling her how bad it really was.

Recent titles by the same author:

AN OFFER TO LOVE

AN INNOCENT DECEIT

Gail Whitiker

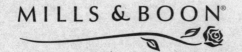

MILLS & BOON®

First published in Great Britain 2000
Harlequin Mills & Boon Limited,
Eton House, 18-24 Paradise Road, Richmond, Surrey TW9 1SR

© Gail Whitiker 2000

ISBN 0 263 82322 9

Set in Times Roman 10½ on 12 pt.
04-1000-78031

Printed and bound in Spain
by Litografia Rosés S.A., Barcelona

Chapter One

'No, my dear, I am very sorry, but I really cannot agree to the idea of your working for the Earl of Carlyle,' Mr Hadley told his daughter regretfully, 'and certainly not in the capacity you have just set forward.'

'But, Papa—'

'Why, only think what your aunt would say if she were to hear of it. Indeed, I wonder what your dear mother would have said, had she lived to see what you were about.'

Miss Antonia Hadley, recipient of this most disappointing news, shook her head in a gesture of mild resignation. While she had not expected this to be easy, neither had she expected her father to be so rigidly opposed to what she considered to be a perfectly splendid idea.

'I venture to say that aunt Ophelia will be shocked and horrified, as no doubt you already suspect, and that she will shake her head and wonder if there is any hope for me at all. But as regards Mama,' Antonia said, her voice softening, 'I believe that she would have *applauded* my ingenuity and commended me to proceed.

As I truly wish you could see your way clear to doing, Papa. After all, we did agree that I had to do something.'

Seated behind his desk Mr Hadley glanced up at his daughter in surprise. 'I beg your pardon?'

'Well, yes. Do you not remember?'

'What I remember is that *you* informed me that it was your intention to seek employment, whereupon *I* informed you that it was neither necessary nor fitting that you do so. Is that not more the way the conversation went?'

Antonia tried not to smile, but failed. Odious man. He might have been able to persuade others of his absent-mindedness, but he had never been able to fool her. He was now, as he had always been, in possession of an annoyingly retentive memory.

'You may be right, now that I come to think of it, Papa,' Antonia allowed grudgingly, 'but that does not alter the fact that I should very much *like* to do something with my time. After all, I am nearly twenty years of age, yet all I seem to do is write letters and pay tedious house calls.'

'Tedious?' Mr Hadley frowned. 'I thought young ladies liked paying house calls.'

'Not every day.'

'Well, then, what about the management of Buntings Hill? Surely that is more than enough to occupy your time, since you do it almost single-handedly.'

'Tosh! Mrs Grenfall is in charge of the household now. All I do is review the accounts and approve the meals, and goodness knows, even that requires little enough of my time. But if I were working for the Earl, I should be required to spend…at least two hours a day at Ashdean. Which is why I think this is the best opportunity to have come along so far.'

'The best opportunity?' Mr Hadley chuckled as he removed his spectacles and wiped them with a remnant of cloth which deposited far more dust than it removed. 'My dear girl, this does not even approach the designation of a *good* opportunity, let alone one deserving of a higher commendation. For a young woman in your position, I would have thought that an offer of employment from the Dowager Countess of Haversham would have been far more worthy of your consideration.'

'Lady Haversham?'

'Yes. She is looking for a companion.'

'What, again? What happened to Miss Marchmaine?'

'I understand the young lady left to take care of her elderly mother.'

'But…she already has two younger sisters at home doing just that.'

Mr Hadley leaned back in his chair, and steepled his fingers in front of his face. 'Perhaps the mother's health took a turn for the worst and the sisters felt compelled to call Miss Marchmaine home. I really do not know, Antonia, that was all Mrs Heath was able to tell me when I chanced to come upon her in the village yesterday. However, I do think it a more appropriate position for a lady than to be a groom in the household of the Earl of Carlyle.'

Antonia's mouth twitched. 'I am not applying to be a groom, Papa. The Earl is looking for someone to teach his daughter how to ride.'

'Semantics. It entails working with horses, does it not?'

'Yes, which is precisely why I wish to apply. You have told me that I am an exceptional rider—'

'Much as I am beginning to wish that I had not—'

'And you know that I enjoy working with children,'

Antonia continued, ignoring his interruption. 'This provides me with an opportunity to do both.'

'Children?' Mr Hadley regarded her with a suddenly hopeful expression. 'My dear, if it is the company of children you seek, perhaps it is Lady Cruikshank's offer you should be considering.'

'Lady Cruikshank? But—' Antonia paled '—surely you *cannot* mean as governess to those five wretched children of hers?'

'Well, yes, actually, I do. Why, what have they done?'

'Only retire three governesses in the past nine months. And last week, even the housekeeper threatened to quit!'

'Good Lord, Mrs Mortonby? Whatever for?'

'It seems that she found a reptile in her bed.'

'A reptile?'

'A snake.'

'Oh, dear. Common garden variety, I hope.'

Antonia blinked. 'Does it matter?'

'Well, yes, my dear, I rather think it does. After all, one would be considerably more alarmed at finding a viper in their bed than a harmless—'

'The fact that she found *any* manner of snake in her bed—and that it was put there by those dreadful children—is reason enough for me to wish to stay well away from them, Papa,' Antonia interrupted, aware that her father was just as like to embark on a biological discussion as he was to give her a straightforward answer. 'Goodness knows, a lady of weaker constitution might have…expired from the discovery of such a creature in her bed.'

'Ah. Well, in that case, I doubt that Mrs Mortonby was in any real danger,' said Mr Hadley as he set the smudged spectacles back on his nose. 'Of the two, I would wager that the snake was the more terrified.

However, given that no one was hurt, I do not see that there is any reason for endowing what was obviously a childish prank with any malicious intent. Certainly, I was not above doing such things when I was their age.'

'Which is the *only* reason I can think of for you to have suggested that I look after them in the first place,' Antonia said wryly. 'I thought I had been a better daughter to you than to warrant being condemned to such a cruel fate as that.'

'You have been the best of daughters, my dear, and I would not knowingly condemn you to any fate but one of your own choosing,' her father replied fondly. 'But in all sincerity, I cannot be happy about this notion of yours to seek a position with the Earl of Carlyle.'

Antonia sighed as she crossed to the window seat and picked up her copy of *La Belle Assemblée*. This was not turning out at all as she had hoped. In her opinion, Lady Cruikshank and Lady Haversham were two of a kind, which was likely the real reason for Miss Marchmaine's departure. Both women possessed an uncanny knack for retiring any and all manner of domestic help with alarming haste and disturbing regularity.

'Well, my dear?' Mr Hadley said. 'You have not yet answered my question. Is it your intention to approach the Earl with regard to this position?'

'I am not sure that I know *what* to do any more, Papa,' Antonia replied in all honesty. 'While teaching the Earl's daughter how to ride would be eminently preferable to serving as a companion to Lady Haversham, or as a governess to Lady Cruikshank, it is obvious that it would cause you more grief than the other two put together, and I certainly have no wish to do that.'

Mr Hadley sighed. 'What grieves me the most, Antonia, is that you feel the need to seek *any* manner of employment. You are a beautiful and accomplished young woman. One whom any man would be proud to call his wife. To my mind, you should be thinking about *marrying* the Earl, not seeking employment in his household!'

'Marry the Earl!' Antonia gasped. 'Gracious, Papa, what an alarming thought.'

'You find the thought of becoming a Countess alarming?'

'I find the thought of becoming *Carlyle*'s Countess alarming,' Antonia replied without hesitation. 'He is a cold and arrogant man who cares little for the feelings of others, and who takes no trouble to conceal it. I cannot think of any man to whom I would less wish to be married.'

'Goodness, a harsh condemnation indeed,' Mr Hadley observed. 'But one, I wonder, which is based upon your *own* assessment of the gentleman's character, or upon the opinions of others? For unless I am mistaken, you have not had occasion even to see Lord Carlyle these past eight years, let alone speak with him.'

Antonia felt her cheeks grow warm. 'It is not always necessary to speak to a gentleman to know the manner of his character. I have heard from more than one source that Lord Carlyle is an exceedingly arrogant man who is very much aware of his position in society, and who prefers not to associate with people of a lesser social consequence as a result. Which means that he is no more likely to notice me than he is…a fly upon his wall.'

The remark brought a smile to her father's face. 'I think that the stories which have reached your ear have been somewhat exaggerated, my dear. I have not heard tales of such colossal arrogance myself. But tell me, if

Lord Carlyle were to notice you, and if he were to seek you out, would you entertain his suit?'

'No.'

'No. You would refuse a peer of the realm simply because of something one of your friends had said?'

'I would refuse him because I do not *like* him, Papa,' Antonia said, wishing she could make her father understand. 'We have absolutely nothing in common. Everyone knows that Lord Carlyle despises the country. He has made no secret of the fact that he prefers to live in London, where he keeps a very fine house and a veritable army of servants to dance attendance upon him. Whereas I, on the other hand, can think of nowhere I would rather live than here at Buntings Hill with you.'

'Bless you for saying so, my child, but the fact that Lord Carlyle prefers to live in London cannot be held against him,' Mr Hadley said reasonably. 'He *is* the Earl, after all, and entitled to the privileges of his rank. I do not see that as being a valid reason to reject him outright.'

'No, but that is not the only reason, Papa.' Antonia turned her eyes towards the lush green hills that were visible through the window, and sighed. 'When you consider that he has no feelings for his child—'

'I beg your pardon? Lord Carlyle not care for Clara? Now that I must take exception to.' Mr Hadley's brows drew downward in a frown. 'Where in the world did you come by such a ridiculous notion as that?'

'It is not ridiculous, nor am I the only one who believes it,' Antonia said in her own defence. 'Lord Carlyle took Clara to Ashdean immediately following his wife's death, and left her there for two years. And in all that time, how many visits has he paid her?'

'Few enough, I admit, but the paucity of his visits

cannot be interpreted as a lack of affection on his part,'
Mr Hadley objected. 'A parent's love for his child
should never be measured by the frequency—or infrequency—of his visits. I am sure that the Earl would have
wished to spend more time with Clara, but for his position in life—'

'His position in life does not justify negligence towards his child,' Antonia said tersely. She rose from the
window seat and began to pace back and forth in front
of her father's desk. 'Your charity does you credit, Papa,
but in this instance, I find I cannot agree with it. If Lord
Carlyle truly cared about his daughter, he would have
found the time to visit her. Instead, he continues to leave
her in the country, all but abandoned to the care of servants, and only makes his presence known when it
pleases him to do so. Hardly commendable behaviour
for a father to my way of thinking!'

Mr Hadley studied his daughter's angry face, whilst
an expression of amusement appeared on his own. 'Antonia, if you dislike the man so intensely, why are you
even thinking about working for him?'

'Because I like his daughter *very* much and I know
that she needs my help.' Antonia's voice gentled as it
always did when she spoke of the Earl of Carlyle's
daughter. 'Lady Clara is a sweet and intelligent child
who is quick to respond and remarkably eager to learn.
But she is lonely, Papa. She lives in that great house all
on her own, with only the servants and her spaniel for
company, and her father seems quite content to leave it
that way. Well, I am not. A six-year-old child needs love
and affection, and I believe that the opportunity of teaching Clara how to ride would be a wonderful experience
for both of us. And that, I can assure you, is the *only*
reason I would consider working for her father.'

'Well, I still think you judge him too harshly, my dear,' Mr Hadley said, returning his attention to the papers on his desk. 'Lord Carlyle has not led a happy life. Have you forgotten that in the space of a few short years, he lost both a father whom he loved *and* a beautiful young wife?'

Antonia shook her head as she gave up pacing to lean against the edge of his desk. 'I have not forgotten. But neither do I believe that his prolonged indifference to Clara can be justified by the tragic events of the past. Lady Carlyle has been gone well over two years. Surely that is long enough for the Earl to have recovered from his grief.'

'Perhaps. But you must remember that not everyone is like you, Antonia,' her father said gently. 'Not everyone behaves in exactly the same way, especially when it comes to matters of the heart. And at such times, you would do well to be more tolerant of those whose behaviours differ from your own. At least until you find yourself in a similar position.'

A quick glance at her father's face assured Antonia that nothing would be gained by prolonging the argument now and, grudgingly accepting defeat, she slowly began to smile. 'Dear Papa. I must be such a strain on your patience. No doubt you are wondering why you were not blessed with an obedient daughter who would have married and had children, and not given you any cause for concern. I would have been a good deal less troublesome, would I not?'

'You would,' her father agreed, 'but then you would not have been my Toni, and I cannot imagine you being any other way than you are. However, I do understand what you are saying. You wish to help the child—without encouraging the father.'

'Precisely.'

'Because you have absolutely no interest in the Earl of Carlyle as a husband.'

'None whatsoever.'

'Fine. Then I suppose there is nothing for it but that we send you up to London for the Season as your aunt has suggested. It is only fair that you be given an opportunity to meet the right kind of gentlemen, and I doubt very much that you will do that here.'

Antonia's face softened. 'Papa, you know that the cost of a Season is well beyond our means at present, and pray do not try to pretend that it is otherwise. I have seen Mr Ludlow come and go any number of times these past few weeks, and I know what that means.'

'The fact that a gentleman speaks to his man of business need not signify that we are under the hatches, Antonia,' her father said wryly.

'No, but I am well aware that our income is no longer sufficient to ensure the adequate maintenance of the property. Only look at the sorry state of the gardens, Papa,' Antonia said, returning to the window and waving her hand in the direction of the gardens which, once immaculate, were now sadly overgrown with grass and weeds. 'We can no longer afford the services of a gardener, and only last week Abbott informed me that a new hole had appeared in the stable roof.'

'I have spoken to Mr Ludlow regarding the roof, and he has assured me that there is money enough to see to its repair. As regards your going up to London for the Season, I intend to speak to Ophelia and—'

'Oh, no, Papa, pray do not!' Antonia said with a groan. 'We both know there will be little enough to be gained for your trouble. Aunt Ophelia will not settle any money on me until I am married, and I certainly do not intend to *rush* into marriage simply to appease her.'

'You must try not to think too harshly of your aunt, my dear. No doubt Ophelia is only doing what she believes to be in your best interests.'

Antonia's lips compressed into a narrow line. Lady Farrington, her mother's eldest sister, was in possession of a considerable sum of money which Antonia's grandmother had set aside for her dowry—money which would have significantly eased the constraints under which she and her father were currently living. Unfortunately, Lady Farrington now seemed reluctant to part with the money, saying that, as Antonia was nearly twenty, and still showing no inclinations towards marriage, it was incumbent upon her to hold on to the money until such time as she felt her niece was responsible enough to look after it herself. Which meant, of course, being married.

As such, Antonia had endeavoured to forget about her inheritance and to look elsewhere for the funds which would support them. This was why the position of riding master to the Earl of Carlyle's six-year-old daughter Clara had appealed so much.

Antonia had met the Earl's daughter a year earlier, at the Christmas party held at the vicarage. Lady Clara, a delicate child with the most astonishing blue eyes Antonia had ever seen, had been brought to the party by her governess in the hopes that the child would meet and mingle with other children her own age. But when Lady Clara had arrived at the entrance to the crowded room and seen upwards of thirty-five little boys and girls, all intent upon their games, she had stopped dead, clearly overwhelmed by the sights and sounds of so many children laughing and playing within.

Fortunately, Antonia had been standing close to the door and had noticed the child's dismay at once. She had wondered at it too—until she had learned that it was the Earl of Carlyle's daughter who stood so timidly in the doorway—and then all had become clear. Lady Clara had never been exposed to a Christmas party like this before and, no doubt after the solitude of Ashdean, it had all seemed rather frightening.

With that in mind, Antonia had quickly made her way to one of the sweet tables and selected a piece of gingerbread which had been baked in the shape of a little boy. After exchanging a few words with the child's governess, Antonia had bent down to greet the Lady Clara, smiling all the while into those wide blue eyes, and had tried to put the child at ease.

At first, Clara had continued to play shy. She had hidden behind her governess's skirts, peeping out at Antonia with reluctant curiosity, and then ducking back behind Eva's skirts again. But when the gingerbread man had tentatively been offered, Clara had slowly come forward. Her glance had gone from the face of the pretty lady, to the pastry and then back again, and when, eventually, a chubby little hand had reached out to take the treat, Clara had glanced up at Antonia with those incredible blue eyes—and smiled.

It was a smile which had brought about Antonia's total capitulation. It had wrapped around her heart, captivating her with its total innocence and convincing her of the child's heart-wrenching need to be loved.

After that, Antonia had taken pains to visit Lady Clara at Ashdean at least once, and sometimes twice, a week. They would sit together in the nursery and read, or go for long walks through the park. Or sometimes they would just sit in the orchard and look at the clouds drifting by overhead. They had laughed together over the silliest of things, and it was during those early days that the bond between Antonia and Clara had truly been forged.

But it was in more recent days that Antonia had discovered something about the child which had given her genuine cause for alarm. Something she had not even guessed at before.

Clara was afraid of horses. On the few occasions they had walked past the stables, or when they had stood watching the gentle cart horses as they grazed peacefully in a field, Antonia had seen the fear in the child's eyes, and the way she had held back.

And that had shaken Antonia. Because she knew all too well what it could mean. She had already witnessed, in the most terrifying and personal way possible, what fear could do to a child. Which was why, when Eva had let slip that his lordship was looking for someone to teach Clara how to ride, there had been no question in Antonia's mind as to what she had to do.

She *had* to secure the position. It was imperative that she be the one to introduce Clara to horses, and to the art of riding them. Because she had to try to banish the child's fear. Antonia shuddered to think what might happen if Clara was to be taught by someone who did not recognise that failing in the child, or who tried to force it out of her.

From a practical point of view, the position also offered Antonia a solution to her other dilemma; namely, the finding of additional funds for the ongoing maintenance of Buntings Hill, a problem which, despite her father's protestations to the contrary, Antonia knew to be of growing concern.

Lastly, it would spare her the tedium of having to sit

as a companion to a fussy old lady like Lady Haversham, or to be responsible for the care of a brood of obnoxious, ill-mannered children like Lady Cruikshank's. Now, if she could only convince her father of its eminent advantages, everything would be just—

'Antonia, are you listening to me?'

'Hmm?' Antonia looked up, and then guiltily shook her head. 'Forgive me, Papa, I was not. What were you saying?'

'I was saying, that, quite apart from *my* reluctance to see you proceed with this, you should be aware that far more formidable objections may arise from the Earl of Carlyle himself. It is well known that he is loathe to take on female servants.'

That was a truism which Antonia had already been forced to consider. Apart from Lady Clara's governess and Mrs Griffiths, the cook, there was not another female servant in the Earl of Carlyle's employ, either here, or at his home in London.

'I realise that the Earl is not generally known for his hiring of female staff,' Antonia conceded, 'but in *this* instance, I cannot help but feel that once he is made aware of all the advantages, he will *have* to recognise the wisdom of hiring me. For one thing, I am already acquainted with his daughter and get on with her exceedingly well. She trusts me, Papa, and you know how important that trust will be if I am to teach her to ride properly.'

'I do not take exception to that, my dear, but that does not mean that Lord Carlyle will see it in a similar light. You must be prepared for the fact that *he* may dash your hopes far more quickly and effectively than I.'

It was an irrefutable point, and one which brought home to Antonia—as reluctant as she was to admit it—

just how slim were the chances of her actually securing the position. She had not had any formal training in the teaching of young children, and it was an undeniable fact that nearly all riding masters were men.

She sighed, and clasped her slender hands together in front of her. 'You are right, Papa. My wishing to work for the Earl does make little sense, and for any number of reasons. It was…foolish of me to bother you with it in the first place.'

'My dear girl, I never said that you were bothering me. And I am certainly not telling you that you may not go and speak to the Earl, if that is truly what you wish to do.'

'You are not?'

'No. Because I know that if I do not allow you to do this, I shall be forced to listen to endless tales of woe regarding Lady Cruikshank's horrible offspring or Lady Haversham's appalling habits. And I think that such a litany of grief would be far more wearing on my patience than forbidding you to try for the position in the first place.' Mr Hadley picked up his pen and fiddled with the nib. 'I simply thought that…given what happened to…Edwina, you would have felt…differently about the position.'

Antonia glanced at her father, and realised that she had finally discovered what lay at the root of his concerns. 'Dearest Papa. It is *because* of what happened to Edwina that I feel so strongly about this. I would hate to think that…but for a lack of training, such a terrible thing could happen to Clara.'

'Yes, I see that, Antonia, and I can only commend your selflessness for wishing to become involved. I know that it will not be easy. That is why I say you may go and approach the Earl. In the end, he shall be the one to make the decision.'

'Thank you, Papa, thank you!' Antonia wrapped her arms around his neck and kissed the top of his head. 'You are truly the *best* of fathers!'

'Yes, well, I am sure there are many who would disagree with your assessment,' he said ruefully. 'I only hope that if your mother is looking down upon me now, she is not shaking her head and wondering at my giving you your way—again.'

Antonia smiled affectionately. 'I do not see how she could be, Papa. You know that Mama always encouraged me to follow my heart. But I promise that you shall have no cause to regret your decision. The Earl is a wealthy man, and if I am fortunate enough to secure the position, I am sure he will be far more generous to his employees than would be either Lady Haversham or Lady Cruikshank.'

'That remains to be seen, Antonia, as does whether or not you will even be invited to apply,' Mr Hadley cautioned her. 'But go and try your luck regardless. I wager I'll hear soon enough what the Earl has to say.'

As Antonia dashed from the room, Mr Hadley paused in his writings and raised his eyes to the full-length portrait of his wife which hung on the wall opposite his desk. It was a particular favourite of his, for it had captured, at the very peak of her beauty, a woman who had loved deeply, and who had been deeply loved in return.

'Yes, she is just like you, my dear. Headstrong and impulsive,' Mr Hadley murmured affectionately. 'Goodness knows, I could never stop you from doing what you truly wanted to either. But have I made a mistake by allowing her this freedom, Elizabeth? For as admirable as Antonia's motives are, I fear that she may be in for something of a disappointment when she comes up against the Earl.' Mr Hadley's brows flickered a little. 'Carlyle is not a happy man, beloved, nor an indulgent one. He has been…changed by the tragic events of the past. And I do believe that he is one gentleman who will *not* allow our dear girl to have her own way, every time she asks for it!'

Not surprisingly, Mr Hadley was not the only one to view his daughter's choice of occupation with apprehension. Antonia's closest friend, the Honourable Catherine Shand, was equally flabbergasted by the notion of Antonia seeking employment in the raffish Earl's household, though for reasons of an entirely different nature.

'Of course your father would be opposed to you working for the Earl,' Catherine said as the two of them sat together in the Rose Room at Shand Hall later that day. 'Apart from the fact that his only daughter is actively seeking employment, he cannot be pleased at knowing that the position she aspires to is in the Earl of Carlyle's household.'

Antonia sighed. 'Yes, I know. The Earl is not inclined towards hiring females.'

'It is not only that, Toni. Lord Carlyle has gained a very bad reputation of late.'

'A reputation? For what?'

Catherine set her cup down on the tray and moved to sit beside Antonia on the settee. 'For wicked and dissolute behaviour!'

Antonia's honey-tipped lashes flew up. 'No!'

'Oh, yes. Apparently, he has taken to staying out until all hours of the night, gambling at the very worst of the hells, and frequenting the most notorious of clubs. There were even rumours about his being challenged to a duel

by a French Count, though details surrounding that particular *contretemps* are very difficult to come by.'

A shaft of late-afternoon sunlight suddenly pierced the
room, bathing Antonia's cap of honey-coloured curls in
a warm golden light. 'Is he still accepted by good
Society?' she asked.

'Oh, to be sure. But when he does attend an event, he
flirts with all of the eligible young ladies, but pays not
a serious mind to any one of them.'

'But why would he do such a thing?' Antonia asked,
not even attempting to hide her surprise. 'Lady Clara
has need of a mother—and Carlyle an heir. Surely he
wishes to marry again. In fact, did I not hear that he was
enamoured of the Lady Helen Cartland?'

'He might be, but not as enamoured as he is reputed
to be of…pretty ballet dancers and actresses,' Catherine
said, blushing hotly.

Antonia gasped. 'Actresses and ballet dancers!
Goodness, Kitty, wherever did you hear such a thing?'

'From Lady Dalrymple, of course. I overheard her
telling Mama that, on her last visit to London, she
chanced to see Lord Carlyle going into Covent Garden.
He was escorting an exceedingly handsome young
woman, but one whose manner of dress and comport-
ment led Lady Dalrymple to believe that she was not a
member of respectable Society.'

'Lady Dalrymple? That old tattlemonger!' Antonia
snapped. 'I sometimes wonder whether she does
not…make up all of her outrageous stories simply in an
attempt to draw attention to herself.'

'I am quite sure that she does, Toni, but not this time
I fear. The very next day, Lady Brocklehurst—who, as
you know, is a great friend of Lady Dalrymple's—happened to encounter the same young woman as she was

coming out of the very shop which Lady Brocklehurst herself was about to enter. Apparently the young woman was wearing an exquisite ruby necklace. A necklace she hinted, quite boldly, had been given to her by her wealthy and very handsome benefactor!'

Antonia's smooth brow furrowed. 'But...if she did not mention Lord Carlyle by name, why would Lady Brocklehurst simply assume that it was the Earl to whom the young woman had been referring? I have heard that many wealthy gentlemen keep—well, that is to say—it could have been any one of a number of...others.'

'It could. Except that Lord Carlyle's penchant for giving rubies to...certain types of young women is well known around London.'

'And I suppose *that* bit of information was also supplied by Lady Dalrymple?'

At her girlfriend's nod, Antonia frowned in irritation. At the moment, she was not sure which of the two people she liked less. Lord knew, she was no admirer of Lady Dalrymple. The woman was an insatiable gabble-grinder who Antonia took pains to avoid meeting in the street. But neither was her opinion of Lord Carlyle improved by the information she had just received. Certainly his predilection for pretty young actresses and ladies of...questionable virtue did nothing to lessen her feelings of contempt towards him. If anything, it only served to strengthen her resolve to try to protect Clara from his influence.

Antonia had never actually been introduced to the handsome Earl of Carlyle. Nor—as her father had pointed out—had she had anything to do with him for the past eight or nine years. The last time she had seen him was when she had been just eleven years old, and he had just returned from London after his marriage to the beautiful Lady Violet Pelham.

At the time, the residents of Upper Tipping had been all agog with the news that the young lord was bringing his new bride to Ashdean. Antonia herself had looked forward to the occasion, though she had little recollection of it now. She did remember that the exquisite young lady who had stepped down from the old Earl's carriage had been dressed all in blue, from the tip of her elegant feathered bonnet to the heels of her soft, kid slippers.

But while the new Viscountess had been undeniably beautiful, it had soon become evident that she was not at all taken with life in the country. She did not like to ride, nor did she enjoy walking along the tree-shaded lanes. Consequently, it had come as no surprise to anyone when, little more than two weeks later, the Viscount and his young wife had packed up their belongings and headed back to Town.

In the years that followed, two significant events had taken place. The first was the death of the old Earl and the ascension of his son to the title. The second was the birth of a daughter to the new Earl and Countess of Carlyle.

The latter news had been greeted with the kind of joy typically reserved for such great occasions, and there had been much celebrating, both in Town and in Upper Tipping. Tragically, however, it was a joy which had been short-lived. The Countess's health had begun to fail. She had endured a difficult and protracted birthing and, frail creature that she was, had never fully recovered from it. Thus, when she had contracted influenza a few years later, the doctors had known that there was little hope. She had died less than six months after, leaving Carlyle, at nine and twenty, solely responsible for the care of his then four-year-old daughter, Clara.

Not surprisingly, Lord Carlyle had returned to the country at once. He had lavished money on the nursery at Ashdean in preparation for the infant's stay, and had hired an army of servants to see to her care. But as soon as all of the arrangements had been made, he had returned to London and stayed there, visiting his daughter only when called upon by duty or necessity to do so.

'Well, I do not care a *fig* for what Lord Carlyle does,' Antonia professed. 'It is his daughter's welfare that I am concerned with, and since Clara is the one to whom I intend to devote my time, the *less* I have to do with her father, the better.'

'I suppose, though he is very handsome, Toni.' Catherine's voice took on a wistful quality. 'Cynthia Prescott told me that she near fainted dead away when she saw him at Almack's, with all that dark, wavy hair and those incredible blue eyes. She said that the colour reminded her of the sky on a summer's day.'

'The sky on a summer—? Really, Kitty, you make Lord Carlyle sound like one of those…heroes in those Gothic novels you are forever reading.'

'I am only repeating what Cynthia told me,' Catherine retorted defensively. 'You can see for yourself when you speak to him about the position.'

Antonia began to fiddle with the lace edging on her sleeve. 'Actually, I am hoping that I shall *not* have to see him about it…at all.'

'Not see him?' Catherine glanced at her best friend in astonishment. 'But how can you possibly avoid it?'

Antonia shrugged. 'I do not think it will be all that difficult, given Lord Carlyle's antipathy for the country.

His steward will likely be handling all of the arrangements.'

'But surely the Earl will at least wish to *see* the applicants before the final selection is made,' Catherine objected. 'He would hardly commit his daughter to the care of someone he hasn't even met.'

'Why not? He was not around much for the first six years of Clara's life, why would he feel compelled to be around for the next few?' Antonia argued. 'All Lord Carlyle requires of a riding master is that he be able to teach his daughter to sit a horse competently and to look good into the bargain. I have no doubt that I can do that as well, or better, than any old riding master from London.'

'And what about Lord Carlyle's refusal to employ women?'

'Ah, now *that* did give me some cause for concern,' Antonia confessed, 'but I do believe I have come up with a rather brilliant idea for circumventing the problem.'

Catherine saw the twinkle in her friend's eye and warily shook her head. 'Toni, what scheme are you concocting now? I know that look, and I know that it bodes no good!'

'Tosh, it is a perfectly splendid idea, and one which will work very well *if*, as I suspect, Lord Carlyle will not be present for the interviews.'

'Are you going to tell me what this perfectly splendid idea is?'

'Not just at the moment. I still have a few more details to work out.'

Clearly disappointed, Catherine's pretty mouth turned downward. 'I think you might at least have given me a hint, Toni. After all, I am your closest friend. But what if Lord Carlyle still finds out the truth of your identity, despite your splendid idea?'

Antonia reached towards the tray and took a plain biscuit. 'I am hoping that by that time, I will have been able to persuade his steward that I am more than capable of filling the position, and that the steward, in turn, will have been able to convince the Earl of the same. Lord Carlyle will not be looking for complications in his life, Kitty. Consequently, it only follows that if matters are proceeding according to plan, and his daughter is happy, it should not matter that the person teaching her how to ride is a woman. Besides which, he is only here for a few days each year.'

'But what if he chances to see you on one of those days?'

Antonia waved aside her friend's objection. 'I shall simply feign an illness and stay at home.'

'That is all very well, but if the Earl does decide to spend more time in the area, I fear that your carefully formulated plan—whatever it is—will go for nought. Lord Carlyle will be none too pleased when he discovers that he has been the object of a clever little deceit.'

'Kitty, we are only talking about the enactment of a simple deception, not a plot to overthrow the King,' Antonia assured her. 'Personally, I do not think his lordship will mind *who* teaches his daughter to ride so long as he does not have to be bothered about it. From what you say, he is much more addicted to Town pleasures anyway and, knowing that, I cannot think of *any* reason why a *non pareil* like Carlyle would suddenly decide to turn feather and retire to the bucolic tranquillity of Upper Tipping!'

Chapter Two

A suffocating yellow fog had descended upon London, blanketing the City, all but immobilising the steady flow of traffic through the already crowded streets. It hung in the night air like a shroud; stinging the eyes of those foolhardy enough to venture outside without suitable covering and making it nearly impossible for anyone to see more than two feet in front of them.

Standing before the drawing-room window of the elegant house in Park Lane, Sebastian Hastings, Earl of Carlyle, stared out into the murky darkness of the night and felt as though the cursed fog had penetrated into the very room in which he stood. Its silence was oppressive; its heaviness permeating into even the most far-flung corners of the house, causing his head to ache, and his already sagging spirits to plummet like a stone.

God, how he hated this house. Hated the unhappy memories associated with it and the wretched way it made him feel. He grew increasingly restless when forced to reside in it for any length of time; assailed by a boredom that was totally out of keeping with his normally ebullient spirits—which was why he endeavoured to spend as much of his time away from it as possible.

But even that did him no good of late, for the moment he stepped through the front door, he felt the familiar malaise begin to return, settling on him much the same way the cursed fog had settled on London. And the most frustrating part of all was that he had absolutely no idea how to go about ridding himself of it.

Turning away from the window, Sebastian walked towards the elegant sideboard situated between the pink and white marble fireplace and the ornate boule cabinet, and poured himself a generous glass of brandy. He swirled the golden liquid in the bowl, impressed neither by the quality of the Venetian crystal nor by the excellent vintage of the wine. These things he took for granted, as he did everything else about the elegant town house in which he lived; a house which meant so little to him, yet which had meant everything to his late wife; the beautiful and desirable Violet, Countess of Carlyle.

At the thought of the woman to whom he had been married, Sebastian tilted the glass to his lips and drank deeply, feeling the fiery spirit burn a path down his throat. Violet. It was hard to believe that she had been dead over two years. At times, he felt like she was still here, her spirit lingering on in the dark corridors of the vast house like a physical presence.

And why would it not linger? Sebastian acknowledged wryly. There was far more of her here than there was of him. The Ming bowls and the other priceless knick-knacks she had been so fond of collecting—indeed, the house itself, with its Italian marble, and its magnificent crystal chandeliers—meant nothing to him. As Sebastian glanced around the opulent drawing room which had been embellished with nearly as much chinoiserie as the Regent's pavilion in Brighton, all he could see were the suffocating crowds Violet had filled it with in her endless quest to become London's most popular and accomplished hostess.

And eventually, she had. But at what cost to him, and to their marriage?

Still, all that was of little consequence now. Sebastian had married the beautiful, but shallow, Lady Violet Pelham, and had elevated her upon his father's death to the exalted rank of Countess, whereupon she had set out to more than make up for the lack of regard her husband seemed to have for the title. And, in doing so, she had lost him.

Perhaps that's what this was all about, he reflected sadly. Perhaps regret was the cause of this…malaise which plagued him; dogging his steps, and causing the mouth which had once moved so easily to laughter to twist so cynically. God knew, he had been living a lie for more years than he cared to admit. A lie which had begun shortly after his marriage…and a marriage which had died shortly after it had begun…

'My lord?'

Sebastian raised the glass to his lips, but he did not turn around. 'What is it, Royce?'

'Mr Bingham asks if you might be able to see him.'

Sebastian's brow furrowed in annoyance. Damn. He wasn't in a mood to see anyone right now, and certainly not the steward of Ashdean. The man knew him too well. He was one of the few people who could see beyond the barricades Sebastian erected, and who could touch on areas, on emotions, that were best left undiscovered.

Unfortunately, Sebastian also knew that there was little to be gained by putting the man off. The business of the estate went on, no matter what his own particular frame of mind. 'Very well.' He downed the rest of the brandy in one mouthful. 'Show him up.'

The butler bowed, and in a few moments, returned with the late-night caller. 'Mr Bingham, my lord.'

'Come in, Paddy.' Sebastian's tone was brusque as he turned to address the steward by name—one of the few people who warranted such treatment. 'Will you have a drink?'

Padrick Douglas Bingham, steward of Ashdean, shook his head as he advanced into the room. He was an ordinary-looking man; tall, with rugged features, a thatch of thick, sandy-coloured hair that styled after no fashion but its own, and green eyes that seemed to sparkle with perpetual mirth. Certainly there was nothing to distinguish him from the hundreds of other men who worked for the Earl.

But there was a difference. Paddy Bingham was one of the few men with whom Carlyle felt truly at ease. He was one of the fewer still who had earned Sebastian's trust.

'Sorry to be stopping by so late, my lord,' Bingham said now as he set a handful of letters on the desk.

Sebastian dismissed the apology with a casual wave of his hand. 'The fault is not yours. No doubt you called earlier and did not find me at home.'

'I would have been surprised if I had.' A knowing smile briefly touched the older man's face. 'You're a very popular gentleman about Town these days.'

Sebastian's face relaxed, as it did when in the company of people he genuinely cared about. 'So I have heard, though for the life of me I cannot think why. My own company is beginning to bore me dreadfully. Sure I cannot tempt you to join me?' he offered, holding up the decanter of brandy again.

'Thank you, my lord, but I stopped at the Crown and Anchor on my way in.'

'The Crown and Anchor.' Sebastian poured himself another brandy. 'Is the fair Mariette still waiting tables there?'

'Aye. With a face that could melt a sailor's heart, and a tongue that could put him to the blush.' Bingham winked knowingly. 'She was asking about you.'

Sebastian smiled but made no reply. He was not surprised that Mariette remembered him. He had spent many a night in her bed since Violet's death, losing himself in the softness of her body and in the forgiving warmth of her arms. But of late, even that had failed to eradicate the blackness which had taken possession of his soul.

He gestured for the steward to sit down. 'So, what brings you out on such a foul night, Paddy? Matters of grave importance?'

'Hardly grave, my lord, though not without some import. I believe I have found a suitable master for the Lady Clara.'

Sebastian stared at him blankly. 'I beg your pardon?'

'A riding master. You asked me to hire one for your daughter.'

Abruptly aware that his latest undertaking had all but slipped his mind, Sebastian's mouth tightened. 'Yes, of course. What have you to tell me?'

'That I received a number of letters in response to the advertisement, and after whittling out the unsuitable ones, I was left with two possibilities.'

'Good God, only two? What was wrong with the rest of them?'

'Any number of things. Dubious work background, not enough experience, suspect reasons for prior dismissals. It doesn't pay to be too careful when it comes to the well-being of the Lady Clara, my lord.'

Sebastian glanced at his man sharply, not sure whether Bingham wasn't bamming him. But one look at the steward's face was enough to assure him that his doubts were both unworthy and unnecessary. Paddy Bingham genuinely cared for the child—which was more than many were willing to say for him, Sebastian reflected guiltily. 'Go on, Paddy, you said you had it down to two gentlemen.'

'Yes, a Mr Henry Huddlesworth and a Mr Tony Davlin. I have both their letters here.'

Sebastian glanced at the letters, but made no move to read them. 'Have you a recommendation?'

'Of the two it would appear that Mr Huddlesworth has more experience in teaching young men and women the skills of riding. However, he is at present living with his ailing mother in Yorkshire.'

Sebastian frowned. 'Rather a long way to come for work, isn't it?'

'It seems that Mr Huddlesworth is quite prepared to move,' Bingham said, 'but I admit I had some concerns as to how often he might need to return to Yorkshire to see to the old lady's health.'

'A valid concern,' Sebastian acknowledged. 'What of Mr Davlin?'

'While Mr Davlin does not seem to have had as much actual teaching experience, I get the impression that he enjoys working with young children a good deal more than does Mr Huddlesworth. And he certainly knows his horses.'

Sebastian glanced at his steward in amusement. 'You gleaned all of that from a letter, Paddy? Upon my word, you are even more astute than I gave you credit for. Very well, this Mr…Davlin,' Sebastian said, wondering why the name should sound vaguely familiar to him. 'Where does he live?'

'In the area,' Bingham informed the Earl. 'He mentions the use of a cottage on Lord Shand's estate.'

'I see. And how would you like to proceed?'

'With your permission, I would like to bring both gentlemen to Ashdean, and have them spend some time with Lady Clara. Once I see how they handle themselves with the little girl, I shall be able to give you a more accurate recommendation.'

'As you will, Paddy. When can they start?'

'Whenever is convenient for you, my lord.' Bingham duly retrieved the letters. 'Neither gentleman is currently employed.'

Sebastian briefly inclined his head, as though weary of the conversation. 'Fine. Make the arrangements. Whichever one you choose may commence as soon as possible.'

Bingham glanced at the Earl in surprise. 'You will not wish to interview them yourself?'

'I hardly think it necessary. Your judgement in matters concerning the estate has always been faultless, Paddy. I am sure that whichever man you choose will be fine with me.'

Bingham flushed at the unexpected compliment. 'It is good of you to say so, my lord.'

'In any event, I have no doubt that I shall see Mr Huddlesworth or Mr Davlin eventually,' Sebastian said carelessly. 'I think it is time that I went down to the country for a while.'

It was difficult to tell who was the more surprised by the unexpected announcement: Mr Bingham upon hearing it, or Sebastian upon uttering it. For, in truth, he had not known that he was even contemplating such an idea until he had heard the words leave his lips. But, once said, the idea began to take hold in his mind.

Yes, perhaps a sojourn in the country was just what he needed. It certainly couldn't be any worse than remaining in Town, Sebastian reflected dimly. And he had always loved Ashdean, the rambling Elizabethan house set in the gently rolling countryside of Kent. Indeed, some of his fondest memories were of growing up in that house. As a child, he had ridden over every hill and explored every valley, coming to love the land which had belonged to his family for centuries. He had even taken his new bride there in the early weeks of their marriage.

Granted, Violet had complained bitterly nearly the entire time they were there until, guilt-ridden, he had dutifully driven her back to Town, but at least there were no memories of bitter fights and long cold silences. Those had come later.

But there was one memory at Ashdean which Sebastian would never be able to forget.

Clara.

Sebastian closed his eyes as he dropped his head forward and pinched the bridge of his nose between his thumb and his forefinger. Good God, was it really a year since he had last visited his daughter? It must be. She had been approaching her sixth birthday at the time, and only two days ago, Bingham had informed him that her seventh birthday was fast approaching. Where had the time gone?

Of course, it wasn't just the time, Sebastian admitted guiltily. He had stayed away, not because he had been reluctant to see Clara, but for reasons which none but himself knew. Reasons which even Paddy had not been privy to. Added to that was the fact that he simply didn't know how to behave around the child. He was not used to children of any age, let alone a six-year-old. Very few of his friends had offspring Clara's age, and those who did were more than happy to leave them to the care of their mothers or nannies.

It was ironic really. For all his adeptness at court, Sebastian found himself painfully at a loss when it came to dealing with the wide-eyed stare of his own child. But then, was it any wonder? He'd had no brothers or sisters of his own, and he had seen Clara less than ten times since she had been born, due mainly to Violet's outright refusal to share the child with him in the early years of her life. She had begun to smother Clara, perhaps in a pathetic attempt to make up for the love that had been missing in her own relationship. It had grown so bad that just the sight of her father was enough to make Clara burst into tears.

Hardly the kind of welcome any new father looked for.

For that reason, and for…others, Sebastian had had virtually nothing to do with the child. After Violet's death, he had seen to it that the nursery at Ashdean had been luxuriously appointed, and had even hired a governess to look after her. But beyond that, the best Sebastian had been able to do was send Clara expensive toys for her birthday and a special box at Christmas; presents usually chosen by Bingham, and sent from an unknown man who called himself her father…

'Yes, I shall go down to the country. Just for a few days, mind,' Sebastian added, aware of a tightness in his throat which had nothing to do with the brandy. 'You may expect me…within the week.'

Taking care to conceal his surprise, Bingham nodded and slowly got to his feet. 'Very good, my lord. I shall inform the household of your impending arrival. And I shall contact Mr Huddlesworth and Mr Davlin to set up interviews.' He paused to glance at the averted face of his employer. 'You are quite sure you do not wish to meet with either of them?'

'Quite sure. There will be many other pressing concerns to which I must address myself.'

'As you wish, my lord. Will there be anything else?'

Sebastian shook his head, his mind already on other matters. 'I think not. Goodnight, Paddy.'

'Goodnight, my lord.'

Alone again, Sebastian sat down at the writing table and stared at the neat pile of papers which dotted its top. A trip to the country? He must be mad. No one travelled to the country when there were still so many things to do in London. And yet, what exactly *was* there for him to do in London? When was the last time he had actually looked *forward* to going to a ball, or to spending an evening at the theatre? When had he ever *anticipated* an afternoon filled with nothing more exciting than going aimlessly from one at-home to the next?

What was there in London that he was truly going to miss?

Nothing. And as the reality of that hit home, Sebastian's mouth began to curve in the first real smile he had experienced in weeks. There was absolutely *nothing* in London that he was going to miss. In fact, the mere thought of getting *out* of it for a few days was enough to lift him out of the dismals. He summoned Royce and informed him of his intentions.

Sebastian did not miss the nearly imperceptible quirk of his servant's left eyebrow. Nor did he fail to recognise that Royce was almost as surprised as Bingham had been. That, if anything, served to convince Sebastian that his actions were long overdue. He had been living the life of a man about Town for too long. It was time he found something else upon which to focus his attention; time he tried to develop some kind of relationship with that little girl in the country—even if he was late in getting started.

He may have failed miserably as a husband, but that did not mean he had to fail at being a father as well! He only hoped that he hadn't left it too late.

'Toni, you did it!' Catherine joyously waved a piece of paper over her head as Antonia walked into the yellow saloon at Shand Hall a few days later. 'The Earl of Carlyle wishes to see you!'

Antonia blanched, and her hand went immediately to her heart. 'He does? Oh, dear! I really had not expected that he would.'

'Well, he does,' Catherine exclaimed, handing her the letter. 'Here. Read it for yourself.'

Antonia set her reticule down on the table and reached for the piece of heavy cream parchment which boldly displayed the Carlyle crest at the top of it, and held it between hands that were visibly shaking.

The letter—which had come to Shand Hall at Antonia's request—was from Carlyle's steward, Mr Bingham, and it informed Tony Davlin that the Earl of Carlyle would be pleased to consider him for the position of riding master to his daughter, the Lady Clara. It further instructed Mr Davlin to be at the stables at Ashdean at two o'clock the following Monday afternoon.

'La, Toni, I can scarce believe it,' Catherine said breathlessly. 'I never thought that you would actually get it.'

Antonia shook her head in wonderment. 'No, nor did I, Kitty.'

Her 'perfectly splendid idea' had been to apply for the position, not as Miss Antonia Hadley, but as Mr Tony Davlin. As she had explained to Catherine, she was not telling a complete lie by using the masculine form of address. If she shortened her first name to Tony, and employed her mother's maiden name of Davlin, she was, for all intents and purposes, Tony Davlin.

And because it was hardly to be expected that Lord Carlyle would entertain a query from a young woman, Antonia felt sure that by representing herself as the highly competent Mr Tony Davlin, she would at least have a chance to meet with the steward and to plead her case. And if she could do that with any degree of competency, was he not then far more likely to recommend *her* for the position than anyone else?

It certainly seemed so. Because here, in her hands, was the proof that she did indeed possess the qualifications the Earl was looking for.

'Nor have I been granted it yet,' Antonia reminded her friend. 'While the letter does not mention my being interviewed by Lord Carlyle himself, it does say that I shall be required to meet with his steward, Mr Bingham.'

'Do you know this Mr Bingham?'

'We have not actually met, but I have seen him when I have gone to visit Clara at Ashdean. Surprisingly, he and Clara seem to be fast friends.'

'Well, I suppose it was too much to hope that you could be hired without having been seen by *anyone*,' Catherine acknowledged, 'but how will you go on at the meeting itself, Toni? It is all very well to fool someone on paper, but there is no disguising the fact that you *are* a young lady when it comes time for the interview. What do you think Mr Bingham will say when he discovers who…or rather *what* you are?'

'I have absolutely no idea,' Antonia answered truthfully as she tapped the letter against her chin. 'I suppose it depends on what *his* feelings are as regards hiring a woman.'

'His feelings may have no bearing on the matter, given Lord Carlyle's antipathy towards women,' Catherine pointed out. 'Still, I suppose there is nothing you can do now but go and give it your best. The fact that you received a reply at all indicates that they were impressed with your qualifications.'

The girls lapsed into silence, each intent upon their own thoughts. For Antonia, the letter's arrival had put her in a definite quandary. To know that she had a genuine chance at the position, solely as a result of her experience with horses and her desire to do the job, was extremely encouraging.

To know that she might lose the position, for no other reason than that she was a woman, was sobering to say the least.

By Friday, Antonia had still not come up with a plan for either avoiding or deceiving Mr Bingham. She had toyed with the idea of dressing up as a man, and had even gone so far as to mention it to Catherine, who had naturally thought it a foolish and outlandish idea. But, friend that she was, Catherine had managed to sneak some of her brother's clothes out of his room for Antonia to try on.

It had soon become apparent, however, that dressing up in a boy's clothes simply wasn't going to work. There was no disguising the feminine curves of Antonia's figure, nor the shapeliness of her legs in the skin-tight pantaloons and tall boots she would be required to wear. Then there was the problem of her face. It was simply…too pretty. The long curving lashes fanning out over soft grey-green eyes could never have belonged to a man, nor could the high, prominent cheekbones or the decidedly feminine mouth.

As Catherine pointed out as they stared at Antonia's reflection in the looking glass in her bedroom, if she and Mr Bingham were to stand at thirty paces and meet by the light of the moon, there might be a slight chance of accomplishing the deceit. But during a face-to-face confrontation in the glaring light of day, there was simply no mistaking Antonia for anything but the lady she was.

'I shall just have to explain the situation to Mr Bingham as best I can,' said Antonia, as she and Catherine shopped for fabric in the village on the following Monday morning. 'It is unlikely that he will not have heard Eva or one of the other servants mention my affection for Lady Clara. Perhaps I can use that as justification for my wishing to secure the post.'

Catherine sighed as she turned her attention towards a particularly fine length of Italian silk. 'You may be able to explain them to Mr Bingham, Toni, but will *he* be able to explain them to the Earl? And even if you are able to avoid meeting the Earl at the initial interview, no doubt you will be forced into an encounter at some time in the not-too-distant future.'

The timing of Catherine's statement could not have been more propitious. As the girls concluded their shopping and made their way along the street, they were stayed by the unmistakable sound of a carriage approaching. And when an impressive looking coach-and-four rounded the corner and drew to a halt in front of the very shop before which they were standing, Antonia's eyes widened in horror.

Carlyle! There could be no mistaking the elaborate coat of arms emblazoned on the coach door or the quality of the four black horses which drew it. Nor could she question that the man who flung open the door and climbed down moments later could be anyone but the omnipotent Earl of Carlyle himself!

'La, Toni, it's *him!*' Catherine squeaked. 'The Earl of Carlyle! Oh, upon my word, Cynthia was right. He *is* handsome!'

For once, Antonia was forced to agree with an assessment made by someone whose opinion she would normally have paid scant attention to. Lord Carlyle *was* handsome; as handsome as any gentleman she had ever seen. Tall and commanding of stature, his features were classically perfect. A slim, aquiline nose was set above an unsmiling mouth that topped a chin that was firm and slightly square, while dark brows drew together under a shock of even blacker hair. He sported a multi-layered cape over a jacket of dark blue superfine and smooth-fitting buff pantaloons, below which Antonia could see the gleam of highly polished Hessians. He wore no jewellery save a signet ring on the ring finger of his right hand.

Not surprisingly, the arrival of the Carlyle coach and the appearance of the dashing Earl were sufficient to cause quite a stir in the tiny main street of Upper Tipping. A small cluster of girls stood giggling together across the street, while some of the more daring ladies began to cast frankly longing glances in Lord Carlyle's direction. But it was not until the town's leading prattle box, Lady Dalrymple, rushed from the mercer's shop opposite and made a beeline for the three of them, that Antonia knew it was too late for her to try to escape.

'Lord Carlyle!' Lady Dalrymple hailed him imperiously. 'My lord, a moment, pray.'

The gentleman glanced up, clearly nonplussed by the sight of a large and bedizened matron steaming towards him at full charge, and did not smile as he doffed his glistening black beaver. 'Madam?'

'Lord Carlyle, how *delighted* I am to see you home again.' Lady Dalrymple, winded by the short run across the road, took a few deep breaths before turning the full force of her countenance upon him. 'I had heard rumours that you were…returning to Upper Tipping, of course, but I had feared them little more than that. One hears so much chatter about Town these days.'

The Earl inclined his head in a gesture that was polite, but nothing more. 'As you can see, they are rumours no longer.'

'No, indeed, and how pleased I am that they are not,' Lady Dalrymple professed heartily. She smiled up into his face—expectantly, it seemed to Antonia—and when no light of recognition dawned in his eyes, added quickly, 'But surely you remember me, Lord Carlyle? Your dear mother and I were the closest of friends.'

'Indeed,' he said, though with no noticeable increase in warmth.

'Oh, yes. Though I was not in London as frequently as I might have liked, we used to spend a great deal of time together whenever she was at Ashdean.'

Still nothing. Lord Carlyle continued to regard the woman with the utmost civility, but with no more insight into who she was than he had upon her arrival. 'Madam, I pray you will forgive me, but—'

'Lady *Dalrymple*, my lord!'

This last bit of information was delivered, to Antonia's way of thinking, with more than a hint of desperation, and its response awaited with equal trepidation. It was clear from the expression on Lady Dalrymple's face that the interview was not turning out at all as she had expected.

Fortunately, it seemed that Lord Carlyle was nothing if not a gentleman. The merest shadow of a smile touched his lips before he bowed to her and said, 'But of course, Lady… Dalrymple. How remiss of me. Mother spoke of you…often.'

Lady Dalrymple's anxiety vanished like a puff of wind. Oblivious to the slight note of sarcasm in the Earl's voice, she beamed her delight and blissfully furthered her perjury. 'Oh, yes, we were the closest of friends, she and I. And as such, I am so very glad that *I* am the one to be on hand to welcome you back.'

'Thank you, Lady Dalrymple. I must say, I had not expected such an…enthusiastic welcome before even reaching my own door,' Lord Carlyle drawled.

Fortunately, Lady Dalrymple was both slow to take offence and quick to take advantage of an opportunity. As the mother of two unmarried daughters, she could ill afford to be otherwise. 'Yes, well, as I said, it is truly fortunate that I happened to be so close. Am I to hope that you will be staying with us for a while, Lord Carlyle?'

'My stay is of an undecided duration,' Lord Carlyle remarked carefully, 'since there are a number of things which I hope to accomplish while I am here.'

'But, that is wonderful,' Lady Dalrymple enthused, convinced by the Earl's carefully worded statement that he *must* be looking for a new wife. 'I was only telling my girls yesterday—lovely girls, both of them unwed—

that it would be such a pleasure to see a Carlyle in permanent residence again.'

'And so you shall. Eventually,' he was quick to point out when he saw the unmistakable look of hope which appeared on her face. 'Though I do not know whether it will be in the near future or not. And now, if you will excuse me, I fear I must be—'

Sebastian broke off in mid-sentence, having turned and found himself staring into one of the loveliest faces he had ever had the pleasure of seeing. A pair of unusual grey-green eyes stared back at him from a face of alabaster perfection, while rose-kissed lips and a delightfully retroussé nose completed the charming visage. The lady's rich, honey-coloured hair had been drawn softly up and back, allowing a few wispy tendrils to escape from beneath the brim of the charming straw bonnet to frame her face. She was wearing a simple gown of pale lemon muslin trimmed with white lace, over which she wore a spencer of a deeper yellow hue. Neither were styled in the first stare of fashion, but there was no denying that the modest outfit more than flattered the feminine curves of its owner.

The young woman standing beside her was also very pretty, but as Sebastian waited for the introductions to be made, he felt his gaze drawn back towards the young lady with the beautiful eyes.

'Lady Dalrymple, perhaps you would be so good as to introduce us,' he said politely, when at length it seemed that no such courtesy was to be extended.

'Hmm? Oh, yes, of course, my lord, forgive me.' Lady Dalrymple quickly made the introductions, taking care to conceal the fact that she wished to do anything *but*.

Both girls curtsied, as was expected. Lord Carlyle bowed first towards Catherine, as was her due, and then turned to address Antonia. 'Hadley,' he repeated thoughtfully. 'Did I hear that correctly?'

Antonia straightened slowly. She was not surprised that the Earl had asked for clarification of her name. Lady Dalrymple had uttered it so quickly as to render it almost unrecognisable. 'You did, my lord.'

'Then…could it be that you are also…Mr Peter Hadley's daughter, and as such, a neighbour of mine?'

Antonia was astonished that he would remember, but took care not to let it show. 'Our property adjoins yours to the south, yes.'

'How strange that we have never met, Miss Hadley.'

'On the contrary, given that I spend so little time in London, and you so little in Kent, it is not surprising at all.'

'Perhaps that is a shortcoming I can remedy by offering to call upon your mother and father at the earliest opportunity.'

Antonia stiffened, and her eyes grew cold. 'My mother died two years ago this November, my lord. Only my father and I reside at Buntings Hill now. I thought you might have heard.'

Beside her, Lady Dalrymple made a faint choking sound but Antonia did not care. The fact that Lord Carlyle was not even aware that her mother—a woman who, by his own admission, was one of his closest neighbours—had passed away that long ago made her exceedingly angry. While he might not choose to live in the country, the very *least* he could have done was to keep abreast of the lives of the families who did.

There was a brief silence as Lord Carlyle gazed down into her face. 'Forgive me, Miss Hadley, I was not aware of your mother's passing. Living in London has left me somewhat…out of touch. I can only say that I shall en-

deavour to set that to rights by paying a call upon you
and your father at the earliest opportunity, in order that
I might express my condolences to you both.'

It was a genuinely offered sentiment and, aware that
Lady Dalrymple was listening to every word, Antonia
managed a small nod of assent. She did not wish news
to travel back to her father that she had been rude to the
Earl—whether he was deserving of it or not. But she
could not bring herself to be any warmer towards him
than that.

'Now I hope I am not rushing my fences, Lord
Carlyle,' Lady Dalrymple said, anxious to regain control
of the conversation, 'but I wonder whether you might
consider joining us on Friday evening, for a small intimate dinner to welcome you back to Upper Tipping.'

The Earl reluctantly returned his attention to the
speaker. 'Thank you, Lady Dalrymple, but I fear I must
decline your kind invitation, simply because I do not
know how long I intend to remain in the area. However,'
he said, observing the crestfallen expression on the
woman's face—and aware that Miss Hadley was watching him closely, 'if I am still in the vicinity and not
otherwise engaged, I would be...pleased to dine with
you.'

It was all the lady needed to hear. 'How very good of
you to say so, Lord Carlyle. I know how busy you must
be, and I shall only say that we would be delighted if
you were able to join us at, shall we say, half past five?'

Lord Carlyle winced and knowing the reason why,
Antonia turned away to hide a smile. In London, she
doubted that the Earl ever sat down to dine before eight.
But this was the country, and here, half past five was
the accepted time.

'Thank you, Lady Dalrymple, I shall...endeavour to

attend,' he said finally. 'But if circumstances warrant a change, I shall send a note round at the earliest opportunity.'

'I hope there will be no need for such a note, my lord. However, *if* you are unable to join us, I know that it will only be as the result of a matter of *extreme* urgency,' Lady Dalrymple said, not wishing to appear too desperate. 'And now, I must be off. I did promise my girls that I would pick up a few items for them. La, there are just that many things to do when one has young, eligible daughters,' she trilled.

Again, Antonia took pains to hide her amusement. Lady Dalrymple was no more likely to buy lace for her daughters than a hare was to sit next to a fox. No doubt the errand she intended to set out upon was the informing of as many of the female residents of the neighbourhood as possible that the handsome and eminently eligible Earl of Carlyle had returned to Upper Tipping *and* of her good fortune in being the first to secure him to dine.

'Interesting woman,' Lord Carlyle remarked carefully as Lady Dalrymple took herself off, her feathered bonnet bristling with excitement. 'Is she always so excitable?'

'I think she was somewhat…overwhelmed by your arrival,' Antonia informed him drily.

She knew that her tone was somewhat sarcastic, and was not at all surprised when he addressed his next remark to Catherine. 'Forgive me, Miss Shand, but I fear my arrival has prevented you from going about your business. May I, perhaps, offer you and Miss Hadley a ride somewhere?'

At the unexpectedly kind gesture, Catherine blushed and promptly forget where they had been going. Antonia, who was far more in control of the situation—

and bothered with an entirely new concern—gave him a polite but dismissive smile. 'Thank you, Lord Carlyle, but our carriage is waiting just there.'

Carlyle stared at her for a moment with eyes that were sharp and assessing. Antonia knew that she had sounded as unimpressed by his arrival—and by him—as Lady Dalrymple had been overwhelmed by it. But whether as a result of breeding—or simply a complete lack of interest as to what she thought—Lord Carlyle merely smiled and offered them a polite bow. 'Then I shall detain you no longer. I bid you good day, ladies.' With that, he walked into the merchant's behind them and disappeared from view.

As the door swung closed behind him, Antonia closed her eyes in relief, aware that her body was trembling all over. Beside her, Catherine merely let out a long, ecstatic sigh. 'La, is he not the most *handsome* of gentlemen, Toni? And so very gallant. He does not seem at all like a rake to me. Does he to you, Toni? Toni!'

'Hmm? Oh, no, I suppose he does not,' Antonia muttered. 'But I cannot *believe* what bad luck our running into him like this is.'

'Bad luck!' Catherine turned to regard her best friend in astonishment. 'Antonia, have you windmills in your head? We have just been amongst the first to be introduced to the Earl of Carlyle upon his return, and you say that it is *bad* luck?'

'Goose! Of course it is! Have you forgotten that I have an *interview* with Mr Bingham this very afternoon? As *Tony Davlin*? What if the Earl should decide to attend?'

Catherine gasped in dismay. 'Oh, dear, yes, I *had* forgotten! But what on earth could have induced Lord Carlyle to come down to the country so early? The Season is not yet over.'

'I have absolutely no idea,' Antonia said thoughtfully as the girls made their way back to Catherine's curricle. 'All I know is that he has chosen an exceedingly awkward time to make his obligatory visit to Ashdean—as if things were not awkward enough before!'

Chapter Three

At precisely fifteen minutes before the hour of two o'clock on Monday afternoon, suitably attired in her most formal habit of dark blue Georgian cloth—and with her stomach tied up in knots—Antonia waited for the stable boy to saddle her dapple grey mare in preparation for the ride over to Ashdean. She had been in a positive fidget all morning. Ever since meeting the Earl of Carlyle in town, Antonia had suffered agonies of uncertainty, wondering what she should do if the Earl chanced to be present for the upcoming interview.

She had toyed with the idea of saying that a friend had written the letter in jest, and that upon discovering the ruse she had felt honour bound to make her presence known to Mr Bingham, and to explain the situation as best she could. Alternately, she had thought to say that she had written the letter on a dare, never for one moment expecting that she would receive a reply, and that she had come to apologise for her imprudent behaviour.

Finally, Antonia decided that the best approach was simply to wait and to see what happened. After all, what was the point in fretting? If the Earl did not appear, then all of her worrying would have been for nought. And if he did…?

Well, as Catherine had said, she would just have to take her chances when the time came. And so, gathering her skirts in one hand, and her whip in the other, Antonia prepared to mount—and to boldly meet whatever Fate held in store for her.

The stables at Ashdean were located well behind the main body of the house. They were accessible only by the road which ran alongside it, or by a path which meandered through the heavily wooded area to the south of it. It was a path which had been cut there years ago, no doubt by neighbouring children who had travelled back and forth between the houses in an effort not to be seen by their elders.

It was this very path which Antonia chose that day, preferring to avoid the main part of the house altogether. She had travelled it many times, and had often found solace in the lush greenery, and its abundance of wild flowers and rich, verdant grass.

Coming to the end of the path, Antonia broke cover about a hundred and fifty feet behind the paddock area, and then quickly headed her mare in the direction of a large clump of trees about forty feet to the left of it. There, her presence concealed by the overhanging branches, Antonia turned her attention to the grassy paddock where Lady Clara was already seated atop her sturdy little Welsh Pony, Teddy, and walking him around the ring. A man was standing in the centre of the paddock. Mr Bingham, Lord Carlyle's steward, leaned against the fence, quietly watching the performance.

The Earl of Carlyle, Antonia noticed with relief, was nowhere in sight.

The man in the centre of the ring was tall and thin, and reasonably well dressed, Antonia noted. He called out a series of instructions to the little girl as she circled, and for the most part, seemed quite competent in the way he conducted himself. But there was something in the tone of his voice that Antonia could not bring herself to like—a feeling evidently shared by Lady Clara. Even at this distance, Antonia could sense the tension in the little girl's body. Her arms and legs were as stiff as pokers. So much so that, if she were to tumble from the pony's back now, Antonia knew that she would hurt herself.

The gentleman also seemed to be having trouble getting Clara to do what he wanted. Antonia was not able to hear exactly what he was saying, but it was clear from the inflection in his voice that he was not pleased. And when he suddenly raised his voice and shouted at her, Clara screwed up her face and burst into tears.

'Right, thank you, Mr Huddlesworth, that will be all,' Mr Bingham said abruptly. His mouth was tight as he vaulted over the low fence and made his way to the little girl's side. 'There, there, Lady Clara, there's no need to cry.' He pulled a large white handkerchief from his pocket and gently dried the child's tears. 'You don't have to ride any more.' Stuffing the handkerchief back in his pocket, he gently lifted Clara out of the saddle. 'Why don't you go and play with Bartholomew while I have a word with Mr Huddlesworth?'

In spite of the tears rolling down her cheeks, the child's huge blue eyes suddenly brightened, and without a word, she ran off to find her puppy, obviously content to leave the irascible pony where he was.

Antonia did not need to hear what the steward was saying to know that he was not pleased with the gentleman's performance. It was apparent from Mr Huddlesworth's posture that he was not being complimented. Nor should he have been, Antonia reflected dimly. The man obviously knew nothing about the instruction of young children. His methods might have worked on older girls, or on boys who were easier to bully, but it certainly wasn't the technique to use on a six-year-old girl who was just getting started.

Fortunately, it seemed that the steward was of the same opinion. After a few minutes more, Mr Huddlesworth turned and left the paddock, his drooping shoulders indicative of his lack of success.

Now, it was her turn.

Taking a deep breath, Antonia gathered the reins in her gloved hands. After casting her eyes about one last time for a glimpse of Lord Carlyle, she lightly flicked the crop against the mare's withers and urged her forward. Once clear of the trees, she pushed Foxfire into an easy canter and made directly for the man who was still standing at the edge of the paddock.

The steward, having turned at the sound of a horse approaching and assuming it to be Mr Davlin, stopped short at the sight of a lovely young woman riding towards him. When he saw who it was, he smiled and respectfully tipped his cap. 'Afternoon, Miss Hadley. Can I help you?'

'I certainly hope so, Mr Bingham. I—'

'Toni!'

The childlike cry of delight rang out before Antonia had a chance to say more, and it caused Mr Bingham to turn around in confusion. 'Tony?'

'Toni's here, Paddy!' Lady Clara cried. She flew down the field towards them with the spaniel yipping noisily at her heels. 'Toni's here.' She came to an abrupt halt next to the steward and then stood gazing up at the lady on the dapple grey mare with an expression of adoration. 'Toni!'

Mr Bingham's expression was considerably more guarded. 'Tony?'

'It's…Antonia, actually,' Antonia stammered, colouring a little. 'And the reason I have come is to see you about the position of…riding master to Lady Clara.'

The steward's eyes narrowed fractionally. 'There must be some mistake, miss. I was expecting a *Mr* Tony Davlin.'

Knowing it was too late to back out now, Antonia offered him a tentative smile. 'Yes, I know. But as strange as this may sound, Mr Bingham, I *am*…Tony Davlin.'

It was quite clear that this was not the explanation Paddy Bingham had been expecting. He took off his cap again and scratched his head until Antonia felt sure he was in danger of rubbing a hole in it. 'Well, I'll be dam—that is, would you mind telling me what this is all about, miss?'

'Yes, I certainly owe you that.' Antonia unhooked her leg from around the crutch and, placing her hand in the one Mr Bingham offered, gracefully slid down from the saddle. After bending to give Lady Clara an affectionate hug, she straightened again, and then looked into the steward's face. 'I think perhaps I should start at the beginning.'

'I think that might be a good idea,' Mr Bingham agreed carefully. 'Shall we take a walk?'

'Before we do, might I ask if…Lord Carlyle is… likely to come down?' Antonia enquired anxiously.

Mr Bingham shook his head. 'His lordship is not at

home this afternoon, miss. I doubt he'll be back before dark.'

More relieved than she cared to admit, Antonia nodded and fell into step beside him. 'Well, you see, Mr Bingham, it all started last Christmas, when I met Lady Clara at the children's party at the vicarage…'

By the time Antonia had finished explaining the situation to Mr Bingham, they had walked fully twice around the ring. The steward had not made any interruption and Antonia had been able to relay her story in a clear and concise manner. At its conclusion, however, she paused and turned to regard the Earl's steward with an expression that was decidedly apprehensive. 'So you see, Mr Bingham, it was not my intention to deceive anyone. I merely wanted an opportunity to speak with you about teaching Lady Clara to ride, and I felt quite sure you would not have entertained a letter from a Miss Antonia Hadley.'

'You're right about that, miss, I wouldn't,' Mr Bingham agreed ruefully. 'Nor do I know that I should even be talking to you about it now. I'm sure I don't have to tell you the reasons why.'

'No, I can appreciate your concerns,' Antonia was quick to assure him. 'But is not the point of this exercise to find someone who has the skills and temperament necessary to teach Lady Clara how to ride?'

'Well, yes, but…'

'And were you impressed with the gentleman you just saw?'

Mr Bingham sniffed disparagingly. 'Not a bit, but…'

'Then will you not at least allow me to *show* you what I can do?' Antonia implored. 'I am a very good rider, Mr Bingham. I have studied with Captain Fozard in

London, and I know that I have the skills to teach Lady Clara how to ride. She likes me, you see. More importantly, she trusts me, and you and I both know how important that is if she is to learn to ride well.'

Antonia glanced towards the little girl who was, even now, giving the pony a wide berth. 'Look there, Mr Bingham. Lady Clara is already afraid of her pony and, if she does not learn to overcome that fear, she may never enjoy riding. That is why she needs to have trust in the person who is going to teach her. She needs to know that she will not be asked to do anything that she is not capable of doing or ready to undertake. And by trusting me, Clara knows that I will not push her.'

'That's all very well, miss, but—'

'Oh, please, Mr Bingham, please say that you will give me a chance. At least let me show you what I can do. Then, if you are still in doubt as to my capabilities, I shall leave and not bother you again. What do you say?'

Mr Bingham, who was nothing if not fair, found himself in a definite quandary. Hiring a lady definitely went against the grain. But if Mr Huddlesworth was, by Bingham's own admission, the best *man* that he could find for the job, did he not owe it to the young lady *and* to himself to see what she could do?

'Lady Clara,' Mr Bingham called. 'Come here a moment, will you, sweetheart?'

Obediently, Clara rose from the grass where she was playing with the brown and white spaniel and hurried to his side. 'Yes, Paddy?'

Slowly, the steward bent down and smiled into the little girl's eyes. 'Now, my little cock sparrow, how would you like Miss…that is, Toni, to take you around the ring on Teddy again?'

In spite of his reassuring voice, Lady Clara glanced
at the pony with a dubious eye. 'I don't think Teddy
likes me, Paddy,' she replied in a small voice. 'He…put
his ears back and pulled the reins away. And then the
man shouted at me.'

'I know,' Mr Bingham said with infinite kindness, 'but
Teddy's fine now, and Mr Huddlesworth is gone.'

'And you know that I am not going to shout at you,
don't you, Clara?' Antonia said gently.

Lady Clara looked up into Antonia's familiar face,
and smiled brightly. 'Yes.'

'Good. Then will you try riding Teddy one more time,
just for me?'

Lady Clara glanced at her pony again, but this time
cautiously nodded her agreement.

Antonia didn't even attempt to hide her relief. 'That's
my girl.'

Mr Bingham resumed his place at the rail while
Antonia led Lady Clara back into the paddock and across
to where the pony stood peacefully grazing. She took up
the reins, but instead of placing the little girl directly on
the pony's back as Mr Huddlesworth had done, Antonia
put the reins in Lady Clara's hands and encouraged her
to lead the pony around the ring, talking to him all the
while. Antonia herself stood at the other side of the
pony's head, just in case it became necessary to quickly
take hold of the bridle.

As it turned out, it was not necessary, because Teddy
behaved like a perfect gentleman. He walked quietly between them, never once tossing his head or pawing at
the ground, until gradually, Antonia saw the look of tension in the little girl's face begin to disappear. She even
started to smile as she realised that the pony was not

going to hurt her, and fed him a carrot which magically appeared from the depths of Antonia's pocket.

In fact, it was not until Antonia felt completely sure that Lady Clara was comfortable at being so close to the pony, that she finally stopped and lifted the child on to its back, settling her gently into the saddle.

By the end of the demonstration, Mr Bingham took off his hat and scratched his head again. 'Well, I'll give you your due, miss. There's no doubt in my mind that you're the one to teach Lady Clara to ride,' he acknowledged as Antonia and Clara walked towards him. 'But I have to warn you, I don't know how the Earl is going to take to this.'

'I know that, Mr Bingham, but does the Earl…have to find out?' Antonia inquired, embarking on what she knew would be the most difficult part of her plan.

Mr Bingham glanced at her sideways. 'Beg pardon, miss, but what exactly are you suggesting?'

Antonia quickly bent down. 'Clara, why don't you walk Teddy around the ring while I talk to Mr Bingham? That way he can cool down a little before we put him back in the stable.'

Sweetly obedient, Clara did as she was asked. As soon as she was out of hearing distance, Antonia turned back to face the steward. 'Mr Bingham, how would it be if you were simply to tell Lord Carlyle that you had hired…Tony Davlin, and leave it at that? You would not be telling him a lie because it is my name—in a manner of speaking. And Lady Clara will confirm it if he asks, though hopefully not with any details. You see how she already calls me Toni.'

'I see that all right, miss, but it's not quite that simple,' Mr Bingham said. 'What happens when his lordship asks to see you? How am I going to explain that *Mr* Tony Davlin is actually a *Miss?*'

'Oh, come now, Mr Bingham. Do you really think the Earl of Carlyle is going to trouble himself over meeting his daughter's new riding master?' Antonia said, trying to make it sound totally implausible. 'I am quite sure that, on the few occasions when the Earl *is* here, he is far more concerned with the business of the estate, or with spending time with his daughter than he is with meeting new servants. And when you consider the infrequency of his visits, is he not far more likely to *cancel* Lady Clara's riding lessons altogether than to encourage them?'

'And what if he doesn't cancel them, miss?' Mr Bingham persisted, having more insight into the Earl's mercurial personality than this young lady ever would. 'What if the Earl not only wishes Lady Clara to continue with her lessons, but insists on coming down to watch?'

'Ah, now that is a problem, Mr Bingham,' Antonia admitted, 'and one with which I am going to need your help. It may be necessary to…vary the timing of Lady Clara's lessons, if you catch my meaning.'

'I'm not sure that I do, miss.'

'Well, the Earl is hardly going to spend all of his time waiting for me to come and give Lady Clara her riding lesson,' Antonia said, 'therefore, if you can keep me apprised of his timetable, and we can schedule Lady Clara's lessons at a time when you *know* he is going to be away, Lord Carlyle and I need never actually…meet.'

'I see. And if he asks to see you at some other time of the day?'

'You shall have to tell him that I have secured…other employment which occupies the remainder of my time,' Antonia said, rapidly thinking it through. 'You can tell him that…I am not available to meet with him at any other time. I am quite sure that he will accept that. And besides, if the Earl knows that *you* are satisfied with my work, surely there will be no need for me to meet with him personally. After all, I shall be nothing more than a paid employee in the Earl's household.'

Mr Bingham winced sharply. *That* nearly made him call the whole thing off then and there. It was madness to think that this scheme could work. There were just too many holes in the fabric of the deception.

'There's one other thing you don't seem to have taken into consideration, miss,' Mr Bingham said, the grooves in his forehead deepening.

'Oh?'

'What if Lord Carlyle happens to pass by when you're giving Lady Clara a lesson? It won't take him long to realise that you're no gentleman.'

Antonia nibbled at her bottom lip. As much as she hated to admit it, this time Mr Bingham had a valid point. What good would all of their planning do if all Lord Carlyle had to do was catch sight of her? She had already attempted to disguise her looks by wearing a boy's clothing, and it hadn't worked. Catherine had told her as much—

Abruptly, Antonia stopped. Yes, Catherine had told her that the disguise would not work. But she had also said that it *could* work, if she was *only to be seen from a distance!*

'I think I can take care of the matter of my appearance, Mr Bingham,' Antonia said slowly, 'and since I can ride side saddle or astride equally well, my presentation on horseback should not prove to be an obstacle either for the brief period of time required. After all, we both know that the Earl seldom spends more than two

or three days here, and I feel confident that we can foo—
that is, make…alternative arrangements for the brief
time necessary. What do you think?'

Mr Bingham sighed. 'I think I must be dicked in the
nob for even *thinking* this will work. If the Earl should
stumble on to any of this, you'll likely be dismissed, and
me right after. I suggest you be very careful that no one,
and I do mean *no one,* hears about it.'

'I shan't tell a soul, Mr Bingham,' Antonia promised.
'Other than my father, of course. And my dearest friend,
Miss Catherine Shand.'

Mr Bingham looked pained. 'That's two more than I
was hoping for. Do you absolutely have to tell them?'

Antonia blushed. 'I am afraid they already know. I
could not proceed without my father's consent, and it
was Miss Shand's idea to give me the fictitious address.
I do, of course, live with my father at Buntings Hill.'

Mr Bingham shook his head again. 'This will never
work. Mark my words, it'll never work. I'll be looking
for a new position, and with not a reference to be had.'

'Now, Paddy, of course it will work,' Antonia said,
not sure why she suddenly felt compelled to address him
by his Christian name. 'With my planning, and your in-
valuable help, I do not see how it can fail. And you have
to believe me when I say that we are not doing this to
deceive the Earl. We are doing it to help Lady Clara.
Oh, please say that you will help me, Paddy,' Antonia
said, bringing all of her persuasive powers to bear. 'Are
we in this together?'

She turned her most dazzling smile on the Earl's steward and, hardened campaigner though he was, Paddy
Bingham was lost. He had never been the recipient of
female cajolery before and, coming now as it did from

the beautiful and sweet Antonia Hadley, he didn't stand a chance.

'We are, though Lord knows I must be cork-brained for saying so. All right, we'll give it a try, miss. Can you be here at quarter past ten next Monday morning?'

Antonia thought for a moment, and then nodded. 'Yes, I'm sure I can be but...why are you waiting a week before we start?'

'Because the Earl doesn't usually spend more than a few days in the country, and I want to make sure he's gone before you conduct your first lesson.'

Antonia nodded happily. 'All right. Then quarter past ten next Monday it is. Thank you, Paddy. Thank you very much!'

'Don't be thanking me just yet, miss. If his lordship should chance to find out about this, there'll be the very devil to pay,' Mr Bingham said ominously. 'And don't say that I didn't warn you!'

As it turned out, Sebastian *was* still in Upper Tipping on Friday, though his reluctance to leave was due more to the presence of the beautiful Miss Antonia Hadley than it was to any matters of business. He was aware of a growing feeling of curiosity about the young woman he had chanced to meet in town, and had been unable to forget the striking loveliness of her face.

He was also hopeful that he would be able to breach the wall of reserve which seemed to have sprung up between them. It had been clear from the tone of her voice that he had offended her by his careless remark about her mother, and he truly wished that he had known of the situation beforehand so that he might have avoided it. But Sebastian refused to believe that Miss Hadley would continue to hold a grudge against him. If he took pains to call upon her and her father, and to make his apologies in a sincere and meaningful way, surely she would relent. He did not like to think that the lady held him in any personal dislike. They had not known each other long enough for that kind of enmity.

The ride to Buntings Hill was not a long one, but Sebastian's thoughts were suitably occupied the entire way there. There were a number of matters which he needed to review in his mind: the cost of improvements to several of the older tenant cottages, the wisdom of clearing another field for the purposes of increased crop production and, of less importance, the commencement of Clara's riding lessons with Mr Tony Davlin.

Bingham had informed him of his decision with regard to the riding master that morning, in fact. He had said that, after watching both of the applicants at work, there had been no doubt in his mind that Davlin was the one more suited to the post. It seemed that Lady Clara too preferred Mr Davlin to the other gentleman, and that they were already on a first-name basis.

Sebastian had been satisfied with his steward's decision, though he had been somewhat surprised at the vagueness with which Bingham had responded to his questions regarding Mr Davlin. It seemed, for example, that Clara's lessons were not to be held at a fixed time each day, but that they would, out of necessity, fluctuate, given that Mr Davlin had suddenly secured other employment.

When questioned as to the nature of this *other* employment, however, Bingham had been rather vague, saying that he had not thought to ask. He was, however, quick to assure the Earl that Davlin was both a conscientious and likeable person, and one whom Bingham felt sure would not disappoint them in any way.

Now, as Sebastian made his way up the long, tree-lined drive leading to Buntings Hill, he could not help but wonder at his steward's peculiar behaviour that morning. It was almost as though he had not wished to discuss the matter. Indeed, when the conversation had ended, Bingham had moved on to the next subject with surprising alacrity.

Still, every man was entitled to his moments, Sebastian conceded. Even the unflappable Paddy Bingham.

Antonia was in the music room when Sebastian arrived to pay his first social call. He was shown into the drawing room upon his arrival, but when he heard the strains of a well-loved sonata, he decided to go in search of the source, suspecting it might be Antonia.

He found her at the instrument soon after, looking absolutely charming in a gown of pale pink muslin, into the bodice of which was tucked a dainty lace fissu. Her gleaming hair was styled in a loose cluster of curls around her face and, as she played, an enchanting smile hovered about her lips.

Sebastian stood in the doorway of the room and silently watched her play. This was no stumbling miss who dutifully learned her music so that she might entertain at *musicales*. This was a truly gifted young woman who played for the sheer pleasure of making music. Her fingers danced nimbly over the keys, never stumbling once as she played the complicated piece completely from memory. It was not until the sonata came to an end and Antonia's fingers stilled, that he finally made his presence known. 'Exceptional, Miss

Hadley,' Sebastian said softly. 'You do the instrument proud.'

Antonia spun around on the bench and gasped. 'Lord Carlyle!' Her cheeks flushed crimson as she quickly got to her feet. 'My lord, forgive me, I had…no idea that you were standing…just there.'

'The fault for which is mine entirely,' Sebastian said smoothly. 'In truth, I did not wish to disturb you for fear that you would not finish the piece. You play exceedingly well, Miss Hadley.'

'Th-thank you,' Antonia said, struggling to regain her composure. 'It is…kind of you to say so, though I am sure that you have heard…far better from the many accomplished ladies in London.'

'In point of fact, I have heard none better,' Sebastian told her. 'You combine a learned skill with a true love of music. That in itself is a rare combination. You must bring a great deal of pleasure to your family and friends.'

'She does indeed, Lord Carlyle, though I would warn you not to compliment her too grandly,' Mr Hadley said upon entering the room. 'I have told my daughter that too much flattery turns the head.' He walked across the carpet to stand in front of their visitor, and bowed. 'We are honoured by your visit, my lord.'

Sebastian inclined his head apologetically. 'Pray forgive my not remaining in the drawing room to greet you, Mr Hadley. When I heard the music, I felt compelled to go in search of it.'

'No apology is necessary; it would not be the first time that Antonia has drawn a crowd.' Mr Hadley's pride and affection for his daughter was evident. 'She is a gifted performer, for all her protestations to the contrary.'

Relieved by her father's arrival, though somewhat embarrassed by his flattery, Antonia moved away from the instrument. 'Now, Papa, you know that it is *you* who are guilty of complimenting me too much. You embarrass me when we are in public by insisting that I play far more than I should, thereby preventing the other ladies from exhibiting their own talents.'

'Had the other ladies any talents which deserved exhibiting, I would be the first to encourage them to do so, my dear,' Mr Hadley told her with a smile. 'But I think I speak the truth when I say that I have yet to hear anyone who is more accomplished than you.'

'I hope I will have the opportunity of adding my compliments to your father's when we are next at a gathering together, Miss Hadley,' Sebastian said. 'I would not wish him to be accused of being your sole devotee.'

He was amused to see that his compliment did nothing to diminish the colour in those lovely cheeks. 'Perhaps we should…adjourn to the drawing room,' Antonia said quickly.

Sebastian inclined his head, and stepped aside to allow Antonia to take the lead. He fell into step beside her father and enjoyed an amiable conversation relating to parliamentary matters and affairs of the church. Once in the cheery parlour, however, he kept the topics more general so as to include Antonia in the discussions.

'Mr Hadley, may I say how very sorry I was to hear about your wife,' Sebastian said as he sank into the wing chair beside the fireplace. 'I truly regret that I was not made aware of her passing until my return a few days ago.'

'It is not to be expected that you would, sir,' said Mr Hadley. 'London is a long way from Upper Tipping in more ways than just distance. But I thank you for the sentiments none the less.'

Aware that her father had echoed her own words,

though in a much more charitable way, Antonia went to preside over the tea things which the servant had just brought in. 'Will you have tea, Lord Carlyle, or would you prefer a glass of wine? I believe Papa has a very fine Madeira which you might enjoy.'

'Thank you, Miss Hadley, but tea will be fine. As you know, I am engaged to dine this evening and I do not think it would do for me to arrive a trifle bosky. I fear I may be feeling that way when I leave, though *not* as a result of anything I might have had to drink,' he said ruefully.

Antonia intercepted her father's quizzical gaze and hastened to explain. 'Lord Carlyle has been invited to dine with Lady Dalrymple this evening, Papa.'

'Lady Dalrymple? Well, in that case, perhaps you *had* best have something stronger,' Mr Hadley advised. 'It will no doubt help you get through an evening spent in the company of Lady Dalrymple and her doleful daughters.'

Antonia gasped. 'Papa, really! Eugenie and Caroline are very…pleasant girls.'

'Yes, I am sure they are, my dear and, in all fairness, Lady Dalrymple does put on an excellent table. Unfortunately, I suspect that a good deal more than just the roast will be sliced up at her table tonight.'

Lord Carlyle's quickly smothered cough sounded suspiciously like a laugh, but there was no hint of humour on his face as he cleared his throat and accepted the cup that Antonia held out to him.

'Papa, did you not caution me just the other day to be mindful of what I said about others?' she reminded him.

'Yes, my dear, I did. And perhaps by informing Lord Carlyle of Lady Dalrymple's propensity towards gossip,

I am guilty of telling tales out of school,' Mr Hadley admitted. 'But you know as well as I do that before the end of the evening, she will have methodically cut up every person she knows—and even a few that she doesn't.'

'Well, yes I know, but it is not the thing to—'

'Miss Hadley, please,' Sebastian interrupted with a laugh, 'there is absolutely no need to reprimand your father on my account. With everything we say so couched in flowery language, it is often difficult to know what is fact and what is not. For myself, I find it refreshing to hear someone speak the truth so openly.'

Suitably absolved, Mr Hadley sat back in his chair and smiled. 'Thank you, Lord Carlyle. You will find that I have little time for hypocrisy, or for those who practise it. However, I will venture away from the topic before my daughter has cause to reprimand me again. But before I do, perhaps you would tell me how Lady Dalrymple managed to secure you to dine so quickly. From what I understand, you have not been in Upper Tipping above a few days.'

Sebastian grimaced in good humour. 'The lady chanced to be in town the very afternoon I arrived. She extended the invitation at that time.'

'Ah. Well, I suppose you cannot fault her for being prompt. With two daughters to settle in marriage, she can hardly afford to be otherwise. Ah, thank you, my dear, nothing like tea to soothe the soul,' Mr Hadley said, accepting the cup his daughter held out to him. 'Well, Lord Carlyle, what are your plans now? Do you intend to stay long in Upper Tipping?'

'To be honest, I have not yet decided, Mr Hadley,' Sebastian admitted. 'I originally came with the intention of spending no more than a few days, but now that I am here, I find there are some problems which require my attention.'

'Oh? Matters concerning the estate?'

'No. Matters concerning…my daughter.'

Antonia's eyes flew up to his. 'Is Lady Clara…not well?'

'On the contrary, she seems to be a healthy enough little thing,' Sebastian said slowly. 'But there is…a reticence in her manner which I find disturbing. I have yet to hear her speak more than ten words in my presence, and when I ask her what she might like to do, I am informed that she would rather stay in the garden and play with her puppy.'

Antonia picked up the plate of biscuits and held it out to him. 'Were you expecting more?'

'I was hoping that she would be more agreeable, yes. And certainly more outgoing.'

Antonia smiled as she set the plate back down. 'Perhaps if you took the time to *know* your daughter better, you would not find her behaviour so… incomprehensible.'

Mr Hadley cleared his throat. 'Antonia, I think that perhaps this is not the time to—'

'No, that is quite all right, Mr Hadley, I am well aware that your daughter is right,' Sebastian said. 'I do not know my daughter well, nor do I pretend to. Unlike others, my life has not lent itself to domestic tranquillity and I have not spent much time with Clara. However, I am hoping that, with time, the problem will resolve itself. Clara seems a pleasant enough child, and I am sure that, with the proper guidance, her more…reclusive tendencies can be eradicated.'

Antonia stiffened. 'My lord, I am surprised that you find your daughter's behaviour so inexplicable. I would have thought that, given the amount of time you spend with her, it is only natural that she would be reserved in your company. You may be her father, but in truth, you are little more than a stranger to her.'

For the first time, Sebastian realised that it wasn't reserve he heard in Miss Hadley's voice, but annoyance. 'I am well aware of that, Miss Hadley, along with the fact that I have not been an ideal father. But I am hardly alone in that respect. Very few gentlemen of my acquaintance having anything to do with the upbringing of their children.'

'And that makes it right?'

'I wonder, my lord,' Mr Hadley said hastily, 'if all Clara needs is a little more time spent in the company of children her own age. In my experience, children who are constantly in the company of adults often become reserved, and perhaps a touch uncommunicative. But when they are surrounded by other children, and are free to laugh and play as children will, there is often a remarkable change in their behaviour. Indeed, Antonia has told me that the Lady Clara can be very chatty on occasion.'

Antonia shot her father a quelling glance—which Sebastian intercepted. 'Really? Am I to understand that you have spent considerable time in my daughter's presence, Miss Hadley?'

'I would not say…considerable time,' Antonia replied, looking decidedly uncomfortable with the direction the conversation had suddenly taken. 'We met at the…children's Christmas party at the church last year. Lady Clara came with her governess. She seemed a little shy in the company of the other children, so I endeavoured to spend some time alone with her.'

'I see. And were you successful in getting her to play with the other children?'

'Eventually. As you say, Lady Clara is a pleasant child and, when left to their own devices, children will naturally draw together. All Lady Clara needed was a gentle…push.'

Sebastian was silent for a moment. Then, suddenly, something akin to recognition flashed in the depths of his eyes. 'Good Lord, why did I not realise it before. You must be Toni.'

Antonia went deathly white. 'T-Toni?'

'Yes. Presumably short for Antonia. Clara has mentioned that name several times of late, and I thought she was referring to her new riding master. Now I realise that she must have been talking about *you* all along.'

Antonia swallowed hard, wishing with all her heart that this dreadful interlude was at an end. She hadn't missed the look on her father's face when Lord Carlyle had mentioned the new riding master, and she wished now that she had told him of her success in securing the position. She went to reach for the teapot—only to think better of it when she saw how badly her hands were shaking. 'It is…possible, I suppose.'

'This…riding master you have hired,' Mr Hadley enquired casually—and without looking at his daughter. 'Wouldn't be a local man, would he?'

'I believe he is, Mr Hadley. My steward did tell me his name, but I'm dashed if I can remember it.'

'But you did say that his first name was…Tony.'

'Yes, that much I remember. Why? Do you know the gentleman?'

Mr Hadley shook his head as he reached for a scone. 'Can't say that I do, my lord. Just curious.' He finally glanced at his daughter and smiled. 'After all, how many riding masters can there be in Upper Tipping with the first name of…Tony?'

Lord Carlyle stayed for the requisite length of time. At the end of twenty minutes, he rose to take his leave, thanking Mr Hadley for his hospitality, and assuring them both that he would call again in the near future.

Antonia escorted him as far as the front hall. What little conversation they exchanged was polite, but reserved. After their discussion in the drawing room, Antonia found that she was not predisposed to chatter in a particularly amiable fashion.

'Thank you for receiving me, Miss Hadley. I enjoyed the opportunity of speaking with you and your father.'

'Thank you, Lord Carlyle. I know that my…father has been most anxious to renew the acquaintance.'

Carlyle smiled cordially as he pulled on his gloves. 'Well, I must make haste. Half past five will be upon me before I know it.'

Briefly taking pity on his plight, Antonia offered him a perfunctory smile. 'Take heart, Lord Carlyle. Lady Dalrymple is not as bad as my father would have you believe. And she does have one of the finest chefs in the county.'

'Then it is to be hoped that the evening will not be a complete loss,' he said, 'for the afternoon has been a most enjoyable forerunner to it. Good afternoon, Miss Hadley.'

Antonia bid him a cool farewell and then returned to the drawing room. Not surprisingly, her father was waiting for her. 'Well, I think that went rather well. Don't you, my dear?'

'Hmm?' Antonia looked up to see an amused expression on her father's face, and forced a smile to her lips. 'Yes, Papa, I believe it did.'

'Quite a surprise, though, learning that Lord Carlyle had already hired someone to teach his daughter how to ride, and that he should have the same first name as you. Rather a coincidence that, don't you think?'

Antonia momentarily weighed the merits of telling her father that she had decided against applying for the position—and then discarded it as utter folly. Her father knew her better than anyone—and after being kind enough to let her try for the position, Antonia knew that the very least she could do was to be honest about it with him in return. 'Actually, it is not a coincidence at all, Papa.'

'Oh?'

Antonia shook her head. 'No.'

'Funny, I thought it might not be,' Mr Hadley said. 'Lord Carlyle's Tony, and my Toni, are one and the same, aren't they, my dear?'

Guilt-ridden, Antonia nodded unhappily. 'Forgive me, Papa. It was not my intention to deceive you. And I was going to tell you that I had secured the position, but I was…waiting for the right time. You are not angry with me, are you?'

'Angry? No, child, I could never be angry with you. I always assume you have the most worthy of reasons for whatever you do. But what of Lord Carlyle? I take it that *he* is not aware that he has just hired my daughter to work for him.'

Antonia bit her lip. 'No. I was interviewed by his steward, Mr Bingham. And he has been ever so helpful, Papa. He has agreed not to tell Lord Carlyle the truth of my identity.'

'Not tell him?' Mr Hadley's smile quickly dissolved

into a frown. 'That does not sound like a very trustworthy fellow to me, my dear. I know that I should be very annoyed if I discovered that someone in my employ was lying to me.'

'Oh, but he is not lying, Papa. At least, not outright. Mr Bingham only refers to me as Toni, so he doesn't actually say whether I am a man or a woman. And I did have to ride and show him that I could work better with Lady Clara than the other candidate. Mr Huddlesworth had the poor child in tears within moments.'

'And what name did *you* use, since it obviously was not Hadley?'

Antonia resumed her chair by the window. 'The only other name I could think of. Davlin.'

'Davlin!' Mr Hadley echoed. 'Good Lord, Antonia, did it never occur to you that Lord Carlyle might have recognised that name as easily as your own?'

'No. Why would he have? Mama was not from Kent.'

'No, her roots were closer to London—which is precisely why I thought Lord Carlyle might have recognised it. Your grandfather was Baron Davlin which, as you know, is one of the reasons your aunt was so dead set against Elizabeth marrying me. She always assured your mother that she could have done better, far better than to marry a penniless teacher.'

'Well, I do not think she could have done *any* better,' Antonia said staunchly, 'because there is no one *I* would rather have as my father. But even if Lord Carlyle were to recognise the name, he would have no reason to connect it with the fictitious Mr Tony Davlin.'

'I hope you are right, my dear,' Mr Hadley said, obviously not as confident about the matter as she was. 'Carlyle will be none too happy when he discovers that he has been deceived.'

Uncomfortably reminded of Catherine's words, Antonia lifted her chin. 'I do not intend that he shall find out, Papa. Mr Bingham and I will be very circumspect in our dealings with him. And in all truth, it should not be all that difficult to make it work. You heard Lord Carlyle say that he was not planning to remain in Upper Tipping for any length of time, and if I can stay out of his way while he is here, I can conduct Lady Clara's riding lessons unhampered. I really do not see there being anything deceitful in that!'

Chapter Four

It was well known by Antonia and her father, that if Lady Farrington was of a mind to pay them one of her all-too-frequent visits, it would likely be on a Sunday when she could be reasonably assured of finding both her brother-in-law and her niece at home. Hence, when Abbott showed the redoubtable lady into the main parlour at Buntings Hill the following Sunday afternoon, Antonia was not overly surprised. But neither was she particularly pleased. Lady Farrington had never been one of her favourite relatives. In Antonia's mind, she was an outspoken and opinionated woman whose sharp tongue had caused them grief on more than one occasion.

Mindful of her duty, however, if not of her own pleasure, Antonia bid her aunt take a comfortable chair and set out to be as charming as possible.

'You look well, aunt Ophelia,' she remarked kindly.

'Stuff and nonsense! I have been abed with megrims this past three days. I've circles under my eyes, cramps in my hands, and at times I can scarce see straight, the pain is so bad. Still, I always say that one must get out and visit one's relations, no matter how it causes one to suffer.' Lady Farrington glanced at her niece disparagingly. 'Family ties are the ties that bind, Antonia. You would do well to remember that.'

'Yes, aunt Ophelia.'

'Speaking of family ties, where is that father of yours?' Lady Farrington's beady eyes darted about the room as if to find Mr Hadley hiding behind a piece of furniture. 'I vow, the man avoids me. How does he expect to resume his place in Society if he does not socialise? He should be out meeting marriageable ladies, not rusticating here in the country. Gracious, does the man plan on mourning Elizabeth for the rest of his life?'

Antonia stiffened. It was an insensitive remark and, in spite of her good intentions, her smile slipped just a little. 'My father does socialise, aunt Ophelia, though not as frequently as you might think appropriate.'

'Humph!' Lady Farrington snorted again. 'And you, young lady, are just as bad. You will never find a husband stuck out here in the depths of the country. You should be in London, moving in the circles that would bring you into contact with the right type of gentlemen. That is what your mother would have wished for you. Had she not gone against my wishes and married beneath her, that is no doubt where you would already be!'

Antonia signalled Abbott with a brief nod. 'I have all the company I require, aunt. My days are full and I am content.'

'Content!' Lady Farrington spat out. 'Lord love us, child, how can you be content when you spend your days visiting sick old women, and handing out sweets at the local vicarage parties. Oh, yes, do not think for one moment that I do not know what you are up to,' Lady Farrington said when she saw Antonia's look of surprise. 'I keep a very close watch on my family. After all, there is a small matter of your dowry with which I must concern myself. A dowry which, as you well know, I would be happy to release if I felt you responsible enough to look after it.'

'Can I interest you in some tea, aunt Ophelia?' Antonia offered as Abbott brought in the tray and set it next to her. 'And perhaps some of Mrs Grenfall's freshly baked scones?'

'Are you being impertinent, girl?' Lady Farrington barked. 'I was speaking to you about matters of importance!'

Antonia affected a look of mild surprise. 'I am well aware of that, aunt, and no, I was not being impertinent. But since we both know that your idea of responsible means my being married, I really did not see that there was any point in continuing the conversation. As I have told you before, I am perfectly content here at Buntings. I may go to London for a Season and if I am fortunate enough to fall in love with a gentleman who is inclined to do the same, perhaps I shall marry him. If I do not, I shall return here at the conclusion of it and feel none the worse for still being single.'

Lady Farrington's eyes narrowed critically, while her lips puckered in the censorious grimace Antonia knew so well. 'That, young lady, is a frightfully misplaced notion, and one you would do well to forget! Your mother trained you to be a lady, and it is your duty to her and to your family to marry—and marry well, I might add. There are precious few avenues open to a young woman who chooses to remain single.'

'I dare say you are correct, aunt,' Antonia agreed in a manner which only seemed to irritate her aunt more. 'But if that is to be the way of things, I shall endeavour to make the best of it.'

'Then you are a foolish young woman, Antonia. And

I shall tell your father as much at the very first opportunity.'

'Tell her father what, Ophelia?' Mr Hadley remarked as he strolled into the room.

Lady Farrington glanced up at her brother-in-law and pursed her thin lips even more. 'Well, so nice of you to honour us with your presence, Peter,' she observed testily. 'I thought perhaps you had locked yourself in the library again.'

'What? And miss an opportunity of spending time with my favourite sister-in-law?'

'Sarcasm does not become you, Peter,' Lady Farrington snapped. 'I came here out of the goodness of my heart to see to my poor sister's family and this is all the thanks I get. I have just been telling your daughter that she is impertinent, but after spending a few minutes in your company, I can see where she comes by it. You will have to change your ways if you ever expect to rejoin Society and marry again.'

Antonia glanced at her father anxiously. No one knew better than she how thin was the line that Lady Farrington was treading.

'I appreciate your concern, Ophelia, but I would thank you to keep your opinions to yourself.' Mr Hadley's voice was deceptively quiet. 'Antonia is in no way impertinent, nor do I intend to be told how to act. Or to be bullied into returning to Society.'

'I was not bullying—' Lady Farrington sputtered.

'Of course you were. The same way you bully us every time you come here. I sometimes wonder if that is the only reason you come at all.'

'Well! I have never—!' Lady Farrington gasped.

'In fact, why don't you just stay down at Farrington Grange and mind your own—'

'The Earl of Carlyle, sir!' Abbott announced abruptly.

Antonia blanched, and turned in her chair so quickly that she nearly dropped the cup of tea she was holding. Mr Hadley, aware that he had been about to say something which would surely have destroyed any remaining chance Antonia might have had of seeing her grandmother's bequest, wisely bit back the rest of his sentence and subsided into silence.

But it was Lady Farrington's reaction which was the most comical of all to behold. She stared wide-eyed at the handsome visitor, clearly rendered speechless by the sight of the illustrious Earl of Carlyle calling at the home of her decidedly provincial brother-in-law.

Antonia was the first to regain her composure. 'My lord, what a pleasant…surprise,' she stammered. 'Pray do come and…join us.'

Sebastian smiled urbanely. He was well aware that he had walked in on some kind of a family argument, but aware that it would be equally bad form to leave solely as a result of it, he inclined his head and strolled forward. 'Thank you, Miss Hadley. I hope my arrival has not come at an inopportune moment.'

Aware that his arrival was probably the *only* thing which had prevented the family gathering from deteriorating into a brawl, Antonia offered him a stiff smile. 'Not at all. As our neighbour, you are always… welcome.'

'I am delighted to hear it. While I do not usually drop by unannounced on a Sunday afternoon, I did want to stop and thank you again for that delightful recital the other afternoon. It was truly a pleasure to watch one so lovely play the instrument so beautifully.'

Antonia coloured furiously. 'It is…good of you to say so, my lord.' She turned towards her aunt, aware that the lady's mouth had not closed since Lord Carlyle had walked into the room. 'Are you acquainted with my aunt?'

Sensing that the autocratic older woman was the source of the problem, Sebastian favoured her with one of his most charming smiles. 'I am indeed. Good afternoon, Lady Farrington. It has been some time since I last saw you, though I think it was at Almack's last year. As I recall, you were in conversation with Lady Jersey.'

Lady Farrington—belatedly aware that she had been staring at one of London's most eligible gentlemen— forced a smile to her lips. 'Yes, I remember the evening, Lord Carlyle. Though, to be perfectly honest, I do not recall having seen you there.'

Sebastian inclined his head. ''Tis not surprising. I arrived just before the doors closed at eleven and did not stay much past midnight. And a lady like yourself could hardly be expected to be aware of the comings and goings of all the guests. But I must confess, I am surprised at finding you here in our rustic little village. I had assumed you to be a lady who would prefer the refinements of Town.'

The fact that she was being complimented by such a noted *non pareil* and confidante of the Regent himself was not lost upon Lady Farrington. She relaxed noticeably, verily purring under his masterful verbal stroking. 'I admit I do enjoy what London has to offer, and I feel quite confident in saying that the scope of entertainment to be found in Town is quite unrivalled anywhere else in England. But, upon occasion, I do enjoy slipping away to the pastoral peacefulness of the English countryside. As I was just saying to my brother-in-law, the country is so…delightful at this time of year,' Lady

Farrington lied effortlessly. 'Would you not agree, Lord Carlyle?'

'Indeed, I would.' Sebastian moved forward to take a seat on the settee beside her. 'The country and, with your arrival, the company.'

Antonia's eyes opened wide as she stared at their visitor. Heavens, he was positively fawning on her aunt. It was almost as though she and her father had ceased to exist. She found the entire performance quite repulsive. But then, why would he not behave in such a manner? Antonia reminded herself. Had she not told her father that Lord Carlyle was an arrogant man who preferred the company of the high born? Only witness his behaviour now. He had obviously called upon them this afternoon as a result of some…misguided sense of obligation, but upon discovering a titled lady in the room, had evidently decided to make her the focus of his attention.

'Your niece is a gifted musician, Lady Farrington,' Lord Carlyle said. 'You must be proud to have such an accomplished and delightful young lady in the family.'

Lady Farrington looked momentarily disconcerted at hearing the Earl of Carlyle single her niece out for such unprecedented praise—until she realised that it could be a blessing in disguise. 'Well, yes, of course I am. In fact, I was only just saying to…dear Antonia that she is a credit to her mother, God rest her soul. As such, I have invited her to stay with me when she comes up to London for the Season.'

Antonia caught her breath, astonished that anyone could do such a *volte face*. She knew full well that no such offer had been made, nor was ever likely to be.

'By the same token,' Lady Farrington continued, satisfied that she had control of the conversation once more,

'I was not aware that *you* had removed to the country, Lord Carlyle. I understood that you were intending to spend the next few months in Town.'

'That had been my intention, yes, though I was moved to change my plans at the last moment. My secretary advised me that there were matters which required my attention here and, as I have not seen much of my daughter over the past few months, I thought a visit might be judicious at this time.'

'Ah, yes, of course, dear little Chloe,' Lady Farrington said.

'Clara.'

'Clara, of course.' Lady Farrington coloured. 'I was confusing her with my other niece, Cassandra.'

'Cassiope,' Antonia whispered.

'What's that, girl?'

'Cassiope,' Antonia repeated softly. 'Your other niece's name is Cassiope.'

For her trouble, Antonia was awarded a chilly stare. 'Yes, that was what I meant to say. Cassiope.' After another speaking glance at her niece, Lady Farrington haughtily turned back towards Lord Carlyle. 'Are you planning to sojourn long in the country, my lord?'

'That is difficult to say at the moment, Lady Farrington,' Sebastian replied easily. 'While my business affairs will necessitate my returning to London shortly, I see no reason why I should not be able to remain at Ashdean for another few weeks yet.'

Antonia choked on a mouthful of tea—and abruptly drew three pairs of eyes towards her.

'Is something wrong, Antonia?' Lady Farrington inquired drily.

''N-no, not at all.' Antonia flicked a nervous glance

towards her father. 'I must have swallowed a...crumb. I am...fine now, thank you.'

'Lord Carlyle, pray forgive my manners, but I have been a most remiss host,' Mr Hadley said, suddenly commandeering the conversation. 'What might I offer you in the way of refreshment? There is tea, of course, but perhaps I could interest you in something stronger? I have a very fine claret of which I am particularly proud.'

Struggling to regain her shattered composure, Antonia silently blessed her father for his intervention. With uncharacteristic aplomb, he had managed to turn the conversation away from her, and to keep it away while she came to grips with this new and startling information.

Lord Carlyle was to stay in the country for a few weeks! But...there must be some mistake, surely. Mr Bingham had not mentioned anything to her about the Earl planning a protracted stay. Dear heavens, she had hoped to be able to maintain her deceit for a few days—but for a few weeks?

When Lady Farrington finally rose to take her leave, Antonia breathed a heartfelt sigh of relief. Her aunt's visits were trying at best, but today's visit had been particularly so. Her only consolation was that the woman left in a much better frame of mind than she had arrived in, due in no small measure to the fact that Lord Carlyle insisted upon escorting her all the way out to her carriage before departing himself.

Returning to the parlour after their guests had left, Mr Hadley sank heavily into his favourite chair and sighed. 'Thank goodness that's over. I hate to say it, Antonia, but I find myself coming to like your aunt less and less with every visit. Which is a great shame, given that she is your mother's only sister.'

'I know, Papa,' Antonia said absently. 'But I like to think that she does not mean to be so objectionable.'

'Ah, well, never mind. I suppose I can learn to put up with her visits, as long as they do not become any more frequent.' Mr Hadley levelled a mischievous glance at his daughter. 'Good thing Lord Carlyle arrived when he did.'

Antonia laughed, though the sound was forced, even to her own ears. 'I dare say we should have been in a fine pickle by now if he hadn't.'

'Bless me if we should not,' Mr Hadley agreed. 'Fortunately, he seemed to know exactly what to say to smooth things over. He must have realised that we had been having…words and purposely set out to be as charming to your aunt as anyone could be.'

Antonia's smile cooled. 'Of course. But as I told you before, Lord Carlyle always has time for those of his own social standing.'

Mr Hadley chuckled. 'As the wife of a lowly knight, your aunt hardly moves in the same circles as the Earl of Carlyle, my dear. I think he was merely trying to divert her attention away from us by flattering her in every way possible. And it worked. I haven't seen Ophelia flutter like that since she was a young woman. Lord Carlyle can be quite the charmer when he sets out to be. Do you not think so?'

Antonia fought to keep her expression as non-committal as possible. Her father's logic made sense, but she was still having trouble casting Lord Carlyle in the part of hero. 'No more than most, I shouldn't think.'

Her father's smile widened, but he let the subject drop and said instead, 'Bit of bad luck for you, though, his deciding to stay on in the area. I imagine that will make things a good deal more difficult.'

Reminded of that less-than-welcome piece of news, Antonia sighed. 'It will make matters a great deal more difficult. The more time Lord Carlyle spends here, the greater the risk of exposure. If he were to discover that I am Tony Davlin, I have no doubt that he would turn me away without a second thought.'

'No doubt he would. And with a few words to go along with it. But I wonder, Antonia? Is it the thought of being turned away from this post, or the possibility of incurring Lord Carlyle's displeasure, that bothers you the most?'

Antonia was helpless to stop the colour from rising to her cheeks. 'I can assure you, Papa, the *only* reason I would come to grief over a decision like that would be because it would take away a position I am very pleased to have. I know what you are thinking and I would thank you to stop it. I have no more interest in Lord Carlyle than he has in me. I have already told you, I am not high enough in the instep for the likes of him. Now if you will excuse me, I have some letters to write.'

Mr Hadley watched his daughter march away, with her back ramrod straight and her pretty head held high. The sight made him smile.

'You may say you have no interest in Lord Carlyle, my dear,' he said into the silence, 'but I am not yet convinced that the gentleman has no interest in you!'

At five minutes of ten Monday morning, Antonia reined in her mare and waited for Mr Bingham to appear. She had taken her position under the shelter of the over-hanging trees and, from a distance, looked for all the world like a well-born young gentleman about to embark on a pleasant morning ride. It was not until one looked closer, however, that it became evident that the fine young gentleman was, in fact, a lovely young lady.

And a very nervous one at that.

Antonia had donned the clothes purloined from Catherine's brother and with her friend's help managed to look quite creditable in the part. Catherine had bound Antonia's chest so that there was little evidence of female breasts, while the jacket of fine worsted wool was large enough to disguise the trimness of her waist. Her hair had been tucked up under a jaunty little cap and, around her throat, a colourful neckcloth had been tied to help to fill out the collar of the shirt which was just a shade too large for her.

Indeed, so complete was her disguise that, for a moment, Bingham was not sure that the person approaching on the dapple grey mare was the same one he had interviewed last week. He walked down the hill from the stable, holding Teddy's reins in one hand and Lady Clara's hand in the other, and peered up at Antonia in frank astonishment.

'Well, I'll be—you were right enough when you said you would take care of your appearance, miss,' Bingham said, chuckling. 'That's quite the outfit. If I didn't know better, I'd swear you were a young man myself.'

Antonia laughed, and the rich, seductive sound immediately destroyed any pretence of a masculine presence. 'Thank you, Paddy. I admit to being rather pleased with the results myself. Do you think it will fool the Earl?'

'From a distance, I dare say it might fool your own father.'

Clara, who had been listening to this exchange with

interest, suddenly looked up at Antonia and squealed her delight. 'Toni, it is you. I thought it was a boy!'

'It's me, Clara.' Antonia swung down from the saddle and bent to kiss the soft, apple blushed cheek. 'I am just dressed like this…so that my skirts do not become a hindrance,' she explained quickly.

Fortunately, Clara accepted the explanation with the unquestioning innocence of a child. 'Can I ride now, Toni?' she asked.

Bingham winked his encouragement. 'There you are, miss. Your pupil awaits. I'll leave the two of you to get on with it.'

Before the lesson began, Bingham briefly drew Antonia aside. 'His lordship shouldn't be back much before noon, so if you want to spend a little extra time with Lady Clara, you can. But keep an eye open. When I expect that Lord Carlyle will be returning, I'll send Eva down to collect Lady Clara and you just cut back through the woods. All right?'

'Yes. And thank you, Paddy,' Antonia said, her eyes warm with gratitude. 'You have been so very kind.'

'Thank me when his lordship goes back to London,' Bingham mumbled ruefully. 'I don't know that I shall rest much before then. This extended visit of his is playing the very devil with my sleep.' Then, sending her another wink, he turned and headed back towards the house, leaving Antonia alone with her charge.

'All right, Clara, shall we begin?' Antonia said brightly. 'I thought we might start by walking Teddy around the ring again.'

The lesson got under way and, in no time at all, Antonia was completely immersed in her work. She was delighted at how quickly Clara responded to her, and at how eager the child was to learn. She was even beginning to show signs that she was overcoming her fear of Teddy, which made it easier for her to follow Antonia's instructions.

There were, of course, the inevitable accidents. Once, when Clara's attention was diverted, Teddy felt the pressure ease off the reins and abruptly put down his head, nearly unseating the little girl as a result. But Antonia turned that into a lesson too, and Clara was not caught daydreaming again.

At first, Antonia kept checking the time on the watch pinned to the front of her jacket, anxious that she not overstay her time. But as the hour wore on, and she became more involved with Clara, the time began to slip by unnoticed. So much so that, when she finally glanced up and saw Eva approaching, Antonia quickly brought the lesson to an end.

'All right, Clara, you have done very well today.' Antonia held the little girl's hands between her own. 'Now, here is Eva come to collect you. I shall see you again tomorrow, all right?'

'All right. Bye, Toni.'

Antonia handed Eva the pony's reins and then watched as the two made their way back up towards the stables. Once she saw Clara turn and wave for the last time, Antonia lightly sprang up into her own saddle and turned Foxfire back towards the woods. Time was of the essence now and she was anxious not to delay her departure. So far, everything had gone according to plan; she had no desire to spoil everything by lingering too long.

Thankfully, she reached the safety of the forest without incident. Casting a quick glance back, she saw no sign of either Mr Bingham or the Earl, and finally allowed herself a sigh of relief.

She was safe. The first lesson had gone without a hitch. Now all she had to do was change back into her regular clothing and head for home.

Antonia drew Foxfire to a halt beside the large oak tree just inside the first glade, and, swinging her right leg over the saddle, easily slid out of the saddle. She had almost forgotten what a pleasure it was to ride astride, though she certainly would never have admitted that to any of her friends. She hurried towards the base of the tree where she had left a small bundle of clothes, and quickly began to change.

Pulling out a long, brown skirt, Antonia slipped it up over her breeches and fastened it a bit higher than was normal to allow for the extra fabric at her waist. Next she replaced the boy's jacket with a loose-fitting spencer, and then draped a long, hooded cape about her shoulders and fastened it beneath her chin. Finally, tugging off the boy's cap, Antonia fluffed her honey-coloured curls before pulling the hood up over her head.

Her transformation taken care of, Antonia led Foxfire to a stump and, putting her left foot in the stirrup, raised herself up, and swung her right leg over Foxfire's back. She was definitely encumbered by the voluminous skirt, but, given that it hid the sight of her breech-clad legs, Antonia was not about to complain. She was not expecting to encounter anyone on the seldom-used path, but if she did, her appearance would at least allow her to pass as a country maid. The fact that she was riding astride would perhaps be a little more difficult to explain, but Antonia decided not to waste time worrying about that until it was necessary.

Of course, once Lord Carlyle returned to London, everything would be so much easier, Antonia reflected. She would be able to wear her stylish riding habits again, and revert to her normal side saddle. For now, however, she would have to make do if she was to see the game through.

Antonia was just about to cross on to the safety of Hadley property, when the unexpected appearance of a horseman in her path caused her to pull up on the reins. When she realised who it was, Antonia caught her breath. 'Lord Carlyle!' she gasped.

'Miss…Hadley?' Sebastian pulled his stallion to a halt, and politely doffed his gleaming black beaver. 'Forgive me for startling you, I had not thought to encounter anyone on this strip of road. Nor, I take it, did you,' he added wryly.

Antonia saw the amusement flickering in the depths of his clear blue eyes and her face grew hot with embarrassment. The thought of the Earl of Carlyle seeing her clad in such casual attire and riding astride nearly caused her courage to desert her altogether, until she realised that there was absolutely no reason for him to connect her present appearance—strange as it might be—with the riding lesson that would have taken place at Ashdean in his absence.

Antonia lifted her chin. 'You owe me no apology, Lord Carlyle. I was not…startled, nor are you wrong in thinking that you would not normally encounter anyone along this path. The only reason you did so today was because I decided to take a…slightly different route back from the home of a…friend that I was visiting. Unfortunately, it would seem that I do not know the path as well as I thought.'

Antonia took some comfort from the fact that she was not telling him a complete untruth, but not wishing to get into a discussion as to why she was employing a gentleman's saddle, said the first thing that popped into her head. 'Did you have a pleasant visit with the vicar, my lord?'

'Yes, it was very—' he glanced at her sharply. 'How did you know that I had been to see the vicar?'

Antonia flushed. 'Actually, I did not know...for certain, but in conversation with Mr Howard at the church yesterday, he mentioned that you had...expressed an interest in seeing the orphanage. I simply assumed that you might have...gone there this morning.'

The excuse sounded feeble even to her own ears, but it was the best Antonia could do. Her fingers were pulling at the reins with such agitation that she actually made Foxfire jump. Thankfully, Lord Carlyle seemed unaware of her distress. His eyes continued to scrutinise her appearance until Antonia was quite sure that he had taken in every detail possible of her clothing, her heightened colour, and of the saddle she was trying so desperately hard to conceal.

'As a matter of fact, I did go up to the orphanage,' he told her idly. 'And the vicar told me that you are a tremendous help to him. He spoke very highly of the good work you do there.'

Antonia managed a faint smile. 'I do what I can, my lord, but at times it seems so inadequate. There are so many children, and their need is so great. I am just thankful that the vicar takes such an interest in their welfare.'

'He also said that you occasionally give the children their lessons.'

'Yes. Mr Howard tries to make sure that the children are given the basic reading and writing skills. Unfortunately, his time and resources are limited, as is usually the case in a small parish like this. And, of course, it is not just the money. The children need so many other things that the vicar cannot provide. Books, for example. I have given them all of my own, but they soon fall into disrepair. I do try to collect books throughout the year, but they are so very expensive.'

Sebastian watched her speak, his gaze lingering pleasurably on the sight of her mouth, and dwelling on the delicate shape of it. Her lips were invitingly pink, reminding him of the petals of a spring rose. He was surprised to find himself wondering how they would feel under his own—

'My lord?'

He started, guiltily aware that he had been caught staring. 'Yes, Miss Hadley?'

'I was saying that, if you find yourself with books you no longer want, the orphanage would be grateful to receive them.'

'Ah. Yes. Books. I shall certainly keep that in mind. Forgive me for keeping you. I am sure that you are anxious to get home.'

'Yes. Papa will be expecting me.'

'Pray give him my regards.'

'Yes, I shall.'

Carlyle doffed his glistening black beaver and set the stallion to an easy canter.

As soon as he was out of sight, Antonia gathered up Foxfire's reins and started in the direction of Buntings Hill, her heart beating wildly. Dear heavens, she had nearly been caught! Had she delayed her departure from Clara but a few minutes longer, Lord Carlyle would have stumbled upon her in the act of changing her clothes.

She could not even begin to imagine how she would have attempted to explain *that*.

Chapter Five

Due to Mr Bingham's careful monitoring of the Earl's schedule, Antonia was able to continue Clara's lessons in relative peace, unobserved by anyone other than the household servants. Thankfully, there were also no repeats of her unfortunate encounter with the Earl in the forest, mainly because Antonia took care to stick to the paths that only she knew about. She also waited until she was actually on Hadley land before changing back into her clothes. It meant that she had to stay dressed as a man longer than she would have liked but, knowing that it also cut down her risk of discovery by Lord Carlyle, Antonia decided it was worth it.

Clara continued to be a willing and able little pupil, gobbling up everything Antonia taught her. Contrary to the belief that a lady need do little more than look good in the saddle, Antonia concentrated on teaching Clara the basics of good horsemanship, stressing that she practise what she learned until it became second nature. But she also insisted that Clara not ride on her own until she had received at least another few months of tuition.

Finally, after two weeks of subterfuge, Mr Bingham informed Antonia that Lord Carlyle had expressed his intention to return to London, and that he would be leaving within the week.

For the first time in days, Antonia actually felt herself begin to relax. Thank goodness. Lord Carlyle's departure would certainly make things easier for her. She would no longer have to pretend to be a man and dress in gentlemen's attire and there would be no need for her to sneak around in the forest and change her clothes before heading back home. It also meant that there would be no more unexpected visits from Lord Carlyle at Buntings Hill, but Antonia had convinced herself that she was happier for it and, as such, did not allow the news of his departure to trouble her unduly.

Others, however, were considerably less sanguine about the news of his imminent return to London. It seemed that, in the brief time Lord Carlyle had been in Upper Tipping, he had begun to earn the respect of the local townspeople. True to his word, he had taken the time to get to know some of the neighbouring families, along with his own tenants, and had made thoughtful and helpful suggestions as to how they might better their crops. He had donated monies to the orphanage, and had made a considerable donation of books from his own library to help augment the reading material of some of the older children.

But it went without saying that the ones most sorry to see him go were the young, single ladies of the community and their anxious mamas. Hence, it came as no surprise to anyone when Catherine's mother, Lady Shand, suggested holding a soirée in Carlyle's honour the night before he was to leave.

Surprisingly, Antonia found herself looking forward to the event. Not because she was anxious to socialise with Lord Carlyle—her feelings in that regard had certainly not changed. But she admitted that she was looking forward to the opportunity of dressing up and of dancing again. Of late, there had been a noticeable dearth of amusing entertainments in the district.

And she would not have been telling the complete truth had she said that she did not care what Lord Carlyle thought of her in her new gown of cream silk trimmed with delicate pink roses. After all, tonight would be the first time that he would have a chance to see her in her finery, rather than in the plain and simple muslins she favoured during the day.

At the appointed hour, Mr Hadley met her at the bottom of the stairs. In honour of the occasion, and in deference to her, he had agreed to attend the Shand soirée, so that when Antonia finally floated down the stairs, it was to find her father looking all the crack in a pair of white satin knee breeches, a dark jacket, and an immaculate white satin waistcoat. His hair, while liberally sprinkled with grey, was still thick and wavy, and Antonia was delighted to observe that it actually fell into some semblance of a fashionable style.

'Well, do I pass muster?' he muttered as Antonia descended the last step.

'Pass it, Father?' Antonia's eyes shone with pride. 'You transcend it. I dare say you shall cut quite a dash this evening.'

Mr Hadley grinned self-consciously. 'I need to, acting as escort to you, my dear. I do not recall having seen that gown before.'

'You have not. Catherine insisted that I have something new for her mother's party.'

'Well, you look absolutely beautiful, my dear,' Mr Hadley told her proudly. 'In fact, you remind me more and more of your mother all the time. I can hardly wait to see Lord Carlyle's face when he catches sight of you.'

An unwelcome blush stole into Antonia's cheeks. 'I care little for what Lord Carlyle thinks, Papa. In fact, I am surprised that he even agreed to come tonight. He is no doubt accustomed to much grander entertainments than those provided by a simple country dance.'

Mr Hadley smiled as he placed the cape over his daughter's shoulders. 'No doubt you are happy to see him leaving, eh poppet? Should make things a deuce more easy for you once he's back in London.'

'Yes, it will,' Antonia replied, refusing to acknowledge the annoying little stab of regret which accompanied the thought. 'Of course, Mr Bingham has been wonderful at scheduling the lessons. But I fear that if Lord Carlyle were to remain much longer our luck would surely run out. In fact, Mr Bingham informed me just yesterday that Lord Carlyle has already begun asking to see Mr Davlin at work.'

Mr Hadley laughed. 'Now, that *would* land you in the suds, my dear. For while I venture to say that Mr Davlin looks quite presentable from a distance, I doubt he would pass for a gentleman at close range.'

Antonia gasped and turned disbelieving eyes towards her parent. 'Papa, you have been spying!'

'Not at all. I merely happened to be passing by the stables when you came home yesterday morning.'

Antonia felt her cheeks burn. 'You might at least have said something. You could have told me that you were there.'

'What? And deprive me of the sight of my beautiful daughter clad in gentlemen's breeches and riding astride? Not on your life. By the by, wherever did you get those clothes?'

'From Catherine's brother.'

'Hmm, I hope they fit him better than they do you. Still, I thank the good Lord that I was the only one around to see it. I dare say we could bid a fond farewell to your dowry if Ophelia were ever to catch you in such a rig.'

The thought of Lady Farrington's horror, and of her subsequent roasting over such a grave transgression, should have brought the gravity of Antonia's deception home to her. Instead, all it did was move both her and her father to laughter, and send them off to the Shand soirée in a spirit of mutual collaboration.

They were met in the main hall by Lord Shand, a tall, dapper-looking man whose enjoyment of life was reflected in his ready smile and his easy manner. 'Peter, how very good to see you again. I was just saying to Maria that I hoped you would come tonight. Where have you been hiding, my old friend?'

'In the library,' Mr Hadley said wryly. 'As usual.'

Lord Shand smiled his understanding. 'Well, you are here now, and very glad I am of it too. Maria, my dear, come and see who has arrived.'

Lady Shand turned away from the couple she had been speaking to and, when she caught sight of Mr Hadley, her round face lit up with pleasure. 'Peter, how wonderful to see you again. I am so delighted that you could come. And, Antonia, my dear, you look lovely.' Lady Shand kissed her affectionately on the cheek. 'Catherine is in the drawing room. Why don't you go in and find her while we steal your father for a few minutes? The three of us have a lot of catching up to do.'

Antonia smiled and brushed Lady Shand's cheek with

her own. 'Thank you,' she whispered so that only that lady might hear. 'He needs to be with his friends again.'

Lady Shand nodded, and pressed Antonia's arm. 'I am so glad you were able to persuade him to come. Now, go and have a good time, and do not worry about your father. Lord Shand and I shall take good care of him.'

Knowing that the lady was as good as her word, Antonia turned and made her way towards the ball room, drawn there by the sounds of laughter and music which emanated from it.

'Toni, there you are!' Catherine cried, hurrying over to greet her friend. 'La, but you look quite the elegant young lady tonight! Your gown is splendid.'

'I should hope so, since you were the one who insisted I have it.'

'Yes, so I did.' Catherine laughed her delight. 'Now do come over here, there are people who are anxious to see you.'

Long before they reached the group of people laughing and chatting in the corner, Antonia had spotted Lord Carlyle. He was standing with two gentlemen, whom Catherine informed her had travelled down from London to stay with her parents for a few days. Antonia recognised that all three gentlemen were similarly well dressed, but it was immediately clear to her that only Carlyle was of the first consequence. His cut-away jacket of midnight blue superfine moulded to his broad shoulders while his snowy white cravat seemed more intricately tied than any of the others. But it was the expression in his eyes which caught and held Antonia's attention. He waited until the general round of greetings had been made before stepping forward to make his own.

'Miss Hadley, may I say how exceptionally lovely you

look this evening. I vow you could take your place in any London gathering looking as you do.'

Antonia opened her fan and plied it to her cheeks. 'You flatter me, my lord. I am sure that the ladies in London dress far more fashionably than this. Indeed, perhaps it is the ladies who are the cause of your leaving us so soon?'

His grin flashed wickedly. 'I would hardly bother to travel all the way to London just for the sight of a pretty face, Miss Hadley. Especially when there is no need.'

A blush ran like a shadow over her cheeks, and Antonia hastily dropped her eyes. She should have known better than to try to flirt with him. She had no experience in the subtle arts the ladies he would be used to dealing with had at their disposal.

Sensing her discomfort, Sebastian reached out and procured a glass of champagne from a passing footman. 'It might interest you to know that I have stayed a good deal longer than I had originally intended, Miss Hadley. And, were it not for business, I would not be rushing back to London now.'

Antonia refused to ask him what type of business had prompted his departure, fearing that he might interpret it as interest on her part. 'You shall be missed,' she commented instead, accepting the glass of champagne he held out to her.

'Shall I?' Sebastian raised an eyebrow expressively. 'By whom, I wonder?'

'By many, I dare say. The vicar is singing your praises, as are most of the residents of Upper Tipping. Your generosity has not gone unnoticed, my lord.'

'I am pleased to hear it, though I had hoped that some-one might have been inclined to miss me on a more… personal level.'

Antonia wielded her fan faster. 'Ah, look, there is Lady Dalrymple trying to catch your attention. By the by, I did not think to ask you how your dinner went that evening.'

Aware that he had been skilfully manoeuvred away from his topic, Sebastian grinned. 'The dinner was memorable and the company much as I had been warned to expect. But tell me, Miss Hadley, are you always so adept at deflecting attention away from yourself?'

Before she had a chance to reply, Lady Dalrymple, magnificent in deep mauve velvet, marched up to them and immediately took control of the conversation.

'Lord Carlyle, I am positively in *despair* of your returning to London. Never say that you are going to leave us just when we were all getting to know you so well. Why, I am acquainted with at least five young ladies who are positively heartbroken at the thought of losing you, my own two gels amongst them.' Lady Dalrymple leaned closer to the Earl and confided, 'I do not think it will come as any surprise, my lord, if I were to tell you that you have made a most favourable impression on my gels.'

Antonia quickly turned away to hide her smile. Lady Dalrymple's daughters *deigning* to approve of Lord Carlyle's acquaintance? It was so outrageous as to invite hilarity. Carlyle, too, seemed amused by the woman's less than tactful comment, but he took care not to show it. 'And I shall certainly miss the ladies of Upper Tipping, Lady Dalrymple. However, I am afraid that business matters necessitate my departure. But I can assure you it will not be long before I return to Upper Tipping again.'

Lady Dalrymple was clearly relieved to hear it, and assured Lord Carlyle that neither of her daughters were likely to commit themselves to any other gentlemen while he was yet single. Then, offering the Earl a fawning smile, she reluctantly moved away.

'*You* do not seem particularly pleased with my intention to return, Miss Hadley,' Sebastian observed when Lady Dalrymple had finally disappeared into the crowd. 'Am I to assume that you are not one of the young ladies who proclaim themselves heartbroken at the thought of my leaving?'

The fact that he had so accurately read what was on her face caused Antonia to blush uncomfortably. 'I cannot imagine why you would think such a thing,' she said. 'I am, of course, sorry to see you return to London. I believe that my father has come to…enjoy your visits immensely.'

'Your father,' Sebastian repeated wryly. 'Yes, I might have known that you would say that.'

Antonia glanced at him quizzically. 'My lord?'

'Miss Hadley, while I am gratified that your father holds me in such esteem, I hope you will forgive me if I tell you that it is *your* feelings I am concerned with, rather than his.'

She gasped. 'Mine?'

'Yes. Because I have the distinct impression that you do not like me.'

Antonia's eyes flew up to his, and then just as quickly away. 'My lord, I cannot…imagine why you would say such a thing. Our acquaintance has not been…of a long enough duration for me to have formed any opinions of you, be they negative or otherwise.'

'Nevertheless, I have been aware of the chill in your voice from the occasion of our first meeting, and I should like very much to know what has put it there. I originally thought that it was as a result of my ignorance of your mother's passing, but now I am not so sure.' His eyes narrowed thoughtfully. 'Have I offended you in some way, Miss Hadley? Were you, perhaps, annoyed that I sought you out in the music room that first time I called at Buntings Hill?'

Knowing that she had allowed too much of herself to show that morning, Antonia strove for a tranquil expression, something made more difficult by the fact that Lord Carlyle had taken a step closer to her. He now stood so near that she could smell the fresh, masculine scent he wore, and see the tiny flecks of gold in his blue eyes; eyes that were regarding her now with a look which had turned unexpectedly sensual. 'Have you no answer for me, Miss Hadley?'

'My lord, I can…assure you, that I was neither offended nor annoyed by your appearance that morning,' Antonia said quickly. 'I was, perhaps, a touch startled when I looked up to see you standing in the doorway, but I did not hold it against you then or now. I…really do not know what else to say except—'

To Antonia's surprise, Carlyle placed the tips of his fingers gently against her lips. 'Then say nothing, Miss Hadley. Because I would far rather imagine that you might miss me, than hear from your lips that you should not.'

Antonia took a quick, sharp breath. His fingers had lingered but a second against her mouth, yet it had been long enough to send a quiver through her entire body. She had never been touched so intimately by a man— and she had no idea how to respond to it.

In silent query, she raised her face to his, her lips slightly parted, her eyes filled with questions.

'Miss Hadley, I swear you are a witch,' Lord Carlyle

whispered huskily, 'for I do not believe that those eyes, or those lips, could belong to a mere mortal woman.'

Antonia's flush deepened to crimson. 'I assure you, my lord, I am…in all ways mortal. It is merely your imagination which imbues them with unearthly charm. And now, if you will…excuse me, there is something I must tell my father.'

Antonia quickly moved away, hoping that Lord Carlyle would not attempt to delay her further. She had to put some distance between them. She could not allow him to shatter her composure further!

'Antonia, my dear,' her father greeted her when she arrived at his side. 'Are you having a good time?'

'Yes, wonderful,' Antonia said, though the reply was purely mechanical. It seemed that she could hear the beating of her heart above everything else. Then, aware that she had interrupted a conversation he seemed to have been having with the lady standing next to him, she hastened to make her apologies. 'Forgive me, Papa, I did not mean to interrupt.'

'You have not, Antonia. As a matter of fact, I was just telling Lady Sheraton about you.' Mr Hadley glanced from his daughter to the lady at his side. 'Are the two of you acquainted?'

'I fear we are not, Mr Hadley,' Lady Sheraton replied in an attractively low-pitched voice. 'Being a good deal older than your daughter, I venture to say that we move in somewhat different circles.'

'I am surprised to find I know anyone, given that I do not move in *any* circles any more,' Mr Hadley admitted ruefully. 'However, that is no one's fault but my own, as my sister-in-law is constantly pointing out. Antonia, I would like you to meet Lady Sheraton. Lady Sheraton, my daughter, Antonia.'

'Good evening, Lady Sheraton.'

'I am very pleased to meet you, Miss Hadley. Your father and I have just been having a delightful conversation about you.'

Antonia glanced at her father in surprise. 'Dear me, I cannot think what he would have been telling you.'

'Amongst other things, he was telling me that you help out at the orphanage,' Lady Sheraton said. 'It is good of you to give of your time so unselfishly.'

'It is easy to be unselfish when the cause is so close to my heart, Lady Sheraton. The children ask for little, and give much in return.'

'Yes, I have always found that to be the case. Perhaps, Miss Hadley, you would be willing to tell me how I might be of service.'

Antonia's lips curved upwards in a smile of delight. 'Well, yes, of course, I should be happy to. The vicar is always anxious to welcome new volunteers. And, please, do call me Antonia.'

'Lady Sheraton has recently come to live in Upper Tipping,' Mr Hadley informed her. 'She resided previously in Devon.'

'Oh, Devon is lovely,' Antonia replied sincerely. 'It has long been one of my favourite parts of England. Next to Kent, of course.'

'I can understand why you would feel that way,' Lady Sheraton said with a smile. 'Everyone has been so very kind to me since I moved here.'

'Where are you living, Lady Sheraton?' Antonia inquired, aware of a genuine desire to know more about her.

'At Newton Spinney, down by the Grange.'

Antonia nodded. She knew it well. Newton Spinney was a charming cottage of rambling proportions, with a thatched roof and one of the prettiest gardens in the area. The previous occupant, Mrs Bainbridge, had recently moved to London to live with her daughter and the cottage had been standing empty for some time. But a few weeks ago, when pretty chintz curtains had gone up at the windows, Antonia had begun to wonder who the new owner might be.

'You are most fortunate, Lady Sheraton,' Antonia said now. 'Newton Spinney is one of the prettiest places I know. And it has a wonderful garden. Mrs Bainbridge often used to let me pick raspberries from her canes at the back. Remember, Papa, Mrs Grenfall's last batch of jam was made from the berries I picked there. And I do recall you saying it was the finest jam she ever made.'

'It was!' Mr Hadley concurred. 'And if there is one thing I do know, it is good jam!'

'Well, I hope you will come and pick all the raspberries you want, Antonia. I know there will be far too many for me.'

'Perhaps you would like a hand with some of the heavier work around the property?' Mr Hadley offered brusquely. 'As I recall, the back garden was pretty well grown over, and I hardly think a delicate lady like yourself should be undertaking such a task.'

Lady Sheraton's laugh was as warm and attractive as everything else about her. 'Rest assured, Mr Hadley, I am stronger than I look. But I would be grateful for the assistance nevertheless. And, of course, I would be happy to pay.'

'Fine. I know of one or two strong young lads in the village who would be grateful for the work. I shall contact them for you tomorrow.'

'Thank you, Mr Hadley, it is very good of you.

Perhaps, once I am more fully settled, you and Antonia would consider calling in for tea.'

Mr Hadley looked pleasantly taken aback. 'We would be delighted to have tea with you, Lady Sheraton. Wouldn't we, Toni?'

Antonia glanced at her father, more in amusement than surprise. She hadn't missed the question in his voice, and knew it had more to do with simply visiting Lady Sheraton. Her father was tacitly asking for her permission to call upon a lady. The first time he had done so since his wife had died.

Impulsively, Antonia squeezed his arm. 'Yes, Papa, I think that would be most delightful indeed!'

Antonia managed to get through the rest of the evening without encountering Lord Carlyle again, though she felt his gaze upon her more than once. And while she pretended not to notice, Antonia had a feeling that the colour which rose in her cheeks gave her away. So it was hardly surprising that, by the time the hour approached one, she was more than ready to leave.

Fortunately, Antonia was spared having to answer any awkward questions from her father about what had transpired during the evening, given that he seemed far more interested in talking about Lady Sheraton. But that did not trouble Antonia either. She was genuinely pleased to hear the way her father spoke of Lady Sheraton, and she listened attentively to everything he said.

Perhaps things were finally starting to change, Antonia reflected as the carriage made its leisurely way home through the quiet woodland. And perhaps, she thought sardonically, her father's behaviour—if not her own— would help to appease Lady Farrington's temper.

* * *

Life quickly reverted to normal once Carlyle returned to London. Antonia's days settled back into a comfortable routine of riding lessons with Clara in the morning, followed by lunch with her pupil at the house, or back home with her father at Buntings Hill, and then any one of a number of pleasant, though innocuous, activities which were normally planned for the afternoon and evening.

Nevertheless, she became aware of a growing feeling of despondency; a sense that...something was missing. The only problem was that she could not isolate what the cause of her dissatisfaction was. Her father's friendship with Lady Sheraton was proceeding well, so it could not be that. And Clara was doing very nicely with her lessons, so it was not as a result of that. Certainly, she refused to countenance that it had *anything* to do with Lord Carlyle's absence—even though she knew that thoughts of him crept into her mind far more often than was right or proper.

What then was the cause of this strange... melancholy? Antonia wondered.

Well, whatever it was, Clara seemed to be suffering from it too. She was quieter than she had been before her father's arrival. It was almost as though, during the brief time Carlyle had been at Ashdean, a fragile bond had started to develop between them, so that for the first time in her young life Clara actually missed her father.

'Do you miss Papa, Toni?' Clara asked her one day. They had finished their lesson and were sitting on the soft grass under the very tree where Antonia had used to wait for Paddy's signal. Now, somewhat startled by the child's question, she purposely fixed a smile on her face and injected a casual note into her voice.

'We all miss your father, Clara. He is a good man, and one much respected in the village.'

'Yes, but do *you* miss him?' Clara repeated ingenuously.

In spite of the fact that she was being questioned by a child, Antonia felt her cheeks begin to glow. 'Well, yes, I miss him, Clara,' she said carefully. 'You see, your father and my father are neighbours. And, occasionally, your father comes to visit us at Buntings Hill.'

Clara lifted puzzled blue eyes to Antonia's face. 'Do you think Papa is nice looking?'

'Nice looking?' This time, Antonia had to bite her lip, not from embarrassment, but in an effort to keep from smiling. It was hardly the type of question a six-year-old asked about her father. 'Why do you ask, Clara? Did you hear someone say that your father was…nice looking?'

Clara nodded. 'Eva said so. So did her sister Nellie when she came to visit Eva. Nellie says Papa makes her feel all…funny inside, but that I'm not to tell him she said so.'

Antonia turned away, fighting the urge to laugh. Trust two silly young girls to speak about the master of the house in front of his own daughter. But then, to be fair, Clara was brighter than most little girls her age. No doubt Eva and her sister had not thought the child old enough to understand or to remember what they were talking about.

'Yes, Clara, your father is…nice looking,' Antonia answered, choosing her words with care. 'Which is one of the reasons why you are so pretty.'

The little girl looked thoughtful for a moment. 'Was Mama pretty, Toni?'

Ah, now that was a question Antonia had been expecting. 'I was not fortunate enough to know her, Clara. She and your father spent most of their time in London after they were married.'

'But was she pretty?' Clara persisted. 'You must have seen her.'

Antonia heard the anguish in the little girl's voice, and felt her heart go out to her. How would she have felt, had her mother died before she was of an age to remember her?

'Yes, Clara, I did see your mother once, long ago. And she was very pretty. She had lovely blonde hair, and pretty blue eyes, just like you. And she was as dainty as one of your dolls.'

Clara nodded, as though her suspicions had been confirmed. 'I have a picture of her, you know,' she informed Antonia solemnly. 'In a gold locket Papa gave me. But it isn't very clear any more.' Clara hesitated for a moment to examine a furry caterpillar that was making its way through the blades of grass. 'Toni?'

'Yes, dearest?'

'Why won't anybody talk to me about Mama? When I ask Eva or Nellie about her, they tell me to hush and give me a sweet.'

Antonia lifted her shoulders in a delicate shrug. 'I think that perhaps they did not know your Mama, Clara. You came to live here after she…went to heaven, so they had no time to get to know her. They only know and love you.'

Clara nodded again with all the innocence of a child. 'I know. Papa told me that Mama was in heaven, and that if I said my prayers at night, she could hear me. But it isn't the same as having her here, is it, Toni?'

Antonia shook her head, aware of a sharp stinging behind her eyes. 'No, dearest, it is not the same. But your Papa was right about your prayers. Your Mama does hear you, and she watches over you all the time. And she shall always be as beautiful as she is in the picture in your locket.'

Clara seemed to think about that for a while, and then raised trusting blue eyes to Antonia. 'Where is your Mama, Toni?'

Antonia smiled sadly. 'In heaven, like yours.'

There was silence for a moment, and then Clara nodded. 'I am glad that they are there together. They can keep each other company. And do you know what else, Toni?'

'What, Clara?'

'I'm glad that…if I cannot have Mama, I have you.'

The childlike sentiment, expressed with such heart-wrenching simplicity, shot straight to Antonia's heart. She had never consciously thought about children, assuming that, like everyone else, she would eventually marry and have some of her own. But as she looked down at the fair head that was nestled so close to her breast, and at the long strands of hair that lay against her brow as soft as corn silk, Antonia suddenly realised that a child of her own body could not have been any dearer to her than Clara.

'Do you know, Clara,' Antonia said, hugging the little girl to her, 'that is one of the nicest things anyone has ever said to me.'

'You're not going to leave me like Mama did, are you, Toni?' Clara whispered.

Antonia shut her eyes tightly and rocked the little girl against her. 'No, Clara, I am not going to leave you. I shall be here…whenever you need me.'

And may God forgive me for saying that, Antonia prayed silently. For she had absolutely no right to do so.

She fervently hoped that Clara would also forgive her when, one day, she did slip out of the little girl's life. Because Antonia knew that eventually that day would come. On the day Lord Carlyle married, Clara would have a new mother, and there would be no more room for Toni in her life.

The thought brought Antonia no joy. She pressed her lips to the child's hair and tried to ignore the sharp stab of pain the thought of Lord Carlyle's marrying caused her. It was terribly wrong of her to think of him as anything but her father's neighbour and her own employer. He was of the first consequence; a gentleman well above the likes of her.

Then why was she thinking about him as…something else? Had she not told her father on more than one occasion that she did not even like the man? That she would not have entertained his suit, even had he had the temerity to ask?

Antonia sighed as she closed her eyes. When had those feelings begun to change?

Padrick Bingham stood by the dining-room window and watched Antonia Hadley and the Earl's daughter as they sat curled up together under the tree. He had made plans to set off for London on the morrow, in response to Lord Carlyle's request, but for the moment he was far more concerned at what he saw going on here than with what might be awaiting him in London.

Miss Hadley and the Earl's daughter were becoming close. Too close, Bingham feared as he slowly let the curtain fall back into place. Clara was starting to see Antonia Hadley as the mother she no longer had, and Miss Hadley…well, there was no mistaking the way she felt about the child. It was written all over her face,

Bingham thought glumly. Which could only lead to trouble and heartache when Lord Carlyle eventually did marry and bring his new wife home to Ashdean.

How would the little girl react? Would she accept another woman stepping into Miss Hadley's place? And what about Miss Hadley? What would it do to her? How would she feel about another woman taking her rightful place as Clara's mother?

Bingham dug his hands into his pockets as a troubled expression shadowed his features. They were questions he had no answers for. But he knew, without a doubt, that there were going to be tears.

Which was probably why he suddenly found himself hoping that, for everyone's sake, the Earl would choose to remain single a good while longer yet!

Chapter Six

The Countess of Clyde was in her glory! Her ball, with a guest list of just over four hundred, was already being hailed as a resounding success. She had gathered together, in one place, some of the most eligible and sought-after *partis* in London. Indeed, she could scarce have prayed for a better turnout, even though she would have been the first to say that the success of any venture could never be left to anything so capricious as luck or prayer.

A superlative hostess, Lady Clyde was nothing if not wise. She knew very well that, in order to attract bees, one must put out honey. And Lady Rosalind Grey was, without doubt, the most honeyed of them all!

Deemed an Incomparable by the *ton*, Lady Rosalind was a dusky, dark-eyed beauty whose propensity for breaking hearts was well known. She was the daughter of an Earl, and had been trained to take her place in a nobleman's house. And there was no question in any one's mind that it was the Earl of Carlyle's house in which she intended to take her place.

Lady Rosalind had seen the tall, good-looking Earl the moment he had entered the ball room and, like a tigress on the prowl, had subtly begun to stalk him. Hence, when they eventually found themselves confronting one another, it seemed to be nothing more than the most casual of coincidences.

'Why, good evening, Lord Carlyle,' Lady Rosalind said, her fine clear voice pitched to an attractively intimate level. 'What a pleasant surprise. I was not aware that you had returned to London.'

Carlyle bowed his head in acknowledgement of her greeting. 'I am only recently returned, Lady Rosalind. This is my first outing since I have been back.'

'Then we must feel honoured that you have chosen this venue with which to mark your return. I fear there are other hostesses who will sorely miss your presence this evening.'

The words were spoken with just the right degree of sincerity, tempered with just the correct amount of constraint, to make a man feel flattered, but not suffocated. Lady Rosalind had perfected the technique, and it seemed that even the self-assured Earl of Carlyle was not immune. 'I feel it is I who have selected well, Lady Rosalind. Shall we?'

Lady Rosalind coloured prettily as she placed one gloved hand lightly upon his arm and fell into step beside him. 'I understand you were visiting the country, my lord.'

'Yes, my country seat at Ashdean.'

'And did you find all well at Ashdean?'

'I did, thank you.'

'But you were there somewhat longer, I think, than you originally intended to be.'

'My delay,' he explained with a smile, 'was brought about by my desire to spend additional time with an utterly charming young lady.'

Lady Rosalind hid her consternation well. Had some-one already stolen a march on her? 'Indeed, my lord. Am I acquainted with this most fortunate young lady?'

'No. She is but six years old and has lived in the country for the past two years. I refer, Lady Rosalind, to my daughter Clara.'

The rush of returning hope was so strong that it nearly caused a draught. 'Your daughter! But of course. Forgive my momentary lapse of memory.' Lady Rosalind laughed, culling her brain for any information she had ever heard about Carlyle's child. 'I do not believe I have heard you speak much about her in the past.'

Lord Carlyle looked decidedly guilty for a moment, a fact which immediately registered in Lady Rosalind's sharp little brain. 'I think it is I who must crave for-giveness,' he said ruefully. 'Until now I have not given my daughter the attention she deserves. But all that has changed now. My time in the country was spent getting to know Clara, and I am delighted to learn that I have such an exceptional child. She is bright and beautiful, and full of laughter. But, forgive me, I run away with myself. I forget that not everyone is as enamoured of her as I.'

Knowing that to be true, Lady Rosalind nevertheless fixed what she hoped was a convincing smile on her face, and set out to sound as maternal as she knew how. 'Never say that, my lord. A child is a wonderful thing, and I am sure that she is every bit as…sweet and loving as you say. And I think it is marvellous that you feel your role as a father so strongly.' Lady Rosalind paused to inject the appropriate note of sorrow into her voice. 'Especially as circumstances have decreed that you be mother and father to her both.'

It was a calculated gamble, and Lady Rosalind held

her breath, waiting to see how Carlyle would react. Though she had heard the rumours that the Earl and his wife had been far from close in the final months—that they had, in fact, been living almost separate lives long before that—Lady Rosalind was smart enough to know that certain memories, especially bad ones, often diminished with time. She had no wish for her statement to arouse anger, rather than regret, on Carlyle's part. Fortunately, it seemed that such was not the case.

'She has not had much of a life, Lady Rosalind,' he said. 'In truth, Clara has known neither mother nor father for much of her life, and I am ashamed to admit that even the daughter of my closest neighbour knows more of her than I.'

That remark also caught Lady Rosalind's attention, and was filed away for possible future reference. 'I understand your tendency towards feeling guilt, my lord,' she said, 'but I assure you that you have absolutely no reason to feel that way. You did what was best for your daughter at the time. After all, how could you adequately care for a child when you were so overset with grief at your wife's death?' she asked. 'And what could you be expected to know of the care of a young child? You did the sensible thing in giving her to the care of others who did know what to do. And now that you are more comfortably settled in your own life, and your daughter is older, I think the time is perfect for you to…re-establish your role as father to her.' Lady Rosalind paused, bracing herself for the big question. 'Are you…planning to bring Lady Clara to London to live with you?'

Carlyle seemed to consider the question. 'To be honest, I have not yet decided,' he said at length. 'My daughter has grown up in the country, and I have cause to wonder how she will feel about London at such a young age. The crowds, the noise, the smells. I've no need to tell you, Lady Rosalind, how different the two environments can be.'

Lady Rosalind shuddered, all too aware of the deficiencies of country life, and marvelling that anyone would actually prefer to live in rural domesticity. But she was certainly not going to tell Carlyle that. He seemed to have developed a partiality for country life himself. 'The country is, of course, a delightful place, my lord, and one which is…worthy of consideration. But one must not overlook the cultural aspects of London, and what it has to offer. The fine museums and the architecture of its old buildings. The theatre, and of course, the music your daughter would be exposed to through any number of venues.'

The thought came unbidden to Sebastian that, at six years old, Clara would hardly be interested in such things as Gothic architecture, or the passionate portrayal of Shylock by Edmund Kean at Drury Lane. Nor did he imagine that Clara could hear music any lovelier than that which he had heard Miss Hadley play.

'You are right, of course,' he acknowledged eventually, 'but I think, before I decide whether to remove Clara from her present surroundings, I shall spend more time with her at Ashdean. I still have much to learn about my daughter, and I cannot help but feel that it will aid the learning to do it in surroundings more familiar and comfortable to her than to me. Once she knows me better, I shall take her anywhere in the world she cares to go.'

Lady Rosalind smiled indulgently. She had no qualms about Lord Carlyle taking his daughter anywhere she wanted to go—just so long as he installed her in a nice boarding school in the country *after* they were married.

'I think that is a wonderful idea,' she concurred, pressing her fingers lightly against his arm. 'But wait, I have just had the most wonderful idea. You mentioned crowds being of concern to Clara?'

Carlyle nodded. 'She has not been exposed to many people in her young life. Apart from the servants at Ashdean, a few village children, and Toni, of course.'

'Toni?' Lady Rosalind asked blankly.

'Forgive me, I meant to say Miss Antonia Hadley, the daughter of my closest neighbour. I fear I have already come to think of her as my daughter does.'

'Toni. What a strange name for a lady,' Lady Rosalind said, her smile not quite reaching her eyes. 'She is a lady, I hope, my lord, if she is exerting any kind of influence on Lady Clara.'

'Miss Hadley is in all ways a lady,' Carlyle replied without hesitation. 'She is a beautiful and accomplished young woman. Clara would do well to emulate her.'

That was definitely not what Lady Rosalind wanted to hear. So, she did have some competition in the country—even if it came in the form of a green girl. Judging by the unexpected warmth in Lord Carlyle's voice when he spoke of her, she would do well not to ignore it.

Lady Rosalind turned her most sympathetic gaze on the Earl. 'Well, if it is exposing Clara to new people that concerns you, why don't you take the opportunity of doing that right in her own surroundings by having a party.'

He glanced at her in bewilderment. 'A party?'

'Yes. It would be a perfect opportunity for everyone to meet Clara,' Lady Rosalind said persuasively. 'And, as you say, the child is bound to feel more comfortable in her own surroundings. That way, when you do bring her up to London, she will already know many of the people with whom you associate and is not likely to be so nervous.'

'Lady Rosalind, that is a splendid idea. In fact, Clara's seventh birthday is just three weeks away. It would make a perfect occasion for a party. And I may just make it into a weekend house party rather than just an evening.'

So much the better, Lady Rosalind thought happily. That would give her more time to get to know the running of Ashdean and work her way into Carlyle's life. Still, she had to tread softly a while longer. 'A birthday party. How lovely.' Lady Rosalind lowered her eyes in a most appealing fashion. 'I look forward to hearing all about it when you return to London.'

'There will be no need to hear about it, Lady Rosalind. It would be the height of bad manners not to invite you when you were the very one to suggest the idea!'

Lady Rosalind kept her triumph carefully hidden. 'I am honoured to be invited, Lord Carlyle. And I hope you will not think it too coming of me to ask who else will be attending. It will allow me to make inquiries as to…whom I may travel with, being that I may not have a carriage at my disposal.' It would also allow her to assess the strength of her competition and prepare beforehand, Lady Rosalind acknowledged shrewdly.

'I shall advise you of the guest list as soon as it is completed,' Carlyle informed her absently, 'though, of course, my own carriage will be at your disposal, should you require it.'

Lady Rosalind's smile flashed brilliantly. Another triumph! Only think how it would look for others to see her receiving such special treatment from Carlyle himself!

'It is very good of you, my lord, and I shall, of course,

bear your very generous offer in mind when I am making my arrangements.'

'Lady Rosalind, pray forgive me, but I think I shall take my leave.' He bowed over her slim white hand. 'My secretary will be in touch to advise you of the arrangements.'

By not so much as a flicker did Lady Rosalind betray her disappointment that Carlyle himself would not deliver the message. Still, it would not do to presume too much. Not yet.

'I eagerly await the invitation.' Lady Rosalind turned her most dazzling smile on him. 'Goodnight, Lord Carlyle.'

'Goodnight, Lady Rosalind. I look forward to introducing you to my little Clara.'

'No more than I look forward to meeting her, my lord,' Lady Rosalind replied sweetly.

On her way home that evening, Rosalind thought long and hard about her conversation with the Earl of Carlyle. There was no doubt in her mind that she wanted to marry him; in fact, she intended to do everything in her power to make it happen, and as soon as possible. Carlyle was exactly what she had been looking for. While her own father might be a member of the aristocracy, his penchant for gambling had long since exhausted the family coffers, and her own financial straits were becoming far too perilous for her liking. Short of having to sell off what few good pieces of jewellery her mother had left her, Rosalind knew she would have little choice but to marry. And soon.

She had contemplated marriage before, of course, but had not been able to find anyone who met all of her stringent requirements. Fortunately, Carlyle, with his old and respected title, his exalted position in society, and his extensive properties both in London and elsewhere, met all of her needs to a nicety. Marriage to Carlyle would elevate her to the position she had so long hungered to achieve. She would be the much envied Countess of Carlyle—with all of the attendant trappings and privileges. And she would have the devastatingly handsome Sebastian Hastings as her husband.

The daughter was another matter, of course, but one which gave Rosalind little cause for concern. She would play along with Carlyle and treat the little girl like gold—until the day she and Carlyle were married. Then she would use every feminine wile at her disposal to persuade Carlyle to send Clara to boarding school.

After all, given the type of lifestyle they would be leading in London, as well as the myriad demands upon her time as a highly fashionable lady and hostess, Rosalind knew that she simply would not have time to look after a child. As she had told Carlyle, there were any number of people better suited to such things. She would pay someone well to take very good care of the little girl.

She planned on being far too busy having a glorious time to attend to such things herself!

Sebastian sent for Mr Bingham early the following afternoon. 'Paddy, we have plans to make. We are going to have a party.'

'Very nice, my lord,' Bingham said, his words accompanied by a genuine smile. 'And what is to be the occasion?'

'Clara's birthday. She is going to be seven on the twenty-fourth and I intend to hold a party for her. It will be the best party she has ever had.'

Neglecting to inform the Earl that it would also be the *first* party she had ever had, Bingham sat down in the chair and prepared to take instruction. 'Would you like me to reserve a room at the Ritz, my lord?'

'Certainly not. I do not intend to hold the party in London, but at Ashdean, and I want you to invite all of the local families to attend. Some of the guests will also be coming down from London and staying over the weekend. Here is a list of their names. You may speak to Cook about the food,' Sebastian continued. 'Hire any additional staff which will be required. My guests will begin arriving on the Friday, so we shall have a special dinner that night, and Clara's ball will be held on the Saturday. Then we shall have to plan something very special for her birthday on Sunday.' Sebastian mentally ticked another item off his list. 'We shall probably have a quiet day on Monday, and hopefully, everyone will be gone by sundown Tuesday. Now, Paddy, I want you to make sure that every manner of sweet and confection that Clara likes is available that weekend. Oh, yes, and I have been giving some thought as to what to buy her for her birthday.' Sebastian grinned. 'What do you think about a horse?'

'A horse, my lord?'

'Yes. I thought perhaps a pretty little mare.'

A furrow appeared in the steward's forehead. 'I don't know that she's outgrown Teddy yet.'

'Nonsense, Teddy is just a child's pony. I want Clara to have a horse of her own. I know,' Sebastian said, snapping his fingers. 'Why don't you get that new riding master to look after it. What's his name, Deblin?'

Bingham started. 'Davlin, my lord.'

'Yes, Davlin. You said the man knows his horseflesh. He might just know of a sound animal in the area.

Failing that, I shall send him to Tatt's and he can pick one up there.' Sebastian paused as another thought suddenly occurred to him. 'By the way, Paddy, I want to see this Mr Davlin the next time I am at Ashdean. Clara seems delighted with him, and I would like to meet the man who is having such a good influence on my daughter.'

Bingham stared at the paper in front of him. 'Yes, my lord, I shall try my best to—'

'I don't expect you to try, Paddy, I expect you to make it happen. And no excuses. You can tell Mr Davlin that if he does not arrange to see me before Clara's ball, he can look elsewhere for employment.' Sebastian's expression hardened. 'I cannot help but think that something is very wrong if a man in my employ cannot meet with me even one day out of two months.'

'Well, yes, I know that, my lord, but—'

'Have I made myself clear, Mr Bingham?'

It was a rhetorical question and Paddy knew it. Carlyle never called him Mr Bingham unless he was annoyed. 'Perfectly, my lord. I shall…speak to Mr Davlin as soon as I arrive at Ashdean.'

'Good. Oh, and while I remember,' Sebastian said in an offhand manner, 'I would like you to make sure that Miss Hadley is included in the guest list for dinner on Friday night. And, of course, for the ball on Saturday.'

This time, Bingham went white. 'Miss…Antonia Hadley?'

'Yes. Clara is always talking about her. At first I thought she was referring to the new riding master, but now I believe that it has been Miss Hadley all along. And if I am not mistaken, Miss Hadley is equally taken with Clara. It will be a pleasure to see the two of them together at the party.'

Because there was nothing else he could do, Bingham dutifully added Antonia's name to the guest list. What a bumble bath this was turning out to be! How in the world were they going to work around the problem of Antonia giving Clara riding lessons when the house was filled with people? And what were they to do about the requested meeting with Tony Davlin?

At length, when Lord Carlyle had finished dictating his instructions for the party, Bingham returned to his chambers and sat down at his desk, his eyes staring blankly at the detailed list in front of him. For once, he had a problem that he had no idea how to go about solving. One way or another, Antonia's plans were going to be upset. Either he would have to fire her for not agreeing to meet Lord Carlyle, or she would run the risk of suffering whatever consequences might befall her if she did risk a meeting, and have her identity exposed.

Either way, Bingham knew they were in for trouble. And at the moment, he couldn't think of any way around it!

'What do you mean you have not heard from him?' Lady Farrington snapped. 'What did you do to drive him away?'

Antonia sighed as she resolutely inserted another rose into the vase. 'I did nothing to drive him away, Aunt, any more than I did anything to attract him. Lord Carlyle was pleasant to me, as I have already told you, but that is all. You are making a mistake in trying to read anything more into his attentions than that.'

'Fustian!' Lady Farrington snorted. 'I do not make mistakes, Antonia. It could not have been any plainer than the nose on my face that Lord Carlyle was taken with you. I saw the way he looked at you. And you would have to be a very foolish young woman not to encourage him. An Earl, with sixty thousand a year? Faith, child, you could not *hope* to do better.' Lady Farrington glanced at her niece and sniffed disdainfully. 'I doubt you shall want the paltry little dowry I am holding for you then. Still,' she amended, 'it would look very shoddy on your part to go to him with nothing at all.'

'Aunt, please! I am not going to anyone, dowry or no,' Antonia replied as firmly as she dared. 'I repeat, Lord Carlyle was pleasant to me but that is all. He did not offer to escort me anywhere, nor have I heard from him since his return to London. No doubt he found himself at loose ends while he was here and thought to…while away a few hours in the company of his neighbour.'

'A few hours with his neighbour! Lord love us, Antonia, even you cannot be that naive, surely.'

'But his reputation—'

'Bother his reputation. A man like Carlyle does not just while away the hours with the daughter of his neighbour. He has more than enough demands on his time. In fact, I do believe he has more to contend with than that fat, dissipated man we call a Regent,' Lady Farrington muttered uncharitably. 'You mark my words, he—'

'Excuse me, miss,' Abbott said, breaking in. 'But this letter just came for you. I was told to deliver it at once.'

'Thank you, Abbott.' Antonia was grateful for the butler's arrival, though whether it was for the letter he delivered or the brief respite his interruption caused she wasn't sure. She took the letter from the platter and her eyes widened in surprise.

The Carlyle family crest stared up at her in bold relief. Unfortunately, Lady Farrington had seen it too. 'Good heavens, it is from Carlyle! Well, hurry up, girl, open it!'

Purposely ignoring her aunt's instructions, Antonia took her time in breaking the seal and opening the missive. But even she could not disguise her shock as she read over the contents of the letter. 'Oh, my!' she gasped, reading it again.

'Well, what does it say?' Lady Farrington barked, thumping her ivory-handled cane on the floor. 'Are you going to keep me in suspense all day, girl, or are you going to tell me?'

Wordlessly, Antonia handed her aunt the letter, and proceeded to watch as Lady Farrington's expression went from curious to incredulous to ecstatic.

'A house party! And you are invited? But this is splendid. There, I knew it!' Lady Farrington said smugly. 'I knew he was harbouring a *tendre* for you. I could tell by the look in his eyes.'

'Tell what by the look in whose eyes, Ophelia?' Mr Hadley enquired, quietly entering the room with an open book in his hands.

'Humph! Trust you not to have any idea. Your daughter has just been invited to the Earl of Carlyle's house party. *And* to be a guest at Lady Clara's birthday party on the twenty-fourth. That is no small honour, brother-in-law. No doubt the pinks of Society shall be coming down from London for the occasion.'

'I am delighted for you, my dear,' Mr Hadley said to his daughter, 'but the question remains—whose eyes are you judging, Ophelia?'

'Well, whose eyes do you think?' Lady Farrington asked in frustration. 'Carlyle's, of course. I was just telling Antonia that I noticed a definite interest on his part the last time I visited, and this invitation confirms it.

Mark my words, if Antonia takes care, she may end up a countess yet!'

Antonia flushed hotly. 'But I am not—'

'And if you tell me one more time that he is only interested in you as a neighbour, my girl, I shall get up and walk right out of that door,' Lady Farrington threatened, unaware of what a very tempting offer she had made. 'Well?' she continued, handing her brother-in-law the letter. 'What have you to say about this, Peter?'

Mr Hadley duly read the letter, but seemed reluctant to draw any conclusions from it. 'I think, Ophelia, that it is very kind of the Earl to include Antonia in his guest list, but I doubt it portends an engagement announcement appearing in *The Times*. Antonia will not be the only lady present.'

'Numbers, dear boy, numbers,' Lady Farrington replied confidently. 'Carlyle is merely trying to divert everyone's attention away from his true purpose. With that many people in the house, he knows that he will be able to conduct a discreet courtship of Antonia with little or no notice taken. Then, when he is ready to announce their engagement—'

'Engagement!' Antonia said aghast.

'Well, yes, girl, what do you think the object of this undertaking is?'

'I think,' Antonia said, all but snatching the letter from her aunt's fingers, 'that the object is to have a party for a little girl whom Lord Carlyle knows I am fond of. And I think he is being considerate of Clara by inviting me to attend.'

'And why would you think that?'

'Imagine how frightening it will be for a child, who has had precious little exposure to large numbers of people, suddenly to be confronted by a house full of strangers, all making a fuss over her. At least if I am there, she will have someone with whom she is familiar.'

Lady Farrington shook her head and rose. 'Very well, Antonia. Play the Bath miss if you wish. Do not heed the wisdom of your aunt. I understand. You would rather bury your head in the sand than admit that Carlyle is in love with you.'

'In love with me!' Antonia gasped, suddenly overcome with a desire to laugh. 'A moment ago you said he was harbouring…a *tendre* for me. When did a *tendre* suddenly blossom into love?'

'It does not take long,' Lady Farrington informed her niece sagely. 'Especially with a man like Carlyle. He makes up his mind about things and he acts upon them. You will not see him shilly-shallying around about love. And if you are smart, my girl, you will keep your wits about you and your eyes open. Opportunities like this do not come along every day!'

'No, I am sure they do not,' Antonia replied, struggling to conceal her exasperation.

'Well, I must take my leave, I have errands to run. Good day, Antonia,' Lady Farrington said, pulling on her soft, kid leather gloves. 'Good day, brother-in-law. By the by, I saw your Lady Sheraton in town yesterday. A fine woman, that. You would do well to mind your manners around her.'

Lady Farrington swept up the skirts of her gown and departed, leaving Antonia feeling as though a gust of wind had ripped through the house. Speechless, she turned to stare at her father, who appeared equally overwhelmed.

'I know, I know,' Mr Hadley said, sinking into the nearest chair. 'There should be a law against women like Ophelia being allowed to call more than twice a month.

Unfortunately, I have a feeling we shall be seeing rather more of my sister-in-law over the next little while than we might like. Especially given the arrival of that auspicious invitation.'

Antonia picked up the single sheet of heavy parchment again and sighed. 'Whatever am I to do, Papa?'

'What do you mean, what are you to do?' Mr Hadley regarded his daughter's tragic face with some amusement. 'Do you not wish to go to Carlyle's party?'

'Well, yes, of course I do, but how *can* I if I am supposed to be giving Clara riding lessons? And how can I pretend to be Tony Davlin with the Earl and a house full of guests milling about?'

'Ah, now that is a coil,' Mr Hadley admitted, chuckling. 'Perhaps you cannot—anymore.'

Deep in thought, Antonia missed the point of her father's remark. 'I know. Perhaps Tony Davlin could become ill. So much so, that he could not…possibly risk exposing himself to a little girl for fear of passing— whatever illness he has along to her. What do you think?'

Mr Hadley eyed his daughter narrowly. 'I think that you are going to get yourself so tangled up in these deceptions that you will forget which way is up. Mayhaps it is time you put an end to this charade.'

'But I can't! Not yet,' Antonia exclaimed. 'It has been going so well until now. And you have to admit, Papa, the extra money has been helping.'

'Yes, it has,' Mr Hadley conceded, 'but I refuse to allow you to continue this escapade at risk to your own reputation, Antonia. I do not like the dishonesty of it.'

Some of the wind seemed to go out of Antonia's sails. 'I know, Papa. In truth, I do not like it very well myself.' She paused for a moment to nibble anxiously at her bottom lip. 'I shall have to talk to Mr Bingham. He always knows what to do.'

'For your sake, I hope he does.' Mr Hadley sat and stared at the tips of his boots in silence for a few minutes. 'Do you know what else bothers me about your aunt?'

'What?'

'The fact that she likes Lady Sheraton. Perhaps I have made a terrible mistake in seeing Eleanor,' he said grimly.

'Papa! How can you say that? Lady Sheraton is a delightful lady. She is gracious, and charming, and warm. In fact, I think she is wonderful. Don't you?'

'As it happens, I do,' her father agreed self-consciously. 'But the fact that Ophelia thinks so too has me definitely worried. I would hate it to be known that, for once, your aunt and I are in complete accord on something!'

Chapter Seven

Unfortunately, Antonia soon discovered that, this time, Mr Bingham did not have a simple solution to her problem. If anything, he seemed to be even more at sixes and sevens than she was.

'But *why* can you not tell Lord Carlyle that Mr Davlin is sick, Paddy?' Antonia asked in a plaintive voice. 'You could simply say that he has something…dreadfully contagious, and that he has been advised to stay in bed. The Earl would believe that, surely?'

But Bingham only shook his head and sighed. 'Not this time, I'm afraid, miss. His lordship specifically asked to see Mr Davlin, and I don't think he'll be taking no for an answer.'

The two of them were sitting in the long grass next to the stables, enjoying the peaceful silence of the balmy summer afternoon. Mr Bingham had arrived back at Ashdean the previous evening and the first thing he had done was send a note round to Buntings Hill, asking Antonia to meet with him at her earliest convenience. 'In fact, he told me that if he wasn't able to meet with Mr Davlin before Clara's party, he would be informing

Mr Davlin that he could look elsewhere for employment.'

'But he can't, Paddy! Tell me that he can't.'

'He can, miss, and no mistake about it. Lord Carlyle made his feelings very clear this last time. He wants to see Tony Davlin, and there was nothing I could say to change his mind. Besides, even if he did buy your story and genuinely believe you to be ill, it wouldn't prevent him from asking again in the future.'

It was Antonia's turn to sigh. Paddy was right, of course. There was nothing she could do to avoid the inevitable. Lord Carlyle was perfectly within his rights to request an interview. In fact, she was very fortunate that she had been able to go this long without being called for one. Which meant that she really had no choice—it was time to give up the deception.

Tony Davlin would have to disappear. If she did not meet with Lord Carlyle, Paddy would have to dismiss her for disobeying the Earl's direct orders. And if she did meet with Lord Carlyle, *he* would dismiss her for pretending to be someone she was not.

What a cull, Antonia thought desperately, as she rode Foxfire back to Buntings Hill. Not only was she losing a paying position, but she would have to watch someone else step in and teach Clara to ride—and possibly undo all of the good she had done.

Still, if that was the way it had to be, so it would be, Antonia admitted sadly. As much as she hated losing the job, there was no question in her mind that she would do that, rather than risk forfeiting Lord Carlyle's good opinion of her. Because when it came to the sticking point, that was far more important to her than anything else.

Antonia was not sure when her feelings towards the

Earl had begun to change. It had not happened in the course of a single afternoon, or as a result of any one particular event. Rather, it had been a slow, day-by-day transition. She had watched Lord Carlyle as he had attempted to get to know his tenants, taking an interest in their lives, and trying to make them better in whatever ways he could. She had seen him donate moneys and books to the orphanage, but refuse to take credit for it, even when the vicar had asked him to stand up and receive the goodwill of the parish.

And she had watched as Lord Carlyle and his daughter had taken their first tentative steps towards one another in an attempt to achieve a more natural father–daughter relationship. Clara had been starved for her father's love and attention, and Carlyle had been astonished by the unconditional love and trust the child had been ready to give him. She had been willing to put aside the past and to start over, as only children were able to do. And Carlyle, having discovered that, with a little effort, he could heal the rift his absence had caused, had taken the time to start being a father.

Yes, all of those things had helped to change her opinion of him, Antonia realised now. And an unwilling affection had blossomed into…something more. Indeed, the very thought of him now filled her with such bittersweet longings that she scarcely knew what to do. She longed to hear the sound of his voice again, and to revel in the rich, rolling melody that was his laughter. She just wanted to be near him. And if something had to be sacrificed in order to make sure that it happened, there was no question in Antonia's mind that it would be her role as Tony Davlin. She could not bear the thought of Sebastian being angry with her. Not any more.

She was falling in love with the Earl of Carlyle, and there was absolutely nothing she could do to stop it.

On the day before Lord Carlyle was due to arrive back in Upper Tipping, Antonia donned her elegant dove grey riding habit and rode over to Ashdean for the last time. The woods were quiet as she guided the mare along one of the less travelled paths, and a hundred different thoughts tumbled about in her head, not the least of which was that, after today, she would no longer be playing the part of Tony Davlin.

In truth, Antonia was sorry to see him go. She had come to like her elusive alter ego. She had never had an opportunity for an adventure like this, and she had found the game of pretending to be someone else rather exciting, even if it had only been for a short time.

Still, she had known all along that it would have to come to an end, and over the last few days she had made her peace with it. Today, she would tell Paddy that Tony Davlin was finished. As of today, he would be leaving the Earl of Carlyle's employ.

Antonia turned the mare on to the grassy path which the village children used as a short cut to the nearby lake—and nearly fainted. Sebastian was riding directly towards her.

'My...lord!' she stammered.

'Why, Miss Hadley. What a pleasant surprise. We do seem to be making a habit of running into each other like this. But are you quite all right? You have gone rather pale.'

Was it any wonder? Antonia reflected weakly. She was on her way to give Lord Carlyle's daughter a riding lesson in the guise of Tony Davlin! Was that not sufficient cause to make anyone pale?

'I—yes, we do. Run into each other, that is. And no, I am…fine.' Dear heavens, she had to stop babbling, lest Carlyle think she had completely lost her wits. 'I was merely…startled by your appearance.' She finally raised her eyes to his—and felt her heart turn over in her breast. Dear Lord, he was so *very* handsome. 'I was…not aware that you were due home until…tomorrow.'

'Really?' Carlyle relaxed in the saddle, and his mouth curved in a sardonic smile. 'I was not aware that it was common knowledge *when* I would be returning.'

'Well, no, of course. That is to say, it is not…likely that it *is* common knowledge…even now,' Antonia stammered. 'But I chanced to meet…Mr Bingham in the village yesterday, and he told me that…you were on your way back.'

'Did he indeed? Well, I shall have to have a word with my steward when I get in. I was hoping to surprise Clara with my return. Now I fear the entire district will already know about it.'

A swathe of dark, wavy hair fell forward across his brow as he spoke, and somehow Antonia resisted the urge to lean over and smooth it back. In a buckskin jacket that did nothing to hide the breadth of his shoulders, and breeches that moulded to his muscular thighs and legs, he was the type of man who could make a lady quite breathless. 'I am certain that Pad—that is, that Mr Bingham would not do anything to spoil your surprise, my lord,' Antonia finally managed to say.

'Why? He has already spoiled any chance I might have had of surprising you.'

The words were spoken in a teasing manner, and unwillingly, Antonia felt a smile work its way to her lips. 'Yes, but then, I am a grown woman, and no longer expectant of surprises. But you must not hold him solely accountable, my lord. I am quite sure that, had he not informed me of your imminent return, Lady Dalrymple most certainly would have.'

'Ah, yes, Lady Dalrymple.' A faint light twinkled in the depth of Carlyle's blue eyes. 'I begin to wonder whether it is possible to surprise *anyone* in Upper Tipping with such a lady keeping watch over the comings and goings of its residents.'

'I would venture to say that it is possible, my lord,' Antonia allowed with a smile, 'albeit exceedingly difficult.'

Carlyle laughed, and the sound of it sent shivers down Antonia's spine. 'Well said, Miss Hadley, well said.' He paused for a moment as his gaze moved over her face, searching her eyes. 'You appear to be heading in the direction of Ashdean. May I accompany you on your ride?'

His question brought the matter of Tony Davlin rushing to the fore, and Antonia's fingers tightened on the reins. What was she to do? She could not ride on to Ashdean now. Clara would be waiting for her lesson, and in doing so, would certainly expose her.

'Actually, I am going to…the orphanage, Lord Carlyle,' Antonia said quickly. 'I thought to turn off at…Chepston Cross and make my way across the fields.'

'Isn't that a rather long way to go?'

'Yes, but it is such a lovely morning that I thought I would take advantage of it and enjoy a longer ride.'

'Ah. Well, then, I shall not delay you further. Good day, Miss Hadley.'

'Lord Carlyle.'

'Oh, Miss Hadley. Since Mr Bingham took the liberty of informing you that I was coming home tomorrow, I expect he also told you that I am planning to hold a ball to celebrate Clara's birthday.'

'As a matter of fact, he did.'

'Good. What he may not have told you is that I should like you to join us for dinner on the Friday evening before.'

Antonia stared at him in astonishment. 'For dinner…my lord?'

'Yes. I have invited some friends down from London and I thought you might enjoy the opportunity of meeting them prior to the ball. They shall be arriving on Friday and staying at Ashdean for a few days.'

'But…surely they will wish to spend time with you—'

'They will be doing that for the better part of five days. I think I can share a little of that time with you, Miss Hadley. Unless that does not meet with your approval, of course.'

His gaze travelled over her face and, as their eyes met, Antonia felt the strangest tingle in the pit of her stomach. What could she say? Quite apart from the fact that she had been granted a considerable honour, she wanted to spend time with him. And was that not what he had just given her an opportunity to do?

'Thank you, Lord Carlyle, I should be…very pleased to attend.'

'Splendid. Shall I send the carriage?'

'No, that is quite all right. I am sure that Abbott can take me in the gig.'

'Very well. Have him bring you round about half past seven. Unlike Lady Dalrymple, *we* dine at eight. Good afternoon, Miss Hadley.'

'Good afternoon, Lord Carlyle.'

'Oh, and Miss Hadley, one more thing.' He smiled broadly. 'A lady like yourself should never consider herself too old for surprises.' Then, doffing his gleaming black beaver, he touched his heels to the stallion's dark flanks and pushed him into an easy canter.

Antonia watched him until he rounded the bend and disappeared from view. Only then did she gather up her own reins and turn her mare back in the direction of Buntings Hill. She could not go to Ashdean, and there was no point in her going to the orphanage. She was far too distracted to be of any use to Mr Howard. The best thing she could do, was to go home and think very carefully about what she had let herself in for.

Imagine accepting an invitation from the Earl of Carlyle to join him for dinner with a group of friends who would no doubt be wealthy, sophisticated, and titled. Antonia smiled in spite of herself. Whatever would aunt Ophelia say about that?

News that the Earl of Carlyle was holding a ball to celebrate his daughter's seventh birthday—along with the fact that there would be guests coming down from London to partake of the festivities—spread throughout the county like wild fire through tinder brush. Most of the prominent families in the area had been invited to attend the Saturday night festivities, but there was much speculation as to the identity of the guests who would be coming to stay at Ashdean for the weekend and for the other entertainments.

It was certainly the most popular topic of conversation at Lady Westerley's *musicale* the following evening, and one made even more so by the arrival of the bright and bubbly Miss Lucy Walters, who announced that she had heard, through an unimpeachable source, the names of some of the guests who would be travelling down from London.

'But however did you find out, Lucy?' Cynthia Prescott demanded.

'Never mind how she found out!' Lady Dalrymple interrupted. 'Are there to be any single gentlemen?'

'Of course,' Lucy informed them in a self-important voice. 'Lord Carlyle has invited Sir Robert Gage and Viscount Edwards—'

'Oh, la, he is *ever* so handsome!' Cynthia professed dreamily.

'Mr Gerald Benbrooke and Mr James Mallett.'

'Both from very respectable families,' Lady Westerley commented with approval.

'And Lord Montague.'

'Montague? Oh, dear. Married, and newly so,' Lady Dalrymple said in disappointment. 'Lady Montague will most certainly be with him.'

'Yes, along with Lady Jane Lytton, Miss Harriet Spencer, Lady Rosalind Grey, and—' Lucy's eyes flashed enviously towards Antonia '—Miss Antonia Hadley is to join them.'

'Antonia!' Lady Dalrymple gasped. 'Faith, child, you have been invited to the Earl of Carlyle's house party and you did not think to tell us?'

'I have not been invited for the entire weekend,' Antonia objected as everyone turned to stare at her. 'Only for the Friday evening dinner.'

'And to Lady Clara's ball on the Saturday,' Lucy reminded her.

'Yes, but so has everyone else in this room!'

'But only *you* have been invited to dine with Lord Carlyle and his friends on Friday evening,' Cynthia grumbled. 'Whatever *have* you done to warrant such special attention, Antonia?'

'She has done nothing,' Lady Farrington announced

to the gathering, 'except to be her own charming self. I was there. I saw it with my own eyes.'

Lady Dalrymple frowned. 'You were where, and saw what?'

'Lord Carlyle, when he called upon my niece at Buntings Hill the Sunday he arrived. I tell you, he could not take his eyes off her.'

'Aunt Ophelia, you know that is not true!'

'Perhaps he was just being polite,' Lady Westerley suggested tactfully.

'Fustian! There are plenty of girls to whom Carlyle has been polite, and they are not on the guest list.'

'Speaking of London, have you heard the latest scandal broth?' Lucy said, anxious to recapture her audience.

'No. Tell us, Lucy!' Cynthia said eagerly.

'Lady Rosalind Grey has been keeping company with Lord Carlyle. In fact, the house party was reputedly *her* idea.'

Lady Westerley tutted. 'A little coming on her part, wouldn't you say?'

'Perhaps, but it does not seem to have worked against her. Lady Rosalind is boasting that Carlyle even offered her the use of his private carriage to bring her to Ashdean.'

A ripple of surprise echoed around the room. Now that *was* an honour.

'She is very beautiful, though,' Catherine allowed generously.

'I suppose,' Lucy said grudgingly. 'But I tend to agree with Lady Westerley, that a lady should never appear too forward. Now, Antonia, you must tell us everything that goes on Friday night. We want to know what everyone wears—'

'And what they say—'

'And who they say it to—'

'Don't forget to see if Lord Edwards pays any attention to—'

'Never mind him, I want to know about Mr Benbrooke and—'

'Excuse me, ladies, but…am I too late?'

The room went deathly silent.

The Earl of Carlyle was standing in the doorway watching them.

'Lord Carlyle!' Lady Westerley hastened towards the door, quite unable to believe her eyes—or her good fortune. 'My lord, this is a most…unexpected pleasure. You do our humble gathering proud.'

'Forgive my coming late, Lady Westerley, but I was unavoidably detained,' Sebastian said as the lady swept him an elegant curtsy. 'I have not, I hope, missed the entertainments?'

'Not at all, my lord. In fact, we were—' Lady Westerley glanced anxiously about the room and found the person she was looking for '—yes, we were just about to begin. Madame Fleurmond, if you would be so kind as to take your place at the piano, we shall commence. Yes, thank you. Ladies, gentlemen, please do take your seats.'

The small cluster of ladies quickly scattered, but not before Sebastian had seen the colour rise to the cheeks of a number of them. He had no doubt that the topic of conversation just before he had entered the room had centred around him and upon the much anticipated house party.

'Lord Carlyle, perhaps you would like to sit here by me,' Lady Farrington offered, feeling a certain superiority over the others as a result of the special treatment she had received at Carlyle's hands at the home of her brother-in-law. 'This will, no doubt, pale in comparison to the quality of the *musicales* we are used to enjoying in London, but it shall serve to pass the evening.'

'It shall indeed, Lady Farrington.'

Sebastian cast his eye about the room for the lady he would have liked to sit beside, and quelled a sigh of disappointment when he saw that she was already seated next to her friend, Miss Shand. It would not do to try to arrange a switch in the seating now. That would call too much attention to both of them.

Hence, dutifully resigned to spending the first part of the *musicale* with Lady Westerley on his right, and Lady Farrington on his left, Sebastian sat down and hoped that the unknown Madame Fleurmond would, indeed, be tolerably entertaining.

In her chair two rows back, Antonia pretended to study the intricate design on her fan and avoided making eye contact with anyone. She had purposely not looked at Lord Carlyle when it had come time to take her seat, because while she had no reason to think that he *would* seek her out, something warned her that it was not entirely impossible that he would not.

'Have you really decided to…bid farewell to Mr Davlin?' Catherine asked in a voice that was barely above a whisper. 'I would not have thought you so willing to give him up, after everything you went through to create him.'

Antonia smiled ruefully. 'Nor did I but, as Mr Bingham pointed out, I really did not have any choice. If Carlyle were to discover who Mr Davlin really was, I would be turned off in a thrice. Dismissed for no good reason. And it really is a shame because Clara was coming along ever so nicely.'

'I hardly think it would be without good reason, Toni,' Catherine observed drily. 'You sent the Earl a letter in which you pretended to be a man, you have been wearing my brother's clothes in order to avoid recognition, and you applied for the position when you knew perfectly well that Lord Carlyle does not hire women. I should think those would be reasons enough to dismiss *anyone.*'

Antonia sighed. 'I suppose, when you put it like that, he does seem to be perfectly within his rights. I only hope that he does not question Mr Bingham at length over it. I should hate him to catch cold over something that I did wrong.'

The music began and the girls lapsed into silence. Antonia sat back in her chair and listened to the opening strains of a minuet, hoping to lose herself in the melody. But thoughts of Sebastian kept buzzing around in her head, until soon Antonia gave up the pretence of enjoying the music at all. Quite apart from the matter of Tony Davlin, she was still troubled by Clara's reaction to her news that she would be ending their lessons. The little girl had been wretchedly disappointed. Her big blue eyes had filled with huge, silver tears, and her little chin had positively quivered.

'But why must my lessons stop, Toni? You said that I was good.'

'And you are, dearest,' Antonia reassured her. 'It is just that…well, you see—'

'It's just that your Papa is going to have some people come and visit him, Lady Clara,' Mr Bingham said helpfully, 'and they are all going to be staying here at the house. So there won't be a lot of time for Toni to give you your lessons.'

'Are the people going to be here long?'

'No. Only for a few days.'

'Then can Toni start teaching me again when every-body has gone?'

Mr Bingham and Antonia quickly exchanged glances. 'That depends, Clara,' Antonia said carefully. 'Things may be…different after everyone leaves.'

'Why?'

Why. Such a simple word, Antonia reflected, yet it could lead to such a host of awkward questions. Like what they would do if Carlyle suddenly decided to start spending a lot more time in the country. Or conversely, what would happen if he decided to take Clara back to London to live with him again?

Or what *she* would do if he announced that he was getting married again…

'Tell you what, my little cock sparrow,' Mr Bingham said brightly. 'Even if someone else has to give you riding lessons, there's no reason why you and Toni can't still go riding together. I know that Toni would like that, wouldn't you, Toni?'

Antonia nodded. 'Yes, I would like that very much. Would that be all right with you, Clara?'

Clara seemed to think about it for a moment, and then sighed in a touchingly adult way. 'Yes, I would like that too, Toni.'

'Good. Then why don't you stop worrying about your lessons, and starting thinking about the lovely surprise your Papa has planned for you instead,' Bingham sug-gested.

That worked like a charm. Clara wiped the tears from her eyes and smiled, causing dimples to appear in her red cheeks. 'Papa has a surprise for me? What is it?'

'If I told you, it wouldn't be a surprise any more.'

'But it is a wonderful surprise, Clara,' Antonia said. 'And it is going to make you a very happy little girl.'

'Do you know what it is too, Toni?'

Antonia glanced at Bingham quickly. 'Y-yes. But only because…Mr Bingham told me. And he made me promise that…I would not tell a soul.'

'And *you* mustn't say a word to your Papa—' Mr Bingham winked at her and grinned '—or I shall be in for a right old ticking off! Shan't I, Toni?'

'Oh, I would most definitely think so,' Antonia murmured.

Fortunately, Clara gave them her solemn promise that she would not breathe a word about it to anyone—not even to her spaniel Bartholomew—and had returned to the house in much better spirits, content to wait and see what the wonderful surprise would be—

'Antonia?'

'Hmm?'

'Antonia?'

It was Catherine's voice which cut into her musings, and the urgency of it which brought Antonia back to the *musicale*. Looking towards the front of the room, she discovered that Madame Fleurmond was no longer sitting at the piano, and that in fact, everyone was looking at her. 'Catherine, what has happened?' she whispered anxiously.

'Madame Fleurmond is taking a rest, and when Lady Westerley asked if there was anyone who might wish to take their turn at the pianoforte, Lord Carlyle suggested that you should!'

Antonia blanched. 'Me? But…I can't!'

'Why not? You play better than anyone else in the room. And if you do not get up, Cynthia Prescott will, and you know how we shall suffer if she starts playing her dreadful funereal pieces.'

'Miss Hadley, will you play for us, or not?' Lady Westerley enquired from the front of the room. She had risen from her chair and was now standing beside the pianoforte. 'I should think you would be honoured that the Earl of Carlyle has specifically requested you to do so.'

Casting a reluctant glance at Lord Carlyle, Antonia felt herself blush as she slowly got to her feet. 'Yes, of course, I should be…delighted to play. Thank you, my lord.'

Carlyle inclined his head. 'The pleasure will be ours, Miss Hadley.'

Aware of the titters from the young ladies around her, Antonia lifted her chin as she made her way to the pianoforte. Normally, she would have been delighted to take a turn at the pianoforte, for Lady Westerley's instrument was an exceptionally fine one. But because Lord Carlyle had singled her out, Antonia felt as though a thousand butterflies had suddenly taken wing in her stomach. She wondered if she would be able to remember a note.

Settling herself gracefully on the bench, Antonia perused the selection of music in front of her. She usually played her pieces from memory, but, deciding that for now it might be wiser to have notes in front of her to follow, she selected a piece by Handel and, taking a slow, deep breath, placed her fingers upon the keys.

It was an indication of her skill that, within moments, Antonia was completely lost in her music. Her nimble fingers danced over the keys, never faltering as she played the complicated piece. And in his comfortable wing chair in the front row, Sebastian finally began to take some enjoyment in the evening. He crossed one leg over the other and relaxed back into the cushions, grateful that the curve of the chair hid his face from the eyes of others. He wanted to be able to study her without fear of observation, because watching Miss Antonia Hadley had become something of a passion of late.

He never tired of looking at her sweet face, with its delightfully retroussé nose, and its pointed chin. Her throat looked warm and shapely above the bodice of the low-cut gown, and Sebastian could just see the gentle swell of her breasts above the lace edging. Her complexion was all pink and white, the dusty rose of her cheeks serving as a warm contrast to the smooth white column of her neck. In the soft light of the candles, her luxurious hair—richly highlighted with strands of copper and gold—shimmered like silk against the backdrop of the creamy walls. One errant curl had dared to escape from the perfection of her upswept style to lay smooth against her forehead, almost inviting touch.

Sebastian sighed. He had never experienced anything like this before. Even in the early days of his courtship with Violet, he had not felt like this. He had never been so…drawn to any one woman that she became…a focal point in his life. From the very first time that he had met Antonia, he had been aware of her allure—even though she had taken pains to be as cool and as distant as possible.

Sebastian smiled. No wonder Clara was so taken with her. It would take a very hard heart indeed to shut out the warmth and goodness of the lovely Miss Antonia Hadley.

The sound of clapping signalled the conclusion of the piece, and roused him from his contemplation of the lady. Sebastian added his appreciation to that of the others. His eyes rested briefly on her face, willing her to look at him. And she did. Not because he believed he had the power to make her look, but because he knew, in his heart, that she was not indifferent to him. The delightful way she coloured every time he came upon her was a sure indication, as was the way she stumbled over her words when he said something to discomfort her. They were indications that either the lady was deathly afraid of him, or she was grudgingly intrigued.

And somehow, Sebastian doubted there was anything Antonia Hadley was afraid of.

'That was wonderful, Miss Hadley, simply wonderful,' Lady Westerley complimented her graciously. 'Might we impose upon you for another?'

'Thank you, Lady Westerley, but I am sure there are…others who would like to take their turn—'

'I wonder, Miss Hadley, if you might honour us with "My Love Lies Sleeping", before you vacate the bench,' Carlyle said unexpectedly.

His request focused every eye in the room on her, and Antonia blushed as the titters began again. The man seemed to be purposely trying to discomfort her. Nevertheless, Antonia lifted her chin and set her fingers back on the keyboard. She needed no music for this piece, and soon, the lilting strains of the old English love song rippled forth.

Abandoning himself to the pleasure of the music, Sebastian closed his eyes and allowed himself to continue his musings about the lovely Miss Hadley. What other depths would he find hidden beneath that calm, collected exterior? he wondered. For how could any woman play with such passion and verve, and be all cool composure underneath?

All too soon the piece came to an end, the final notes

drifting into silence. Sebastian joined in the applause, but this time, he did not attempt to make her stay when she got up from the bench and returned to her seat. Fortunately, Lady Westerley—who had observed that Cynthia Prescott was about to make *her* way to the pianoforte—decided that it was time to call an interlude. She refused to have the Earl of Carlyle leave her house as a result of the painful pounding of the keys Cynthia called playing.

'Ladies and gentlemen, refreshments are served. Shall we adjourn?'

Antonia did not immediately join the other guests in the partaking of refreshments. Desperate for a few moments alone, she slipped quietly out of the drawing room and into the adjoining saloon, where tall French doors opened out on to a small garden. Checking to see that no one had observed her flight, Antonia opened one of the doors and went outside.

The night air felt blissfully cool against her cheeks, and making her way to a small, stone bench located at the edge of the garden, Antonia sat down. She needed some time to review what had been happening, and how she felt about it. Like the remark Lucy Walters had made this evening about Lord Carlyle and his supposed interest in Lady Rosalind Grey.

Was it just a supposed interest? Antonia wondered. She had heard of the lady's great beauty, of course, and of her grace and refinement, but until tonight she had not been aware that Carlyle might be…interested in her.

And yet, who better than Lady Rosalind to be his countess? Antonia asked herself. Indeed, she possessed all of the qualities a nobleman would be looking for in a wife. Was that one of the reasons Lady Rosalind had been invited to Ashdean? So that she might become…acquainted with the house she was possibly to be mistress over?

'You seem to be in something of a brown study, Miss Hadley,' an all-too-familiar voice said from the direction of the French doors. 'I hope I have not blotted my copy book by singling you out for attention again.'

Antonia drew a sharp breath. 'Lord Carlyle! I…did not hear you approach.'

'Nor were you meant to. Please resume your seat, Miss Hadley, it was not my wish to discomfort you.' With a deliberately casual movement, Sebastian pushed himself away from the door and advanced a few steps closer. 'You are not angry with me for asking you to play, I hope?'

Antonia sank back down upon the stone bench, thankful for the darkness which hid her blushes. 'Not at all. Why would you think so?'

'Because sometimes one is able to glean a great deal more from a face unaware of observation, than through lips which would volunteer all.'

Antonia's golden lashes flew up. 'Rest assured, my lord, though I was…startled by your request, I was neither alarmed nor angered by it. I have been asked to play too many times to profess a shyness at doing so now.'

'And yet, I think there were those inside who found the fact that I specifically asked you to play amusing?'

Antonia lifted her shoulders in a pretty shrug. 'It is the nature of some to see amusement in everything.'

'But not you, I think, Miss Hadley,' Sebastian observed quietly. 'I think that there must be considerably more to something before you would express amusement over it.'

'You make me sound…far more formidable than I

am, Lord Carlyle. I can be as easily amused as the next lady.'

'Perhaps.' Sebastian reached out to finger the tender curl which still lay invitingly against her forehead. 'But I do not believe it. There is more depth to you than most, Miss Hadley. The matters which are closest to your heart would not be of concern to many of the young ladies inside.'

The casual touch of his hand caused Antonia's pulse to skitter alarmingly. 'I think you judge them too harshly, Lord Carlyle. There is no reason to believe that they are any less concerned with important matters than I—'

'But that is just my point. Are the matters with which they concern themselves important? Do they worry about the welfare of the children at the orphanage, I wonder? Do they try to find ways to acquire more books, or devote any of their time to teaching the young ones how to enjoy the ones they have so that they might make a better life for themselves? Does Miss Prescott think to take a jar of home-made jam to the elderly lady down the street who cannot go about for herself? Would Miss Walters trouble herself with a shy child who, though well born, had no more skills than a new-born when it came to playing with children her own age?'

'I...really could not say, my lord.'

'Could you not?' Sebastian's eyes found hers and held them firm. 'I think you could, Miss Hadley. Because I think you have more compassion than any woman in that room.'

The sound of Lady Farrington's imperious voice cut through the silence of the garden and jerked Antonia out of the hypnotic web his words had begun to weave around her. 'My lord, I must…return to the drawing room. My aunt—'

Sebastian swore softly under his breath, but he did not try to persuade her to stay. 'Yes, your aunt. It would not do for her to find you here alone with me.'

Antonia went to walk by him, and was stayed by the light but gentle pressure of his hand on her arm. 'Miss Hadley, I trust I have not offended you in any way? Because I can assure you, I care…too much for your good opinion to risk losing it.'

Tempted at first to look away, Antonia abruptly changed her mind. She tilted her head back to look at him, and felt her lips curve in a soft smile. 'No, Lord Carlyle. You have not offended me. Indeed, I am flattered that you have singled me out for such attention, and for such praise. I can think of no reason why…any woman would be offended by that.' With that, Antonia picked up her skirts and walked gracefully back into the house.

Left deep in thought by her remark, it was some time before Sebastian followed.

Chapter Eight

The guests began to arrive on the following Friday.

For the better part of a day, a steady stream of carriages turned in through Ashdean's massive stone gates and rolled up the long gravelled drive, groaning under the weight of trunks and portmanteaus filled with everything necessary for a weekend stay in the country.

Because Carlyle had purposely been vague about the type of entertainments he had planned for the weekend, the ladies—shuddering at the thought of not being suitably attired for *any* manner of festivity—had frantically instructed their maids to pack absolutely everything which might be required: everything from formal ball gowns and day dresses in light weight muslins and silks, to velvet riding habits, along with all the necessary fripperies and falderals.

Hence, it was hardly surprising that it took considerable time and effort on the part of the Ashdean footmen to unload all of the ladies' trunks, and for the butler to see the ladies comfortably settled in their assigned rooms.

The gentlemen, of course, being able to get by with considerably less clothing and quite happy to leave the management of it to their valets, gathered in the library with Carlyle, content to enjoy a few hours of masculine companionship before the ladies joined them.

Sebastian had decided not to introduce Lady Clara to his guests straight away. He was of the opinion that the visitors might not be at their best after the tiring trip down from London, and so had decided to wait until the following day. As a result, he planned dinner on the Friday for later in the evening, and joined Clara for an early tea in the cosy atmosphere of the schoolroom.

Antonia arrived slightly after seven o'clock. Since Carlyle had told her that dinner would be at eight, she instructed Abbott to return with the gig some time around midnight. Then, walking up the impressive stone steps to the porticoed entrance, she was greeted at the door by the butler and led towards the green salon where, judging by the sounds of light-hearted conversation and laughter, most of the guests had already gathered.

Sebastian was there. He looked so dashing and aristocratic in his formal clothes that, for a moment, Antonia found herself quite at a loss for words. His compelling blue eyes, and the confident set of his shoulders, identified him as a man who was used to being obeyed and, for an instant, Antonia felt the great social gulf that existed between them. Then, as he turned to smile at her, the distance seemed to vanish.

'Miss Hadley, how very pleased I am to see you,' he said, crossing the room to welcome her. 'Thank you again for accepting my invitation to join us. And may I say how very lovely you look this evening.'

A rush of pink stained Antonia's cheeks. She had known that tonight she would be dressing, not only for Sebastian, but for the very refined and sophisticated company in which he moved, and now, as she glanced around the room and saw the elegantly dressed ladies and gentlemen occupying it, she was thankful for the extra time Lucille had taken with her appearance. Her gown of ivory silk, trimmed with matching lace and delicate beading on the bodice, was—if not as elaborate—certainly as elegant as any of the other dresses in the room. 'Thank you, my lord. I am…grateful for the invitation.'

'Now I know this may seem a little daunting at first,' Sebastian whispered in her ear as he escorted her into the room, 'but I shall try to make the introductions as painless as possible. And take heart if you do not remember everyone's name at first. By the end of the weekend, you shall know them as well as you know me.'

Surprised by his unexpected compassion, Antonia smiled up at him with an expression that was much warmer than she realised. 'Thank you, my lord. I shall endeavour to apply a simple technique which I tell the children at the orphanage to use when they are trying to remember something new.'

'Oh?' Sebastian smiled in amusement. 'And what might that be?'

'To look for something unique or distinguishing about the person or thing. A characteristic, or a descriptive word that conjures up a memory of who or what they are trying to connect it to.'

'Ah, I see. As in…using the colour of an elderly lady's hair to remember that her name is…Mrs Snow?'

Antonia smiled her delight. 'Precisely. Or by using a physical feature to recall an aspect of their appearance.'

'Such as their height, as in the case of Lord Tallbrook,' Sebastian suggested.

'Or by their shape, like Mrs Dumpleton.'

'Or by thinking of a chicken when I wish to remember Lady Dalrymple.'

Antonia looked at him askance. 'A chicken, my lord?'

'Yes. Because they are forever scratching around in the dirt, trying to uncover what is hidden just below the surface. It reminds me of Lady Dalrymple.'

It was an outrageous thing to say, but when Antonia saw the merriment brimming in Sebastian's eyes, she could not help but laugh herself. The image conjured up by his words was far more apt than she cared to admit.

Unfortunately, Lady Rosalind Grey, who had also been watching for the new arrival, seemed none too pleased by the moment of shared laughter. Nor was her temper improved by the fact that the green girl she had been expecting to see was far more lovely and refined than she would have wished.

Blissfully unaware of Lady Rosalind's displeasure, however, Antonia turned to Sebastian as he commenced the introductions. 'Miss Antonia Hadley, may I present Miss Harriet Spencer and Mr James Mallett,' he said, beginning with the couple standing by the fireplace. 'And, to their left, Lord Edwards and Mr Gerald Benbrooke.'

Antonia smiled, and tried to commit the names to memory. She knew the Honourable Gerald Benbrooke, having seen him once before at a soirée in London. He was a good-looking young man, with fair, almost white hair, and very pale blue eyes. He was the eldest son of Viscount Benbrooke, and was considered by many to be an extremely good catch.

Mr James Mallett, whose name she also had a vague recollection of, was likewise an Honourable, his father being the rather formidable James Stewart Mallett, fifth Baron Mallett of Teasdale. Antonia had heard her own father speak in less than complimentary terms of the outspoken Baron, and hoped that his son would be more amiable company. Certainly he did not have the romantic appearance of Gerald Benbrooke. Mr Mallett's features were in no way remarkable, and there was a slight thickness about his middle which indicated a decided fondness for sweets. But he was amiable of nature and not in the least intimidating. And as he was also heir to a considerable fortune, he was no doubt looked upon as eligible for that reason, if for no other.

Lord Edwards, who appeared closer in age to Sebastian than either Gerald Benbrooke or James Mallett, was known to Antonia only by name. He had a rather stern air, but his face lightened considerably when he laughed. Miss Harriet Spencer was also unknown to her, but when that lady smiled back in response to Antonia's greeting, her pretty face totally devoid of guile, Antonia had warmed to her immediately.

'Miss Hadley, how very nice to meet you,' Harriet said now. 'I understand from Lord Carlyle that you and Lady Clara are fast friends.'

'I like to think so,' Antonia replied, surprised that Sebastian would have bothered to tell his guests anything about her. 'She is a thoroughly delightful little girl. Have you not met her?'

'Actually, I thought it better to wait until the party tomorrow,' Sebastian explained. 'I feared all the excitement might keep Clara up.'

Antonia was touched by his unexpected consideration for the child he had so recently come to know, and nodded. 'Yes, it takes very little in the way of excitement to keep a child awake at night.'

'You sound as though you know your way around children, Miss Hadley,' observed a very elegant and attractive young woman who was seated on the brocade settee. 'Have you perhaps younger brothers and sisters at home?'

Sebastian introduced the young woman as Lady Montague, and the man who was sitting across from her as her husband, Lord Montague. Antonia smiled at them both in greeting, remembering what Lady Dalrymple had said about the Viscount and his wife having only recently been married. Was Lady Montague anxious, perhaps, to have children of her own?

'I am afraid not, Lady Montague,' Antonia demurred, 'but I do help out at the orphanage here, so I am not unfamiliar with the ways of young children. In fact, it was there I first met Lady Clara.'

'Yes. Clara kept mentioning a "Toni",' Sebastian said with a smile, 'and at first, I thought she was referring to Tony Davlin, the gentleman I hired to give Clara riding instruction. At least I did, until Miss Hadley informed me that she and my daughter had met at a Christmas party last year.'

'Well, having seen Miss Hadley, I hardly think anyone could confuse one for the other,' Lord Edwards drawled. 'Miss Hadley bears no more resemblance to a man than I do to the Princess Caroline.'

'Thankfully, neither do any other ladies of my acquaintance,' Gerald Benbrooke quipped. 'If they did, I fear I should find myself remaining a bachelor for the rest of my days. And I wouldn't want to see that happen, would I, my dear, dear Jane?'

Mr Benbrooke's comment was addressed to the petite young woman sitting next to Lady Montague on the settee. She was an exquisitely lovely girl with a head of shimmering blonde curls that framed an oval face, enchanting blue eyes that were set above a delicately turned-up nose, and a figure that would set any young buck's heart to racing. The most appealing quality about Lady Jane Lytton, however, was the fact that she seemed blissfully unaware of her own allure.

'I do not imagine for a moment that it would, Mr Benbrooke.' Lady Jane's voice was soft, but her blue eyes sparkled mischievously. 'However, I feel quite secure in saying that, if by some chance you did remain single, it would not be due to the fact that you could not find handsome enough women, but rather that you would not be able to choose from amongst them.'

'Ho, Gerald! You have been put in your place,' Lord Montague chortled. 'I believe your reputation for fickleness precedes you.'

Gerald Benbrooke, who had, in fact, fallen hopelessly in love any number of times—and just as quickly out again—had the decency to blush. 'That was in my younger days, Montague. I have not proclaimed my heart lost—save to one—' he glanced pointedly at Lady Jane '—this many months. Have I, Gage?'

This was addressed to the gentleman sitting in the green velvet wing chair, who Sebastian introduced as Sir Robert Gage. He looked to be somewhere in his early forties. His thick, dark hair was just starting to grey at the temples, but his teeth were very white against a face bronzed by the sun. Clearly a man who enjoyed being outdoors, Antonia decided.

'I am not getting into this one, Benbrooke,' Sir Robert said after politely greeting Antonia. 'But history must speak for itself, I'm afraid.'

Amidst the outburst of laughter which followed, Antonia saw the last remaining lady in the room walk slowly towards her, and knew that she was looking at

Lady Rosalind Grey. The woman's striking beauty was identification enough.

'Am I not to be introduced to your country neighbour, my lord?' the Diamond asked in a seductively husky voice. 'For I believe I am the only one to have escaped your notice thus far.'

'As if you could escape anyone's notice for long, Lady Rosalind,' Mr Mallett commented in adoration.

'Easy, James,' Benbrooke warned. 'Lest you be awarded the same sobriquet as I.'

'*That* will hardly happen,' the rotund little man replied disdainfully. 'I do not cast my eyes upon so many stars in the night sky. I save my regard for one who outshines all others.'

'Oh, my. How terribly eloquent, James!' Lady Montague observed with a charming laugh. 'I do not think Mr Byron could have been any more poetic. Are you not terribly flattered, Rosalind?'

'Terribly,' Lady Rosalind replied, but in a tone so withering as to reduce poor Mr Mallett to a blushing bundle of nerves. Then, to Antonia's surprise, she tucked her hand into the crook of Lord Carlyle's arm and her sarcasm disappeared completely. 'My lord?'

'My apologies, Lady Rosalind. Lady Rosalind Grey, may I present Miss Antonia Hadley.'

Antonia curtsied prettily. 'Lady Rosalind.'

The smile which formed upon Lady Rosalind's lips was polite, but cool. 'Miss Hadley. I am surprised that we have not met before. I assume you were in London for the Season?'

'Not these past two, as I was still in mourning for my mother, but I was there prior to that. Of course, given the crowds which attend most of the functions, I am not surprised that we did not meet.'

'That is very true, Miss Hadley.' Harriet Spencer nodded her agreement. 'I shudder at the thought of them. They truly are such a dreadful crush. And the rooms get so uncomfortably warm.'

Lady Rosalind favoured Harriet with an equally patronising stare. 'Really. No doubt you are both more used to the bucolic pleasures of the country. Personally, I enjoy the excitement of Town. So many people to see, so many things to hear—'

'So many boring parties to attend,' Lady Montague interrupted disparagingly.

'You find the parties boring?' Lady Rosalind actually sounded incredulous.

'I do. Like Miss Spencer, I find the crowding of four and five hundred people into a house exceedingly oppressive, not to mention the tedium of having to mingle with all those pompous dandies parading about in their vile coloured waistcoats and ridiculous collar points. And the nonsense they do spout. Frankly, Rosalind, I haven't the patience to listen to them. Especially since most of what they say is rife with rumour and gossip besides!'

Harriet flashed Antonia a knowing grin. Lady Montague's remark had certainly put Lady Rosalind in her place, and at the moment, the beauty was looking extremely put out. Her hold on Carlyle's arm tightened, and she said so that everyone could hear, 'By the by, Lord Carlyle, I would like to thank you again for the generous use of your carriage. It was so very considerate of you to send it all the way up to London just for me.'

'Not at all,' Sebastian replied easily. 'It would have been a shame to deprive the party of your company simply because you were unable to arrange transportation.'

'But...I thought you said you were bringing your father's carriage, Lady Rosalind,' Mr Mallett said, frowning. 'Was that not your reason for turning down my own offer of an escort?'

Lady Rosalind flushed. 'I had fully intended to use my father's carriage, Mr Mallett, as I told you, but after a…last-minute inspection, I was informed that the carriage was…sadly in need of repair. And by that time, I assumed you would have made other arrangements and I did not wish to…trouble you. Lord Carlyle learned of my dilemma and kindly offered me the use of his own carriage. Otherwise, I should have been…delighted to travel with you,' she finished sweetly.

The timely arrival of Hildegarde to announce dinner saved Mr Mallett from the necessity of a reply, and brightening because of it, Lady Rosalind favoured Carlyle with one of her most breathtaking smiles. 'Shall we go in, my lord?'

Sebastian bowed, but offered no comment as he gave the lady his arm. 'By all means.' The rest of the group made their own arrangements and fell in behind according to rank and marital status. Lord Montague escorted his wife, while Gerald Benbrooke, trying to make his way to Lady Jane, but being beaten to the gate by Lord Edwards, had to settle for Miss Spencer. James Mallett, his elusive Rosalind having been squired by their host, breathed a remorseful sigh and wandered in alone, while Sir Robert graciously made up for Mr Mallett's lack of manners by offering his arm to Antonia.

Not surprisingly, the conversation over dinner was lively and entertaining. It soon became apparent to Antonia where the various affections lay, and it was with a great deal of enjoyment that she watched Gerald Benbrooke, who by good fortune had ended up being seated next to Lady Jane, vie for her attention with Lord

Edwards who was seated on her left, and who seemed to be receiving the lion's share of the lady's regard.

Mr Mallett, much to his delight, had been seated next to his adored Lady Rosalind, and spent much of the meal trying to divert her attention away from Sebastian. That, unfortunately, proved to be a futile exercise, since it was evident that Lady Rosalind was far more interested in conversing with her host than she was with anyone else. Poor Mr Mallett had to be content with speaking to Harriet, who was seated to his left. Lord and Lady Montague acted very much the part of the newlywed couple, but they did adhere to the rules of etiquette, and frequently directed their conversation to the people around them.

Antonia was very satisfied with her dinner placement, having found herself between Sir Robert and Miss Spencer, a placement which allowed her to further her acquaintance with the good-natured Harriet.

It was indeed a lavish feast which Carlyle presented to his guests that first evening. Each dish was perfectly prepared and, as expected, beautifully arranged and served. A selection of desserts followed, exquisitely arranged on silver trays and presented to each guest for their selection.

'My compliments to your chef, Carlyle,' Lord Montague said at the conclusion of the meal. He leaned back in his chair and patted his stomach. 'That is as fine a meal as I have eaten in many a day.'

'Come now, Monte, never tell me that a newly married man is suffering such a fate.' Sebastian winked at Lady Montague. 'I am quite sure that you eat every bit as well as this at home.'

'Besides, I wasn't aware that food was supposed to

be one of the main concerns of the newly married man,' Lord Edwards observed drily.

The somewhat risqué remark elicited knowing laughter from the gentlemen, and brought a delicate blush to the female cheeks present. Lady Montague, deciding that it was time to leave the gentlemen to their port and conversation—gave the signal and, as one, the ladies rose and gracefully withdrew.

Whether it was due to the lack of male companionship, however, or the combined effect of a long day's travel and the advanced hour, conversation amongst the ladies was desultory, so that by the time the gentlemen did finally rejoin them, a few of the ladies begged leave to retire.

Antonia was one of them. Aware that Abbott would be arriving shortly to collect her, she made her way to Sebastian's side to say her goodnights. She was pleasantly surprised when he seemed genuinely sorry to see her go. 'Miss Hadley, I fear I have not had much opportunity to speak with you this evening. I hope you are not slighted by the fact.'

'On the contrary, Lord Carlyle, as host to a room full of people, you could not have spent more time with any one guest than another. I am honoured that you thought to include me.' Antonia glanced at him shyly from under lowered lashes. 'I am well aware that our acquaintance is not as long standing as that of most of your other guests.'

'Be that as it may, Miss Hadley, you are here at my invitation, and I had hoped to spend more time with you. I shall endeavour to make up for my lack of attention tomorrow.' His gaze was as soft as a caress as it lingered on her face. 'I hope that meets with your approval?'

It did meet with Antonia's approval, though it cer-

tainly did not with Lady Rosalind's, who just happened
to be standing close enough to catch the end of their
conversation.

'Ah, there you are, my lord. Miss Hadley.' She moved
towards them in a rustle of perfumed silk. 'Perhaps the
two of you would care to make up a table for whist?'

'Thank you, Lady Rosalind, but I was just leaving,'
Antonia replied. 'Abbott is waiting for me even now.'

'What a pity. Lord Carlyle?'

'Yes, I shall be there directly, Rosalind. Oh, Miss
Hadley, before you go—I was planning to take a party
into Canterbury for a few hours tomorrow afternoon. I
thought perhaps the ladies might enjoy walking around
the Cathedral grounds, and no doubt the gentlemen will
find other activities with which to amuse themselves.
Would you care to join us?'

Exceedingly flattered by his request, Antonia regretfully shook her head. 'I very much wish I could, Lord
Carlyle, but I promised Lady Sheraton that I would take
her down to visit the orphanage. She has kindly expressed an interest in helping out.'

'Oh, what a shame,' Lady Rosalind purred, sounding
more relieved than dismayed. 'But it would equally be
a shame to deprive such a worthy cause of your attention, Miss Hadley. Do you not think so, my lord?'

'It is a worthy cause indeed,' Sebastian agreed slowly,
'and Lady Sheraton is a lovely woman. But I am truly
sorry that it will deny us the pleasure of your company,
Miss Hadley.'

Lady Rosalind's smile dimmed slightly at the warmth
of Carlyle's tone, but she bid Antonia a pleasant goodnight and then returned to the drawing room where the
remaining guests were preparing to play cards.

'You will be free in time to come for Clara's ball

tomorrow evening I hope, Miss Hadley,' Sebastian said. 'I know she would be dreadfully disappointed were you not here to celebrate her birthday with her. As would I.'

His voice was like silk over steel and Antonia felt a pulse begin to beat at the base of her throat. 'I would not miss it for the world, my lord,' she said, meaning every word.

To her surprise, Sebastian actually seemed relieved. 'Good. And now, I suppose I too must return to my guests.' To Antonia's surprise, he raised her hand to his lips and pressed a tender kiss to the back of it. 'Until tomorrow.'

Antonia's heart thudded once and then settled back into its normal rhythm. She murmured something appropriate before turning and making her way outside to where Abbott was waiting with the gig, thankful once again for the darkness which hid the rosy colour in her cheeks. And as they set off down the long drive, Antonia couldn't resist turning around to steal a quick glance behind her.

She was surprised to see that Sebastian was still standing on the steps watching her. She would have been even more surprised had she known that he continued to stand there long after the carriage rounded the last bend in the driveway and disappeared from sight.

In spite of the fact that she would very much liked to have joined Sebastian and his guests for an afternoon visit to Canterbury, Antonia spent a most delightful day in the company of Lady Sheraton. She soon came to realise that the lady was possessed of both a warm, giving nature and a delightful sense of humour.

When they had finished their tour of the orphanage, Lady Sheraton stopped back to see the vicar, assuring him that she was most anxious to be of help and adjuring him to call upon her whenever necessary. That completed, the two ladies headed back outside to where Lady Sheraton's smart barouche awaited.

'Poor little dears,' Lady Sheraton murmured when they were both comfortably seated. 'I wanted to take all of them home with me. Especially the little ones.'

Antonia nodded sympathetically. 'I know. I feel that way every time I go there. They all look up at you with such longing in their eyes.'

'Yes, as if to ask by what cruel twist of fate they found themselves in such a place.'

Antonia heard the note of recrimination in the older woman's voice and hastened to reassure her. 'You must not think badly of the place, Lady Sheraton. The orphanage is clean and well maintained. Far better than most, I think.'

'I suppose. The children seem healthy enough, and they do have adequate clothing. But what of their education, Antonia? Have they anyone to teach them?'

'Not on a permanent basis, but the vicar has set up a kind of volunteer group that helps when it can. I go in Tuesday and Thursday afternoons, and Mrs Howard, the vicar's wife, visits Mondays and Fridays. Then, on Sunday, they are all brought to the church and after service, are given a hot meal by Mrs Howard.'

'It is very good of her—and of you, to go to the trouble. I think perhaps that is how I could best be of service too. I shall go and see Mr Howard and tell him that I would like to volunteer my services. Particularly in the area of reading, I think. I was very pleased to see such an assortment of books.'

'Those were donated by a number of people, including Lord Carlyle,' Antonia told her. 'In fact, he has been

most generous since his return to Upper Tipping. As well
as the books, he has given the vicar a substantial amount
of money to go towards paying for the repairs and up-
keep of the building, with a promise of more, should it
be required.'

'I am not surprised,' Lady Sheraton said. 'Sebastian
has always been very generous towards those in need.'

Sebastian? Antonia glanced at her companion in surprise. 'Are you...well acquainted with the Earl, Lady
Sheraton?'

'Yes, quite well. Oh, no, dear, not like that!' Lady
Sheraton said when she saw the look which appeared on
Antonia's face. 'I am definitely too old for the likes of
Carlyle. But we are friends. And I did happen to notice
the other evening that you and he seemed, well...close.'
Lady Sheraton glanced at her shrewdly. 'Is there perhaps
an...understanding between the two of you?'

Antonia's cheeks burned, even as her eyes were suddenly filled with a curious longing. 'No, my lady, there
is not. As I told my father, Lord Carlyle has been very
pleasant to me, but that is all. There is nothing between
us beyond that.'

'No? Pity,' Lady Sheraton said, her brief sideways
glance alight with amusement. 'He is one of the most
handsome gentlemen I have ever had the pleasure of
knowing, do you not think?'

Antonia hesitated, feeling suddenly tongue-tied. 'Yes,
I...suppose he is.'

'Yes, indeed,' Lady Sheraton agreed, trying to hide
the laughter in her eyes.

The rest of the afternoon passed all too quickly, and
both ladies were genuinely sorry when it came to an end.
Antonia did persuade Lady Sheraton to come in for a

cup of tea and one of Mrs Grenfall's excellent home-made scones before setting off for Newton Spinney.

'I really should not, you know,' Lady Sheraton said, reluctantly accompanying Antonia into Buntings Hill. 'I have a terrible sweet tooth, and I did have that dish of plum pudding after lunch.'

'Fudge! You are as trim as a debutante. I really cannot credit that you have anything to worry about.'

'My dear, you are terribly flattering,' Lady Sheraton replied, laughing. 'I think I shall endeavour to come here more often.'

'Now that's a fine idea if ever I heard one,' Mr Hadley said, emerging from library at the sound of the feminine chatter.

Lady Sheraton, whose poise and refinement were two of the qualities Antonia admired most about her, suddenly started to blush like a schoolgirl. 'Mr Hadley, what a pleasant surprise,' she said breathlessly. 'I hope it is not an inconvenience, but Antonia convinced me that I must come in and try one of your cook's famous scones before returning home.'

Mr Hadley glanced at his daughter shrewdly. 'Did she, indeed? Well, I have always held it to be true that Mrs Grenfall's currant scones were reason enough to put off going almost anywhere. I am doubly glad that it was reason enough to persuade you to join us today.'

Lady Sheraton continued to blush prettily as she followed Mr Hadley and Antonia into the drawing room. Momentarily, Abbott arrived with a tempting array of the highly touted scones, along with currant buns and delicate cream cakes.

'Lady Sheraton, I wonder if I might impose upon you to pour,' Antonia asked, as Abbott went to set the tray down beside her.

'Antonia?' Mr Hadley glanced up at his daughter in surprise.

'Forgive me, Papa, but with your permission I should like to retire to my room for a while. Lady Clara's party is this evening, and I would like to rest. No doubt it will be a very late night.'

Antonia was amused to see the blush deepen in Lady Sheraton's cheeks, and the knowing twinkle which suddenly appeared in her father's eye. 'I see. And I take it that you do not feel that we older folk, who will also be attending this very late evening, will be in need of rest as well?'

'I feel sure that you and Lady Sheraton are much more used to these types of diversions,' Antonia said innocently, 'and are, as such, better able to cope with the strain of them.' She saw the laughter trembling on her father's lips, and hastily looked away. 'Thank you for a lovely day, Lady Sheraton. I hope we shall be able to do it again very soon.'

'I look forward to it, Antonia,' Lady Sheraton said, her bright blue eyes brimming with merriment. Clearly, she was not fooled by the excuse either.

'Papa?'

'You may be excused, Antonia,' Mr Hadley said wryly, well aware that he and Lady Sheraton had been victims of a plot—albeit a well-meaning one. 'By the by, are you intending to accompany me to Ashdean this evening—if and when you are sufficiently well rested? Or have you secured other means of transport?'

'If it is not inconvenient, I should like to travel with you, Papa,' Antonia said, fondly bestowing a kiss on her father's brow before she turned to leave. 'Good afternoon, Lady Sheraton.'

'Thank you again for the pleasure of your company,

Antonia,' Lady Sheraton said warmly. 'And I look forward to seeing you at the ball this evening.'

Upstairs, in the privacy of her bedroom, Antonia thought about the two people in the drawing room below, and smiled. It was strange but, for a long time after her mother had died, Antonia had dreaded the thought of her father becoming involved with another woman. She had found it impossible to imagine anyone else stepping into that role, and had thought that she would have been resentful of any lady trying to steal her father's affection.

And yet, since meeting Lady Sheraton and seeing the change it had wrought in her father, Antonia could feel nothing but happiness. Lady Sheraton was a lady in every sense of the word, and she was exactly what her father needed. There was nothing invasive or forward about her. She was a kind and gentle woman; considerate of her friends, and sensitive to the needs of others.

But there was spirit there too, Antonia admitted, thinking back on their visit to the orphanage. The kind of spirit that made a lady speak out on the issues of child welfare, including the abolishment of the dreadful practice of sending young boys up sooty chimneys, and of child labour in the mills.

Yes, she was a woman Antonia could admire in so many ways. And she was exactly the type of woman who could give her father's life meaning again.

Would that *she* could have that type of effect on someone's life, Antonia thought wistfully.

Chapter Nine

True to his word, Sebastian spared no expense in ensuring that his daughter's seventh birthday would be one to remember. While the weekend house party had been planned with a limited number of guests in mind, Clara's birthday celebration had been extended to include many of the local people as well; consequently, the house had been decorated no less than it would have been for a gala ball.

The servants were up before dawn, hard at work polishing the brass and the silverware, sweeping the floors and making sure that the floor in the ballroom was as highly polished as it could be, and attending to a thousand and one other details which inevitably accompanied a gala event.

Finally, when the time was right, Sebastian proudly led his daughter into the glittering ballroom where everyone was waiting for her. In honour of the occasion, Clara was wearing a beautiful new dress; a fairy-tale confection of white and silver gauze, guaranteed to make any little girl feel like a princess. The dress had been a special gift from her father, along with the dainty silver slippers and the pretty pearl necklace.

Antonia stood beside Lady Montague and Catherine Shand as Sebastian and his daughter made their descent. She watched the pair weave their way through the crowded room, and felt that her heart would surely burst from happiness. Clara might not be her own child, but at the moment Antonia could not have been more proud if she had. The little girl hesitated at the bottom of the stairs, momentarily alarmed by the unexpected sight of so many beautifully dressed ladies and handsome gentlemen smiling at her, but soon began to relax as Sebastian slowly made his way through the crowd and began introducing her.

'Lord Carlyle looks very happy this evening, Miss Hadley,' Lady Montague whispered, looking exceedingly lovely in a gown of lavender silk with matching gloves and fan. 'I cannot recall ever having seen him look so…content.'

'I think discovering his daughter was the best thing that could have happened to him, Lady Montague.'

'Certainly, he does not look at all like a rake now,' Catherine put in.

Antonia caught her bottom lip between her teeth. 'Lady Montague, was Lord Carlyle…truly that much of a rake? That is to say, I have heard rumours about his…behaviour while he was in London, but seeing him the way he is now, and indeed the way he has behaved ever since returning to Upper Tipping, it is difficult to believe that he was so very wicked.'

Lady Montague smiled, and her eyes were warmly affectionate as they rested on their host. 'I do not think it was wickedness at all, Miss Hadley. If those were the stories you heard, I fear they were somewhat…exaggerated. Carlyle was lonely and he was bored. I think he sought to bury his loneliness in...reckless behaviour. Yes, he frequented the hells, but what blue-blooded man has not at some time in his life? As for his behaviour with the ladies, well, I suppose that too is to be expected.' Lady Montague glanced at Antonia and her eyes sparkled. 'I hope I do not you to the blush, Miss Hadley, but it is a well known fact that most men—not all, but most...amuse themselves with certain types of women at different times in their lives. Carlyle was no different. But at least he did not indulge himself with married ladies, or toy with the affections of those who might have been considered candidates for the role of countess. I know of other men who have, and who felt no compunction about it whatsoever.'

Antonia nodded, irrationally pleased to discover that the tales Lady Dalrymple had been spreading were just that. For surely Lady Montague, who had been with Sebastian in London and would have seen him at his worst, would be a far more reliable source of information.

There were a number of other questions Antonia would have liked to ask Lady Montague, but suddenly, Sebastian and Clara were standing in front of them. Impulsively, Clara flung open her arms. 'Toni, you look beautiful,' the little girl breathed. 'Doesn't Toni look beautiful, Papa?'

'Yes, Clara, she does.'

Antonia felt the warmth creep up into her cheeks at his unexpected compliment, and hastily averted her eyes. She certainly wasn't dressed as elegantly as Lady Montague, nor did she have the kind of jewellery many of the other ladies had but, nevertheless, she had tried to make the best of her appearance. She had not wanted to appear a plain little wren amongst a garden of exotic birds. Fortunately, she knew that her pure white gown, over which lay a shimmering net of silver gauze, was one of her prettiest, and that it became her very well. Long white gloves covered her arms, and skilfully wound through her hair were a strand of pure white pearls. Her mother's pearl and diamond necklace and matching ear bobs were her only other accessories.

Needing something to say, Antonia abruptly directed her attention back to Clara. 'You did not think I would miss your birthday, did you, Clara?'

Clara dimpled and shook her head, making the golden ringlets bob and dance. 'No. Because you came to my last one too.'

Sebastian's dark eyebrows drew together in a frown. 'There was a party for Clara last year?'

'Yes, we held it at the vicarage,' Antonia explained quietly. 'Actually, it was also the birthday of one of the other little girls the same day, so we decided to celebrate both at the same time.'

'And no one thought to tell me about it?'

Antonia glanced up at him in surprise, surprised by the quick flash of anger she saw in his eyes. 'We saw no reason to advise you, my lord. Eva told me beforehand that you had already sent a gift to Clara, with a note, apologising for the fact that you would not be able to be with her. And knowing that, I did not see any point in advising you of a simple children's party that was being held at the orphanage.'

Antonia saw a muscle jump in Sebastian's jaw, and realised in surprise that he was angry. But what was the point? There was nothing he could do about the years of Clara's childhood that he had missed, whether he regretted them or not.

'Lord Carlyle, pray do not dwell on what you cannot change,' Antonia said gently. 'The past is over and done.

But Clara will have many birthdays to look forward to, and you will be there for all of them. Just think how much more memorable they will be because you have chosen to be a part of them.'

Sebastian was astonished to find himself at a loss for words. As illogical as it sounded, he *had* been angry that someone had held a party for Clara, and not told him about it. He was her father, wasn't he? And yet, as Antonia had pointed out, why would they have told him? What difference would it have made to him last year? Would he have made the effort to travel down to the country, just to celebrate a party being held at the orphanage?

Knowing the answer, Sebastian swallowed the lump which suddenly formed in his throat, and nodded. 'It is good of you to say so, Miss Hadley. And you may rest assured that every birthday *will* be more special than the last. I shall make sure of it!'

In spite of all the excitement, it wasn't long before Clara's eyelids began to droop—she was, after all, a very little girl. Aware that she would not be able to stay awake much longer, Sebastian gently picked her up and walked her around the room so that everyone had an opportunity to wish her a happy birthday. Finally, at the bottom of the stairs, he turned to allow her to wave a sleepy goodbye to her guests, before tenderly handing her into Eva's care.

'What a charming little girl,' Harriet Spencer said as she and Gerald Benbrooke came to join them.

'Yes, she is. Oh, Harriet, Mr Benbrooke, I would like to introduce my dear friend, Miss Catherine Shand,' Antonia said. 'Catherine, this is Miss Harriet Spencer and Mr Gerald Benbrooke.'

The two ladies curtsied, each smiling warmly upon

the other, before Catherine turned to find Gerald Benbrooke watching her with interest. 'Are you a close neighbour of Lord Carlyle's, Miss Shand?' he enquired smoothly.

Catherine blushed prettily. 'Not as close as Miss Hadley. My parents live on the other side of Upper Tipping,' she informed him. 'At Willow Wood.'

'Willow Wood! But what a coincidence. My father did some shooting there last fall, I am almost certain of it,' Gerald said.

'Yes, in all likelihood he did. Papa often has gentlemen in for the sport.'

'But of course. I've heard my father speak of Lord Shand. Apparently he is something of a crack shot.' He grinned at her rather wickedly. 'Do you share your father's interests?'

Catherine blushed prettily. 'Not when it comes to hunting, sir.'

'But I have seen her knock an acorn from a branch at fifty paces,' Antonia told him.

Mr Benbrooke was entranced. 'Perhaps I could persuade you to join me for a stroll about the room, Miss Shand, in order that you might tell me more about your…skills?'

Catherine's lovely eyes sparkled. 'Thank you, Mr Benbrooke. I should quite enjoy that.'

'What a very pretty girl,' Harriet commented wistfully as the two moved away. 'I wish I looked like that. Or like you, Antonia.'

In conversation, Antonia had discovered that Harriet was the eldest daughter of Lord Spencer, and heiress to a considerable fortune. Unfortunately, she had neither the looks of Lady Jane nor the composure of Lady

Montague. But she was possessed of a lovely, quiet nature. Antonia found her very pleasant company indeed.

'Now, Harriet, you must not say such things about yourself,' Antonia admonished. 'You have the most wonderful auburn hair and quite the prettiest eyes I have ever seen. I am sure that any number of gentlemen in this room think so too.'

'Do you really think so, Miss Hadley?'

'I do indeed.'

Pleased that Antonia should say so, Harriet beamed and, temporarily mollified, moved away to speak to Lady Jane and Sir Robert Gage.

'Well, I am surprised at finding you alone, Miss Hadley,' Sebastian whispered close to Antonia's ear. 'Being as beautiful as you are, I would hardly have expected to find you without male companionship at all times.'

Feeling a return of the breathlessness which always accompanied his arrival, Antonia opened her fan with a practised flick of her wrist, and tried not to let him see how strongly his presence affected her. 'Lady Clara's party is going splendidly, do you not think?'

Sebastian's mouth twisted ruefully. 'What I think is that I have been put off again. But no matter, I shall not hold it against you. And, yes, thank you, I do think the party is going rather well.'

They stood together in silence for a few moments, before Sebastian turned back to Antonia and said, 'You truly care about my daughter, don't you, Miss Hadley?'

'Do you find that so surprising, my lord, now that you have come to know her for yourself?'

Sebastian shook his head. 'No. I admit that I find her delightful in every way. Just as I do my neighbour,' he added wickedly. 'In fact, I cannot think why I have not taken the time to get to know both of them, long before now.'

Antonia wielded the fan more quickly. 'I think that has much to do with your predilection for remaining in Town, and mine for staying in the country. Indeed, my aunt believes me to be dreadfully provincial.'

'Provincial? You?' Abruptly, Sebastian threw back his head and laughed. 'There is nothing in the least countrified about you, Miss Hadley. You possess all the grace and refinement of a London lady, but with none of the artifice. You have a depth of compassion that is quite uncommon in my experience, and you are as talented as any young lady of my acquaintance. Indeed, better than most. Speaking of which, I wonder if I might impose upon you to play for us a little later, Miss Hadley? I am sure that my friends would be delighted to hear you.'

Antonia inclined her head. 'I should be pleased to, my lord.'

Sebastian's eyes swept over her face approvingly. 'Good. I shall try not to clap the longest, or the loudest.'

Antonia met his gaze, and for a moment, the sounds of the party suddenly seemed to fade into the background. They might have been the only two people in the room. Was this what it was to be in love? Antonia wondered dreamily. Was this…breathless giddiness, and racing pulse, all part of it?

'Lord Carlyle, there you are. I thought that perhaps you had gone upstairs with your daughter.'

The cool voice brought Antonia back to earth with a thump. She turned to find herself looking into the very cold, very unfriendly eyes of Lady Rosalind Grey.

'Forgive me, Miss Hadley, I did not mean to intrude upon your conversation.'

Aware that Lady Rosalind had expressly intended to

intrude, Antonia graciously inclined her head, and then excused herself. She was in no mood to cross swords with Lady Rosalind tonight, nor to draw barbs from her in front of Sebastian. If the lady wished to play that game, she could do it with someone else. Instead, Antonia walked across the room to where her father and Lady Sheraton stood talking together, that lady looking quite splendid in a gown of pomona green satin with matching gloves and an elegant turban.

'Antonia, my dear,' Mr Hadley greeted her, looking younger than Antonia had seen him in years. 'Lady Sheraton was just telling me the most delightful story. Did you know that Mrs Bainbridge used to set out food for a tame deer in the garden at Newton Spinney?'

'A deer?' Antonia shook her head. 'No, I did not. Perhaps that was why she had to put covers over her garden rather than just around it.'

'Probably,' Lady Sheraton agreed, laughing. 'The doe is a fleet little creature. No doubt she would be up and over the top in no time.'

'Yes, no doubt,' Antonia murmured, her smile somewhat distracted.

Mr Hadley glanced at his daughter. 'Toni, is everything all right?'

'Hmm? Oh, yes, Papa, of course. I am just a little tired.'

'What? After spending most of the afternoon resting?'

Antonia smiled absently, and chanced to glance back to where Sebastian and Lady Rosalind were still standing together in conversation. She was just in time to see the lady lay a delicate white hand on Sebastian's sleeve, then lean closer to whisper something in his ear. Antonia felt her heart turn over at the sight of the slow, attractive smile which spread across Sebastian's face in response.

They looked so very good together. Indeed, almost as though they belonged that way.

Abruptly, she closed her eyes and looked away.

'Take heart, my dear. Things are not always what they seem,' Lady Sheraton whispered in Antonia's ear.

Mortified that her casual observation of Lord Carlyle had been witnessed, Antonia straightened. 'I cannot think what you mean, Lady Sheraton. I was merely… glancing in that direction. My thoughts were elsewhere entirely, I can assure you.'

'Yes, of course they were,' Lady Sheraton agreed. 'Pray forgive my mistake.'

Lady Sheraton's gentle apology only served to make Antonia feel worse, and she blushed uncomfortably. 'Will you both excuse me?'

It seemed to Antonia that, after that, she spent most of the evening excusing herself from one person or another, because everywhere she went she seemed to see Sebastian talking to one young lady or another—and all too frequently to the beautiful and self-assured Lady Rosalind Grey.

Worse, everyone seemed anxious to draw conclusions as to the likelihood of Lady Rosalind becoming the next Countess of Carlyle. They even went so far as to speculate whether Carlyle would ask her to marry him *before* she went back to London or whether he would wait until his own return to Town. And when it was pointed out that Carlyle seemed predisposed to remain in the country a little while longer, the money was bet on the offer being made before the end of the weekend.

For Antonia, the rest of the evening was tedious at best. She was given no further opportunity for conversation alone with Sebastian, thanks in large part to Lady Rosalind. The woman was always there, hovering close by, watching Antonia with that coolly superior smile that seemed to say, don't waste your time—he's mine.

Determined to pretend an indifference to the whole situation, Antonia smiled brightly and chatted with the other guests as though she hadn't a care in the world. She laughed with Harriet Spencer over tales of that young lady's eccentric aunt, she teased Catherine about how taken Mr Gerald Benbrooke seemed to be with her. She even answered Lady Montague's questions about the behaviour of young children, confirming her opinion that the newly married Viscountess was eager to start a family.

Eventually, however, the act of maintaining a brave face took its toll. Antonia's mouth was stiff from smiling, and around midnight she pleaded a headache and asked her father if Abbott could take her home.

'But I am surprised that you wish to leave so early, my dear.' Mr Hadley glanced at her flushed face anxiously. 'You are not feeling ill, I hope?'

'No, but I have a touch of the headache, and the heat and the crowds are not helping.'

Antonia feared that he was about to press, when Lady Sheraton unexpectedly came to her rescue. 'Yes, it is very warm,' she said, placing a gentle hand on his arm. 'Besides, the hour is late. Surely there is no harm in Antonia leaving ahead of us. You are more than welcome to make use of my carriage for the ride home.'

Mr Hadley hesitated, and then smiled into the lovely face upturned towards his. 'Thank you, Lady Sheraton, I am most obliged for your offer. And, yes, perhaps it is best that you go home, Antonia. I would not want you to stay if you are not feeling up to snuff.' He leaned forward and placed a gentle kiss on her forehead. 'I shall see you in the morning.'

Antonia breathed a sigh of relief and, smiling gratefully at Lady Sheraton, quickly turned and made her way towards the front door.

She was stayed by the unexpected touch of a hand on her arm.

'Miss Hadley, surely you are not leaving us so soon?'

Sebastian.

An involuntary shudder passed through Antonia's body. How could she face him when her emotions were so raw? How could she hide what she was feeling? He would see through her in an instant.

'I fear I must, my lord,' Antonia said, keeping her eyes averted. 'The headache is upon me.'

'I am very sorry to hear that.' Sebastian's voice was low, and caring. 'We have not yet had a chance to hear you play. Or, at least, the others have not.'

Antonia felt her heart hammering against her ribs. Oh, why had he chosen such an awkward time to leave Lady Rosalind? She had hoped to slip away without arousing his notice. 'Perhaps…another time.'

'Yes, perhaps.' Sebastian continued to watch her, his eyes narrowed. 'I hope you will feel up to joining us tomorrow. I have planned a picnic down by Silver Lake.'

Silver Lake was the name given the shimmering body of water which comprised part of the border between her father's land and Lord Carlyle's. Antonia had ridden by it many times, and had always stopped to admire its tranquil setting with its graceful weeping willows and sweeping views. Indeed, he could not have chosen a lovelier spot for an al fresco meal.

'Naturally, as it is the actual day of Clara's birthday, she will be the guest of honour,' Sebastian continued, 'and I know how much she will be looking forward to seeing you there.'

Antonia smiled wearily. He always knew exactly what to say to get around her.

'Thank you, Lord Carlyle, that would be lovely. I would be…pleased to make up one of the party.'

'Splendid. But, I do have a small favour to ask you before you go,' Sebastian said.

Antonia waited. 'And that is?'

'That you help me keep an eye on Clara tomorrow.'

Antonia blinked, surprised that he would ask. 'I hardly think Lady Clara will give you any trouble, my lord. She is an extremely well-mannered and biddable child.'

'Nevertheless, with that many people around, I will not always be able to look out for her,' Sebastian explained. 'And I know that I shall rest easier knowing that someone like yourself is watching her as well.'

It seemed a reasonable enough request, Antonia decided. As host to eight other people, it would be difficult for Carlyle to watch his daughter every moment. And the lake was reputed to be quite deep. 'Yes, of course, I would be happy to watch Lady Clara.'

'Good. Then I shall send the carriage for you at one, and you may tell Mr Hadley that I will personally escort you home after the picnic. Will that be satisfactory, Miss Hadley?'

Antonia felt the warmth creep into her cheeks and stay there. 'It is more than satisfactory, Lord Carlyle. Indeed, there is really no need for you to go to all that bother. I can have Abbott drive—'

'Please believe me when I say that is no bother, Miss Hadley,' Sebastian assured her quickly. 'In fact, it will be much easier than trying to guess what time to tell poor Abbott to be here to take you home. If the day is fine, who knows what time we shall return?'

As always, his logic made perfect sense, and Antonia

found herself agreeing to the suggestion—just as she knew she would.

'Until tomorrow then, Miss Hadley,' Sebastian said, the sparkle in his eyes leaving Antonia in no doubt as to his satisfaction with the arrangements.

At half past eight the following morning, Sebastian stood in front of the window in the library and gazed out across the lush green fields in the direction of Buntings Hill. He had passed a restless night, and risen early as a result. And not surprisingly, his first thoughts upon waking had been of Antonia Hadley.

He wondered how she was feeling this morning, and if the headache was still upon her. He found himself wondering how she looked in the morning, when she first opened those beautiful eyes and gazed about her at the new day.

And he wondered how she looked last thing at night, when she lay down upon her bed and prepared to drift away to sleep, her hair spilling over the pillow, her skin as white and smooth as the sheets upon which she lay…

'Good morning, my lord. You wished to see me?'

The disturbingly sensual image of Antonia dissolved, but not his longing for her, and Sebastian drew a deep breath. 'Yes, Paddy, I did.' He turned away from the window and moved towards his desk. 'Is everything ready for the outing this afternoon?'

'Yes, my lord. Just like you asked.'

'And Clara's new mare?'

'Is safely in the stable and ready to ride.' Bingham's face creased in a smile. 'She's a little beauty, my lord. I don't think I could have done any better myself.'

Sebastian's mouth curved in wry amusement. 'Thank

you, Paddy, I'm flattered to know that I have been able
to meet your exacting standards.'

At the last minute, Sebastian had decided not to send
anyone else to buy Clara a horse, but to undertake the
purchase himself. Hence, before leaving London, he had
spent an afternoon at Tattersall's and chosen what he
considered to be the best he could find. The little dapple
grey mare, with her dark mane and tail, her soft mouth
and gentle brown eyes, would be perfect.

Sebastian nodded his satisfaction. 'Good. Just before
we set off for the lake, you can bring her around to the
front of the house and I shall give her to Clara. She can
ride her instead of—' Sebastian broke off at the expression on his steward's face. 'Something wrong, Paddy?'

'Well, not exactly wrong, my lord. It's just that…well,
this new mare's a good bit bigger than Teddy, and I
wonder if Clara shouldn't have some time to get used to
her.'

Sebastian smiled. 'If I were suggesting a neck-or-
nothing gallop over field and hedge, I would be the first
to agree with you, Paddy, but given that a trot is likely
the fastest gait we shall achieve, I hardly think Clara is
in any danger. In fact, I expect that she will walk the
mare most of the way to the lake and back. And as I
have asked Miss Hadley to help keep an eye on her, I
doubt there'll be any cause for concern.'

Bingham glanced up quickly. 'Miss Hadley, you say?'

'Yes. She is very fond of Clara. More to the point,
she is an accomplished rider, and one who would set a
good example for Clara. I expect that Mr Davlin is
teaching her the basics of riding, but I think that watching someone like Miss Hadley would be equally valuable.'

Bingham began to fidget. 'Yes, my lord.'

'Speaking of which, when have you arranged for me to meet with Mr Davlin, Paddy?'

Bingham breathed a heavy sigh. 'I'm afraid I have some bad news in that regard, my lord.'

Sebastian's face darkened. 'Don't tell me that Mr Davlin hasn't time to meet with me?'

'No, my lord, it isn't that. I regret to tell you that…Mr Davlin is…no longer in your employ.'

'I beg your pardon?'

'He left, my lord. Came to me about…a week ago and told me that he was moving on.'

'Moving where?'

'He didn't say. Just that he was…leaving.'

Sebastian's brows drew together in an angry frown. 'Why did you not tell me about this before?'

The steward cleared his throat. 'Well, what with everything that was going on, I didn't think it was all that important.'

'It might not be to you, but it will be to Clara. How did she take the news of his leaving?'

'She was…sad and disappointed, of course,' Bingham said, hating the fact that he had to keep lying, 'but I told her that she was going to be getting a lovely surprise for her birthday, and I think that helped a lot.'

'I see,' Sebastian said quietly. He was startled to hear that Davlin had left. He paid his staff good wages. Indeed, better than most. And he was not used to them just…up and moving on, which was why the news disturbed him so much. That, and the fact that…something about this whole Tony Davlin situation just didn't add up.

'Would you like me to make enquiries about a new riding master, once your guests leave?' Bingham asked.

Sebastian shook his head. 'No. Hold off on that for

now, Paddy. I do not know what is going to be happening in the near future. I have been giving some thought as to what is best for Clara's future. I may want to take her to London with me, in which case I shall arrange for someone to continue her lessons there. But I am not happy about this situation with Davlin, Paddy, and I don't mind telling you so.'

Bingham shook his head. 'No, my lord, nor am I.'

There was a brief silence. Then Sebastian got up. 'Well, I suppose there is nothing to be done about it now. Besides, Clara is young. A lot of people will come and go in her life. I am sure in a few months time, she won't even remember who Mr Davlin was.'

'Yes, my lord.'

'And, as you say, she is going to have a very nice surprise this afternoon. Hopefully, that will do the trick.'

Bingham sighed. 'Aye, my lord. I certainly hope that it will.'

As promised, a carriage did arrive from Ashdean to pick Antonia up that afternoon—but it was not the one she had been expecting. At precisely half past twelve, an elegant phaeton drawn by two perfectly matched blacks advanced at a smart pace up the gravelled drive at Buntings Hill. And tooling the ribbons was none other than the Earl of Carlyle himself!

'My lord!' Antonia gasped as he pulled the high-stepping blacks to a halt. 'What are you doing here?'

Sebastian grinned boyishly as he swung down from the rather precarious seat. 'Picking you up, Miss Hadley, as I told you I would.'

'You told me you were sending a carriage for me, my lord, not that *you* would be driving it,' Antonia objected. 'Should you not be at home attending to your guests?'

Sebastian smiled as he swept a connoisseur's eye over Antonia's appearance, making her very glad that she had chosen the gown of jonquil silk, with a Venetian bonnet trimmed with ribands of deeper yellow. 'Pray do not trouble yourself about such matters, Miss Hadley. When I set off from Ashdean, most of the ladies were still in their rooms, and the gentlemen who were down were enjoying a late breakfast. I guarantee that we shall be back before they even notice I am gone. Besides,' he said as he helped Antonia up into the high seat, 'I *am* attending to my guests. Last evening, I promised one of them that I would arrange transportation for her, and that is precisely what I am doing.' Sebastian settled himself in the driver's seat and smiled down at her wickedly. 'Do you object so strongly to the manner of the arrangements, Miss Hadley?'

His voice, deep and sensual, sent a ripple of awareness through her—as did the touch of his thigh against hers in the close confines of the seat. 'N-not in the least, my lord. I was merely…surprised that you would take the time to come all the way over here yourself.'

Sebastian chuckled softly, but said nothing. Then, cracking the whip with an experienced flick of his wrist, he set the matched pair off at a brisk trot towards Ashdean.

'I trust you are feeling better this morning, Miss Hadley?' Sebastian enquired when they were on the main road.

'Much better, thank you.' Antonia risked a glance at him from beneath the shadow of her lashes. 'I regret that I had to leave so…precipitously last night.'

'Your apologies are not necessary,' Sebastian assured her. 'I was simply sorry to be deprived of the pleasure of your company.'

Antonia blushed at the warmth in his tone. 'I fear I am becoming...more like my father every day. We have both kept so much to ourselves these past two years, that neither of us are really comfortable in society any more. Papa says it is the crowds which bother him. After last night, it would seem that...they bother me too.'

'I wonder if it is so much the crowds, as the pressure of being in a situation you are not entirely comfortable with,' Sebastian said intuitively. 'We are creatures of habit, Miss Hadley, and when something happens to disturb the nature of our routine, we grow naturally upset.'

Antonia smiled. What would he say, she wondered, if he knew just how upset her routine had been, both by him and as a result of the deception she had been enacting?

'That is true, my lord, and yet I do not think that we enjoy being mired in habit day after day. What would be the pleasure in getting up each morning, if we knew that nothing different was going to happen that day, than had happened the day before? I think life would become a very dull affair indeed.'

Sebastian studied her face, watching the breeze tug at the loose curls at her temples, and ruffle the lace at her throat. 'I do not think you would ever be bored with life, Miss Hadley,' he said softly. 'You enjoy it too much. You are not satisfied with the mundane, and I doubt you will ever be willing to settle for the ordinary.'

Antonia smiled, remembering the conversation she had had with her father not so long ago. 'It does not make for a complacent life, my lord, but I think it makes for a far more interesting one. I have never done what people expect me to. In truth, I cannot imagine anything more tedious.'

Sebastian turned to capture her gaze with his. 'Nor can I, Miss Hadley. Nor can I.'

Sebastian's assurances that none of his guests would miss him proved to be incorrect. As he drew the team to a prancing halt in front of Ashdean, Antonia saw a very agitated Lady Rosalind, and an attendant Mr Mallett, standing on the front steps waiting for them.

'There you are, my lord.' Lady Rosalind's eyes narrowed at the sight of Antonia sitting next to him on the narrow seat. 'We were beginning to worry about you. You left without leaving word with anyone as to where you were going.'

'As you can see, there was no need for concern,' Sebastian said easily. He sprang down from the phaeton and turned to help Antonia alight. 'I promised Miss Hadley that I would send a carriage for her this morning, and was making arrangements to do so, when I discovered that young Collins was already out exercising one of the horses. Accordingly, I decided to ride over to Buntings Hill myself. I really did not think that my absence would be greatly noticed.'

Lady Rosalind smiled and shook her head. 'No one could help but miss the presence of such a charming and gracious host, my lord.'

'Papa! Toni!'

Lady Clara's excited cry spared Sebastian the trouble of answering. Instead, he held out his arms and a moment later was lifting the child high into the air. 'Well, if it isn't the lady of the house. Good morning, my dear. Did you sleep well?'

'Yes, Papa,' Lady Clara replied. Happily, she turned and reached towards Antonia. 'Toni's here.'

'Yes, I am here, Lady Clara.' Antonia took the child's

hand in hers and held it, unaware of the charming picture the three of them formed.

'Clara, do you know what today is?' Sebastian asked softly.

Clara giggled, and nodded. 'It's my birthday.'

'Yes, it is. And how would you like to come on a picnic with us, as our very special guest of honour? We are going to Silver Lake.'

Clara's face lit up. 'Oh, yes, Papa, I should like that very much. May I try to catch the little fish that come up to the edge of the water?'

Lady Rosalind laughed, and Clara, suddenly shy in the presence of strangers, buried her face against her father's neck.

'My lord, she is absolutely adorable,' Lady Rosalind crooned. 'You are very fortunate.'

'Yes, I think so,' Sebastian said proudly. Setting the little girl down, he said, 'Clara, are you going to say good morning to Lady Rosalind and Mr Mallett?'

Clara glanced uncertainly at the strangers, and then hid her face against her father's leg.

'Poor little mite's a tad shy, I think,' Mr Mallett said in a surprisingly gentle voice. 'I've a niece about her age. Get on with her rather well, in fact.'

Antonia bent down and said in a soft voice, 'Clara? Will you not say hello to Lady Rosalind and Mr Mallett? They have both come a long way to be with you on your birthday, and they shall be very unhappy if you do not speak to them.'

Clara turned to look at Antonia for a moment. Then, seeing her nod of encouragement, she glanced up at the two adults. 'Hello,' she said shyly.

Purposely imitating Antonia's action, Lady Rosalind bent down so that she was level with the little girl's face.

'Happy birthday, Lady Clara. How lovely you look in your new dress.'

Clara studied the face close to hers, and smiled. 'You're pretty.'

She could not have said anything more destined to please. The child's unexpected expression of affection was exactly what Lady Rosalind wanted to hear—especially within Carlyle's hearing.

'Well, thank you, Lady Clara. Sweet child. Would you like to ride up in the carriage next to me?' Lady Rosalind offered magnanimously.

Clara glanced towards her father. 'Are you riding in the carriage, Papa?'

'No, my dear. I shall be riding Apollo.'

Clara's eyes grew wide with sudden hope. 'Oh, then please may I ride Teddy to the picnic?'

Sebastian glanced at his daughter in amusement. 'Teddy is just a pony, Clara. Surely you would like to ride a pretty little mare of your own.'

'But I don't have a mare,' Clara said quietly. 'I only ride Teddy. But I could ride him to the picnic, because I don't fall off any more. Toni says that I ride very well. Don't I, Toni?'

Antonia blanched. Her gaze went quickly to Sebastian. 'Y-yes, Clara, you do.'

Lady Rosalind looked momentarily confused. 'But I thought…Tony was a man?' She, too, looked to Carlyle for clarification. 'Did you not tell me that Clara's riding instructor was a gentleman?'

'Tony Davlin is a man,' Sebastian replied easily, 'but I think that in this case, my daughter is referring to Miss Hadley, who has also seen her ride.'

'But I still do not understand. Why would she refer to Miss Hadley as…Tony?'

'Because that happens to be my name, Lady Rosalind,' Antonia said quietly. The few minutes during which Lady Rosalind and Sebastian had been speaking had allowed her to regain her shaken composure. 'Lady Clara calls me Toni, because Antonia is too difficult for her to pronounce.'

'Ah, I see.' Lady Rosalind smiled, but the gaze she levelled at Antonia was patronising in the extreme. 'I had momentarily forgotten that you and Lady Clara were so *close*.'

'Papa, may I ride Teddy?' Clara repeated urgently. 'I promise I won't fall off.'

Sebastian smiled. 'I think you can do better than Teddy, my dear. Mr Bingham, are you there?'

'I am, my lord,' came the steward's voice. Then, from around the side of the house, Mr Bingham suddenly appeared. He was leading a lovely, dapple grey mare, and his face was wreathed in smiles. 'Look what I found down by the stables.'

Clara gazed at the horse in adoration. 'Oh, Papa, she is beautiful.'

Sebastian smiled. 'Do you think so, Clara?'

The child nodded enthusiastically. 'What is her name?'

'She hasn't one yet,' Sebastian said softly. 'Why don't you give her one now?'

Clara thought about that for a moment. Then, she laughed and clapped her hands together. 'Ariana. Like the princess in my book. She was beautiful too.'

'Now, wouldn't you rather ride…Ariana to the lake than Teddy?' Sebastian asked.

'Oh, yes, Papa, I should like that above all.'

'Good. Because Ariana is my birthday present to you,

dearest. Now, why don't you go over and get to know her a little better.'

Antonia held her breath as Clara ran towards the horse. In her excitement, the child had forgotten what she had been told about horses being easy to startle.

'Clara, walk slowly towards her,' Antonia called out. 'Ariana will not be happy if you frighten her.'

Clara did slow down, but even so, the mare jumped. Watching her, Mr Mallett said, 'I say, Carlyle, how far away is this lake?'

'No more than a fifteen-minute ride, I shouldn't think.'

'I would be happy to ride alongside the young lady, if it would make you feel better.'

Sebastian glanced at Mr Mallett with approval. 'Thank you, James, that is very generous of you. As long as Miss Hadley agrees.'

Antonia glanced up, startled. 'Me?'

'Of course. Well, apart from Mr Bingham, you are the only one here who has seen Clara ride. Which means that you are the only other one qualified to offer an opinion on her abilities. Do you think Clara is competent enough to ride her new mare down to Silver Lake?'

Antonia suffered a moment of indecision. Would Clara be able to control the mare? Ariana was a good bit bigger than Teddy, which meant that her gait would be different, as would her stride. And if she had habits that Clara was not familiar with, it could prove unsettling to the child.

Still, if Mr Mallett and Sebastian would be riding alongside her, surely the chances of anything happening were extremely remote. 'I am sure that Lady Clara will be just fine riding Ariana to Silver Lake, Lord Carlyle,' Antonia said. 'I had initially thought that she might be too big, but I am sure that, if Clara takes extra care, she will be fine.'

'Good. Then it is settled.'

Clara's eyes widened in delight as she reached out to stroke the mare's velvety soft nose. 'Oh, thank you, Papa!'

'And look, here is Miss Spencer come to join us. Will you say hello to Miss Spencer, Clara?'

'Hello,' Clara said softly, before hiding her face against his leg again.

'Now what's all this—?'

'That's quite all right, Lord Carlyle,' Harriet interrupted him gently. 'I am sure that Lady Clara is not used to being the centre of attention, and is just being shy.'

'Yes, you have no need to concern yourself, my lord,' Lady Rosalind purred, very much aware of the need to reassert her presence over both Harriet and that insufferably sweet neighbour, who seemed to be having far too much influence on the family as a whole. 'By this afternoon, Lady Clara will be laughing and playing for all to see. Miss Spencer is right. Lady Clara simply needs a little time to adjust to all of these extra people.'

Antonia glanced at Lady Rosalind in surprise. She had not credited the Town beauty with knowing the first thing about children, and this unexpected show of maternal intuition startled her. Or it did—until Antonia caught the mocking expression on the woman's face, and the malice in the beauty's eyes.

'I wonder, Lord Carlyle,' Lady Rosalind began coolly, 'if it is wise to encourage Lady Clara to address servants in such an informal manner.'

'Servants?'

'Yes, this riding master, for example.'

'I really don't see that it is likely to do her any harm,'

Mr Mallett piped up. 'I called my governess Betty for years, and I do not think I suffered because of it.'

'Be that as it may, it does not do for the daughter of an Earl to become too familiar with those beneath her,' Lady Rosalind said. 'And in this case, I should think it is even more confusing, given Miss Hadley's name.'

'Confusing, Lady Rosalind?' Antonia replied quietly.

'Well, yes. By addressing you with the familiarity that would normally be reserved for a servant, Lady Clara might lose sight of the fact that you are not a servant, nor even a relative. In fact, perhaps you would do better to encourage more formality between the two of you, Miss Hadley.'

Antonia met Lady Rosalind's eyes without flinching. 'I hardly think that encouraging Lady Clara to call me Miss Hadley would serve any useful purpose, Lady Rosalind, other than to make her feel ill at ease with me.'

'But as Lord Carlyle's neighbour, surely there is no need for Lady Clara to feel *at* ease with you,' Lady Rosalind said, the smile on her lips masking the sting behind the words. 'In fact, I wonder, my lord, if it would not be in Lady Clara's best interests to spend more time in the company of other children.'

'I understand that Clara does play with the village children,' Sebastian informed her. 'Is that not correct, Miss Hadley?'

'Indeed. Clara makes friends very quickly.'

'Village children?' The disdain in Lady Rosalind's voice was patent. 'I was referring to the children of other fine, aristocratic families.'

Antonia felt a swift rush of anger at the woman's condescending tone. 'Children do not concern themselves with such matters, Lady Rosalind.'

'Of course they do not,' Lady Rosalind replied haughtily, 'which is precisely why we must choose their companions for them. It would not do for Lady Clara to mistakenly assume that she is one of them, any more than it would do for one of them to believe that they are on a level with her. After all, she *is* the daughter of an Earl,' Lady Rosalind finished dramatically.

'Yes, she is,' Sebastian interrupted, his tone ominously quiet. 'And as such, it is even more important that she learn to deal with people at all levels—not just her own. I see nothing wrong with Clara addressing Miss Hadley as Toni, nor in her calling a riding master by his first name. And I certainly do not intend to remove her from the presence of other children, simply as a result of her birth. Now, I suggest that we put an end to the conversation and make our preparations to set off. We have a very busy afternoon ahead of us, and I, for one, am anxious to get underway.'

With that, Sebastian walked away, leaving Lady Rosalind turning a most unbecoming shade of red. Even Mr Mallett regarded her with pity before he too drifted away.

Lady Rosalind turned back to Antonia, her thin smile flashing like a rapier. 'Well, thank you, Miss Hadley. You have just made me look a complete fool in front of the Earl. It would seem that you have a champion in Lady Clara. How very convenient for you. Perhaps that is the secret to your success. Perhaps I should spend less time cultivating the father, and more time getting close to the daughter.'

With that, Lady Rosalind turned and marched away, leaving Antonia in no doubt that she had just made a very dangerous and bitter enemy!

Chapter Ten

By one o'clock, all of the guests were finally down-stairs and assembled at the front of the house. They had arranged to take two carriages: Lord and Lady Montague, Lord Edwards and Miss Spencer in the first, and Lady Jane, Lady Rosalind, Mr Benbrooke and Antonia in the second. Sir Robert Gage and Mr Mallett had asked for and been provided with mounts and, like Sebastian, had chosen to ride alongside the carriages.

Clara rode too, looking very much the proper little lady on her new mare. Mr Mallett had taken his position beside them and kept a close eye on the pair but, every now and then, found time to glance at his lovely Lady Rosalind, who was looking particularly fetching in a sprigged muslin gown, and carrying a dainty white-fringed parasol.

On Sebastian's signal, the entourage moved off. Antonia watched Lady Clara pay close attention to her new mare on the slight incline leading down to the first gate, while Mr Mallett paid close attention to her. Once they were on flat ground, however, the riders spread out, the gentlemen urging their horses to a leisurely canter and circling back when they got too far ahead of the carriages.

Mr Mallett began telling Clara about one of his young nieces and her little pony, Penny Farthing, so that it wasn't long before the two of them were chatting away like old friends; a fact which only added to Antonia's enjoyment of the day. Now, there would be three of them watching out for the little girl. And she knew, judging by the affection she glimpsed in Mr Mallett's eyes, that he would be every bit as attentive to Clara as she or Sebastian, who was even now doubling back to check on his daughter's progress.

Antonia let her eyes linger on Sebastian for a moment, admiring the way he sat tall and proud in the saddle, and felt a different kind of awareness impinge upon her senses. He was an extremely virile man with those compelling blue eyes and more than a hint of sensuality in his firm features. His broad shoulders strained at the fabric of his jacket, while the smooth-fitting breeches accentuated the muscular strength of his legs. And yet, for all his masculinity, there were traces of humour around his mouth and eyes, softening the harsh edges, and making him appear so very human.

Antonia sighed. She could well understand why Lady Rosalind was so taken with him.

The carriages arrived at Silver Lake in good time. The servants were already there, and were setting out colourful blankets and unpacking the bulging picnic hampers. The spot Sebastian had chosen for the meal was a particularly lovely one, set amidst a bower of graceful willows with trailing branches that hung down almost to the surface of the water. Around one side of the lake, a wooden walkway had been constructed to facilitate strolling, while further along a number of small boats were pulled up to shore, their brightly painted sides reflecting in the crystal clear water. It was to these little boats that Antonia was eventually drawn. She had seen them during her numerous rides past the lake, but she had never actually stopped to take a closer look at them.

'Do you enjoy boating, Miss Hadley?'

Antonia was not aware that Sebastian had followed her down to the water but, pleased by the fact that he had, she smiled as she turned to look up at him. 'Yes, very much. Though I have not been in a boat this many years, I remember it as being a most peaceful pastime. Especially when the weather was as lovely as this. Unfortunately, I do confess to a certain nervousness of the water itself.'

'You surprise me, Miss Hadley,' Sebastian said. 'You do not strike me as the type of woman who would be nervous of anything at all. Or is it just your aura of confidence which makes it seem so?'

Antonia blushed, but laughed none the less. 'In truth, there are many things which discomfort me, my lord. I simply try not to let them show.'

Sebastian was silent for a moment, and then he smiled too. 'Well, if it is not a very great fear, perhaps I could persuade you to join me for a row around the lake after lunch. It has been a long time since I indulged in such pleasurable pastimes myself.'

There was a wistful quality to his voice and Antonia wondered what had put it there. Was it the sight of the little boats bobbing in the water that conjured up memories of his past? Had he perhaps, enjoyed such things with his wife when they had first been courting? Or was it merely that he was finally coming to appreciate the simpler pleasures of life in the country?

'Papa, Toni, are you coming?' Clara cried, running

down the field towards them. 'Mr Mallett says that we are not to start without you.' Her cheeks were shining like two polished apples and it was evident that she was having a marvellous time. One of her new hair ribbons had already come undone, and there was a small smudge of dirt on her nose. 'Miss Spencer told me that I could have a chocolate biscuit if I found you. And I have found you. So please may I have a biscuit, Papa?'

'You may have one, but not before lunch, Clara,' Sebastian said, trying to be firm. But when he saw the disappointment in those huge blue eyes, he knew he was lost. 'Oh, very well, since it is your birthday, I suppose you may have a biscuit,' he relented. 'In fact, you may have two!'

The transformation in Clara's face was a delight to behold and, holding on to each of their hands, she happily led Antonia and her father back up to the picnic grounds where a veritable feast had been laid out for them. It seemed to Antonia that there was something to tempt even the most jaded of palates, from joints of roast pheasant and jugged hare, to chicken pasties and cold turkey. Certainly no one could go away hungry from such a banquet.

The guests broke into smaller groups to eat, the arrangement of which Antonia could only wonder at given the amount of time the occupants of one blanket spent glancing at the occupants of another. Lord and Lady Montague, and Lady Jane, sat together on one blanket; Lady Rosalind, Lord Edwards and Mr Benbrooke occupied another, while Miss Spencer, Antonia and Sir Robert claimed a third.

Lady Clara, who was, by now, fast friends with Mr Mallett, was drawing him towards the blanket upon which Antonia and Harriet were seated, and indicated that he should sit down beside her. Mr Mallett gallantly complied, causing Antonia to warm to him even further as a result. She was quite sure that he would have preferred to sit next to Lady Rosalind, but it was equally clear that he had no intention of disappointing the little girl. Hence, sitting down between Harriet and Lady Clara, he contented himself with casting longing glances towards the fair Rosalind.

Meanwhile, Harriet Spencer gazed with evident adoration at Gerald Benbrooke, while that gentleman tried unsuccessfully to catch Lady Jane's eye. Sir Robert watched the entire proceedings with an expression of sardonic amusement on his handsome features, and Lord Edwards tucked into his meal with seemingly no romantic inclinations towards anyone.

Sebastian, Antonia noted with interest, did not settle with one party or another, but moved randomly throughout his guests. This was clearly not to Lady Rosalind's liking, but as there was nothing she could do about it, she grudgingly accepted the situation, and bestowed the most radiant of smiles upon him whenever he chanced to pass by.

As the sun rose higher in the sky and warmed the afternoon air, the mood of the party grew quite languorous. Harriet drew out a pad and set to sketching the lovely vista all around them, while Lady Montague nestled comfortably against her husband's side and drew out a volume of poetry. Obviously content with the arrangement, Lord Montague closed his eyes and rested his chin against his wife's shining dark hair.

'I say, Jane,' Benbrooke said, hastily moving to that lady's side once the remnants of the meal had been cleared away, 'could I interest you in a turn about the lake? I've a mind to stretch my legs after all that food.'

'Oh, I am sorry, Mr Benbrooke,' Lady Jane replied sweetly, 'but Lord Edwards has just asked me if *he* might escort me around the lake.'

'Has he, by Jove?' Benbrooke slanted Lord Edwards a look of irritation. 'Accepted him, have you?'

Lady Jane smiled coquettishly at her dejected swain. 'Yes, but perhaps you would care to join us?'

While it was clear that neither gentleman wished to be in the company of the other, it was also clear that neither wished to be left behind. That being the case, Lady Jane set off with not one, but two, gentlemen in tow, and endeavoured to place herself in the middle so as to keep them a safe distance apart.

Sebastian, who had been strolling around the field with Clara, now returned to the picnic area and stopped beside Antonia. 'Could I interest you in that row now, Miss Hadley? Or would you prefer to rest in the shade with Lady Montague and Miss Spencer?'

Antonia shook her head as she rose gracefully to her feet, pleased that he had not forgotten. 'On the contrary, Lord Carlyle, I should quite enjoy an outing on the lake.'

'I say, Carlyle,' Mr Mallett piped up. 'Perhaps Lady Rosalind and I might join you. After that splendid repast, I feel in need of some activity. That is, if you feel up to it, Lady Rosalind,' he added solicitously.

Lady Rosalind agreed with an alacrity that Antonia suspected had more to do with her desire to remain in Sebastian's eye than it did to be at the side of Mr Mallett, but she refused to let it to dampen her enthusiasm for the outing. After all, when all was said and done, it was *her* company Sebastian had sought, not Lady Rosalind's.

She duly waited beside the other woman as the gentlemen proceeded to prepare the boats.

'I would not put too much stock in Lord Carlyle's attentions if I were you, Miss Hadley,' Lady Rosalind said, even as her eyes rested on the Earl. 'While I can understand his feelings of…gratitude towards you for the affection you have shown his daughter, it would be foolish of you to think that it stems from anything more serious than that. Carlyle is suffering a certain amount of…fatherly guilt at the moment, and I think he is prone to look kindly upon anyone Clara holds in esteem. I am sure that, in time, the feelings will pass.'

It was a cutting remark, and Antonia knew that the woman had made it to embarrass and discomfort her. Fortunately, she was made of sterner stuff than that. 'Thank you, Lady Rosalind, but I can assure you that no such warnings are necessary. Lord Carlyle is an acquaintance and a neighbour of mine, and he treats me with the courtesy any gentleman would extend towards a lady. I certainly do not read anything more into it than that. As regards his daughter, I find her to be a dear little girl whom I would care about whether her father was around or not.'

'Yes, so you have told us on more than one occasion,' Lady Rosalind drawled. 'But I repeat, it will not do you any good in the long run. Trying to get to Lord Carlyle through his daughter will eventually wear thin. When the Earl does choose a wife, it will be a decision based upon the lady's suitability to be the next Countess, not on how fond she is of his child.'

Antonia lifted one eyebrow in surprise. 'Are you saying that Lord Carlyle will not care if the lady he wishes to marry has no fondness for his child?'

Lady Rosalind shrugged her lovely shoulders. 'Clara is, as you say, a sweet child, but she is of an age where she demands a great deal of attention. And Lord Carlyle has been a widower these past two years. I feel sure that he will wish to spend more time with his new wife than with his daughter in the early days of his marriage. For that reason, I suspect that other arrangements will likely be made.'

Antonia stiffened. Lady Rosalind's animosity towards her was one thing. Her lightly veiled threats with regard to Clara's future were something else entirely. 'What *other* arrangements?'

'Oh, come, Miss Hadley, surely you cannot be as naive as all that. Everyone knows that it is quite common for children of the aristocracy to be sent away for their schooling.'

'You mean…to a boarding school?'

'Of course.' Lady Rosalind turned to regard Antonia with a haughty look. 'Clara would benefit from the opportunity of spending time with girls of her own age and class.'

'But she is so young,' Antonia objected. 'And she has so little knowledge of her father. Surely it is more important that she spend time with him now.'

The smile Lady Rosalind gave her was filled with condescension. 'I think *that* will be a decision made between Lord Carlyle and his new wife. Do you not agree, Miss Hadley?'

Antonia stared at the cold-eyed beauty and knew that she was wasting her time. Lady Rosalind might wish to marry the Earl of Carlyle, but she had no intention of playing a devoted mother to his child. The only thought that would likely be spared for Clara was how quickly she could be dispatched to a boarding school, and how far away from London it would be.

'All right, ladies, I think we are ready to go.' Sebastian and Mr Mallett returned to the spot where the ladies stood waiting for them. 'Would you care to step aboard?'

'But of course, my lord, we are anxious to get underway.'

Giving Antonia the benefit of a bright and totally false smile, Lady Rosalind put her gloved hand in Mr Mallett's and followed him down to the edge of the water. She allowed him to help her into the boat, and waited as he dutifully arranged the cushions behind her back to ensure that she was entirely comfortable.

Sebastian did the same for Antonia. Unfortunately, the sides of the boat which he had chosen were slightly higher than Mr Mallett's, and Antonia was forced to lift her skirt a bit higher in order to step over it. Sebastian gallantly looked away, but not before Antonia feared he had been given a tempting view of her ankle and lower leg. He said nothing, however, as he helped her into the bow and settled the cushions behind her back.

Soon both boats were pushing away from the grassy bank and gliding smoothly over the surface of the pristine lake. It really was lovely, Antonia reflected as she relaxed back against the cushions. The air was warm but a light breeze kept it from becoming oppressive, while tiny birds flitted amongst the branches of the trees, filling the afternoon air with their sweet songs. The only other sounds to be heard were the gentle dipping of the oars into the water, and the occasional creak of the wooden boats.

Antonia watched Sebastian as he worked, marvelling at how easy he made it look. His hands curved lightly around the smooth wooden handles, while his strong arms pulled on the oars to propel them through the water. He had discarded his jacket, and his shirt gleamed a blinding white in the afternoon sun. A gust of wind ruffled his dark hair, and once again, it was all Antonia could do not to reach out and smooth that errant lock back into place.

'A penny for them, Miss Hadley,' Sebastian said in a teasing voice, 'or shall I have to pay more?'

Blushing at the very thought of his knowing, Antonia smiled and shook her head. 'They are hardly worth the trouble, my lord. I am far too at ease to be harbouring any thoughts that would be worth selling.'

'Well, if you will not share them with me, I hope that you will at least tell me that you are enjoying yourself,' Sebastian said. 'I should hate to think that I am the only one deriving any pleasure from our outing.'

'On the contrary, I am enjoying it very much indeed. I only hope that you do not find the weather too warm for such exertion.' Antonia glanced back towards the occupants of the other boat and bit her lip. Lady Rosalind seemed to be urging Mr Mallett to catch them up, while poor Mr Mallett grew redder in the face in an attempt to accommodate her. 'I do not think Mr Mallett is having as easy a time of it as you.'

'No, but that is because *you* are not of a mind to push me beyond my capabilities,' Sebastian said, his eyes bright with humour. 'Fortunately, I am also more fit than my associate, and do not find rowing a lovely lady around the lake at all fatiguing.'

Antonia dimpled as she turned back to face him. 'Are you an avid sportsman, Lord Carlyle?'

'I enjoy most of the sports which are available to gentlemen. Shooting, boxing, fencing, and the like. I have always believed that physical activity strengthens both the mind and the body, Miss Hadley. Sadly, I believe it is the nature of society to be indolent.'

Antonia nodded her agreement. 'Yes. Certainly, it is easy for ladies to grow complacent.'

'Is that one of the reasons you ride?'

Antonia tensed slightly. 'I…beg your pardon?'

'Well, you have mentioned on more than one occasion that you spend a good deal of time on horseback. That day I met you in the woods, for example, you said you were taking the longer route to the orphanage because you wished to enjoy a longer ride. I wondered if riding was a way of getting exercise, or merely an opportunity for enjoying the scenery?'

Relieved, Antonia slowly settled back against the cushions. She had obviously read more into his words than he had intended. 'Yes, I suppose I do enjoy riding for the exercise it provides but, to be truthful, I think I enjoy the solitude even more. There is nothing so liberating as a gallop across an open field. I feel as though I am…a creature of the wind; freed from the restrictions of the polite world. I feel as though—' Antonia suddenly broke off, aware that her companion had started to smile. 'Forgive me, my lord. You must think me…somewhat flighty to be harbouring such strange sentiments.'

'Flighty is the last word I would use to describe you, Miss Hadley,' Sebastian said. 'In fact, I do believe that you are one of the most charming and refreshing young women I have ever had the pleasure of meeting.'

Antonia coloured and quickly looked away, shaken by the softly spoken sentiment. She had been the recipient of flattery before, but it had never affected her like this. Perhaps because there was…a sincerity to Sebastian's words that made his compliments so much more meaningful than anyone else's. Antonia found herself wishing that they could remain like this forever; just the two of them, floating peacefully on the stillness of the lake. She wished that he would go on speaking to her, whispering sweet words of affection; words that intensified this strange fluttery feeling in her heart, and the delicious tingling all over her body.

To tell her, in words and with looks, that he loved her as much as she loved him.

'You know, my father used to talk about your mother when I was a young boy,' Sebastian said casually. 'He told me that she was one of the finest equestriennes he had ever seen. Said she had better hands than most of the gentlemen he knew. I think you must have inherited her skills.'

Antonia froze, her peaceful idyll shattering like glass. Was it possible that Sebastian knew that her mother's maiden name had been Davlin?

No, he couldn't have. Otherwise, he would certainly have made comment upon the fact that her name and that of Clara's riding master were so similar.

'Yes, I do enjoy riding…very much,' Antonia stammered, reluctant to meet his gaze, 'but I do not claim to replicate my mother's ability. She was…quite rare in that respect.'

'So I have heard, though I confess, I do not find the daughter all that different,' Sebastian said quietly. 'In fact, I find her to be…a rather rare and special woman too.' He paused for a moment, and then cleared his throat. 'Miss Hadley, I wonder if you would consider—'

The rest of the question went unspoken, cut off by a high, terrified scream that shattered the peaceful afternoon silence.

'Good God, what was that?' Sebastian's head whipped round towards shore. Seconds later, he blanched. 'Sweet Jesus! *Clara!*'

The horror in his voice caused Antonia to look towards shore—and her blood to turn to ice. Clara's little mare was galloping full out across the field. The reins were dangling loose around her neck and her ears were laid back flat. And there on her back was Clara, hanging on to the crutch of the saddle for everything she was worth!

With a strangled gasp, Sebastian dropped the oars back into the water. He began to row like a man possessed, his face set, his mouth pulled tight and unsmiling. Helpless to do anything but watch, Antonia clung to the edge of the boat, fear twisting in her stomach like a snake. The mare had the bit between her teeth and she was running with it. Lord only knew how long Clara would be able to stay in the saddle.

Hold on, Clara, Antonia whispered fervently as hot tears sprang to her eyes. *Dear God, please hold on.*

On the shore, other members of the party were rushing to do what they could. Sir Robert made a dash for his mount, while Benbrooke and Lord Edwards went after the pair on foot. Sebastian pulled harder at the oars, sweat beading on his forehead as he fought to close the distance between them and the shore.

Antonia kept her eyes locked on Clara, sensing the terror in her body. The little girl would not have the strength to hold on much longer. 'My lord, we are not going to make it!'

'We have to make it,' Sebastian said grimly. The front of his shirt was soaked with perspiration, but his strokes never flagged. Seconds later, he ploughed the bow of the boat into the grassy bank and jumped out, stopping only long enough to help Antonia disembark. Then, the two of them began to run towards the field.

Suddenly, Sir Robert Gage appeared on the horizon, galloping at right angles towards Clara and the mare. He rode low over his mount's neck, urging him ever closer to the runaway horse, until no more than twenty feet separated them. Antonia held her breath. He was trying to head the mare off, but would he be able to do it in time?

Then, it happened. The mare, feeling the stallion closing in, suddenly swung around to the right, heading back in the very direction from which she'd come.

Straight into Sebastian's path.

'Benbrooke, Edwards, stand ready!' Sebastian shouted. 'I'll make a grab for the reins. If I'm successful, Clara will be thrown from the saddle. I'll need you on either side of me to try to catch her.'

Antonia felt as though a hand suddenly closed around her throat. The manoeuvre Sebastian was attempting was horribly dangerous. It called for split-second timing and nerves of steel. It was all she could do to watch.

But watch she did, heart in her mouth as the three men took up their positions in front of the charging horse.

The thunder of hooves echoed down the hill. Sebastian crouched, readying himself to spring. The mare's ears pricked forward, spying the three men standing directly ahead of her. For the space of a heart beat, she slowed.

It was all the time Sebastian needed. He lunged—making a wild grab for the dangling rein and grasping it firmly in both hands as he dug in his heels. The mare came to a juddering halt, her shrill whinny of protest echoing through the still afternoon air as her head went down and around.

As expected, the sudden stop ripped Clara from the saddle. She screamed as her hands were wrenched free and she flew out over the mare's shoulder—straight into

Benbrooke's arms. But it was not an easy landing. Antonia watched in horror as Benbrooke staggered backwards, fighting to keep his balance. In the end, it was more than he could manage. As one, they fell to the ground, Clara crying out in pain as her left arm twisted awkwardly beneath Benbrooke's back.

'Clara!' Antonia cried.

Sebastian tossed the mare's reins to Lord Edwards and dropped to his knees in the grass. 'Clara, darling, are you all right?'

'My arm,' Clara whimpered as huge tears rolled down her cheeks. 'Hurts!'

Sebastian glanced at his daughter's arm, and his expression was grim. The awkward angle at which it lay told him all he needed to know.

'Gage, bring one of the carriages around,' he said quietly to Sir Robert. 'Gerald, are you all right?'

Benbrooke winced, but nodded gamely. 'A touch…winded, but that's all. How's…Clara?'

Sebastian's face was set. 'I'm taking her home. She'll need a doctor's care. The ladies can take the other carriage back to Ashdean. The gentlemen will have to ride.'

'Let me go with you, my lord,' Antonia said quickly. 'You will not be able to drive and look after Clara, especially if, as I suspect, her arm is broken.'

Sebastian nodded, dimly aware that Antonia's face was even whiter than his daughter's. 'Thank you, Miss Hadley, your assistance would be…most appreciated.'

'Perhaps I should ride back in the carriage with you as well, Lord Carlyle,' Lady Rosalind said hastily. 'That will leave more room in the carriage for the others.'

Sebastian shook his head as he gently lifted Clara from Benbrooke's arms. 'Thank you, Rosalind, but there will be room enough. Speed now is of the essence. Mr

Mallett, would you see that the mare is taken to the stables immediately upon your arrival at Ashdean?'

'Of course, my lord.'

'Thank you. Miss Hadley, are you ready?'

Antonia nodded as Sir Robert brought the carriage to a halt. She climbed up into the seat, then waited as Sebastian carefully settled Clara in her lap.

'You're going to be all right, Clara,' Sebastian whispered to the little girl, gently brushing back the blonde hair which had fallen forward across her face. 'Everything is going to be fine.'

'Will you c-come with us, Papa?' Clara said tearfully.

Sebastian swallowed hard. 'Yes, of course. Take the ribbons, Gage. I shall sit back here with Clara and Miss Hadley.'

Sir Robert nodded. Then, waiting only until Sebastian was settled in the seat across from Antonia, he set the horses at a brisk trot towards Ashdean.

Sebastian said little on the ride home. Antonia sat in the seat across from him, with Clara's head resting in her lap, and wished she could offer some soothing words of comfort. She could only imagine the thoughts that were going through his head. His face was drawn, his eyes so dark as to appear almost black.

Upon reaching the courtyard at Ashdean, Sebastian sprang down and shouted for a servant to ride for the doctor. Then, handling Clara as though she were the most fragile of flowers, he carried her into the house and up to her room, there laying her gently on the bed.

'I should have listened to you,' Sebastian said as Antonia slipped off the child's boots and put her to bed. 'You said the mare was too big for her, and I should have listened. I have…no one to blame for Clara's accident but myself.'

Antonia shook her head as she tucked the covers around Clara. The child's eyes were closed and had been for some time. 'The accident was not your fault, my lord. Nor is the mare's size to blame. Something frightened her, and caused her to bolt. No one could have foreseen that.'

Sebastian stared down at his daughter's white face. 'I would not have believed it possible to feel this way about…one's own child. When I think of all the years I stayed away from her…all the things I missed—' He clenched his hands by his sides, and turned away.

Sensing his despair, Antonia got up to follow him. 'Do not reproach yourself for the mistakes of the past, my lord. You must look instead to the future, and to the many years you will have with Clara. The memory of this will grow dim as time passes. For both of you.'

'T-Toni?'

Antonia spun around to face the bed. Clara's eyes were open and shimmering with tears.

'Yes, Clara, I'm here.' Antonia dropped to the floor beside the bed. She smoothed her fingers across the child's forehead and tried to smile. 'How do you feel, dearest?'

'It…hurts,' Clara said as the huge tears began to fall again. 'My arm…hurts.'

The pain in the child's voice tore at Antonia's heart, but she did her best to keep it from showing in her face. 'I know, sweetheart, but the doctor is on his way and he is going to make it all better.'

'Is…Papa here?'

'Yes, Clara, I'm here.' Sebastian leaned over the bed

and smiled down into his daughter's face. 'And I am going to stay right here until the doctor comes.'

The little girl swallowed. 'Is…Ariana…all right?'

'Ariana is just fine. Mr Mallett has taken her down to the stables and is looking after her.'

'It wasn't her fault,' Clara whispered tremulously. 'There was…a rabbit. It jumped out…and scared her. Then she…pulled the reins out of my hand and started to run. I c-couldn't get them back.' Her face began to crumple and fresh tears to fall. 'I'm so sorry, Toni.'

Antonia was dismayed to feel tears stinging her own eyes. 'Sorry? But you have nothing to be sorry for, Clara, it was not your fault.'

'But it was. You told me…never to ride unless… someone was with me. You told me that…at our very first lesson.'

'It's all right, Clara, you are confusing Miss Hadley with someone else.' Sebastian gently wiped away her tears. 'Mr Davlin is the gentleman Mr Bingham hired to teach you, not Toni.'

'No. Toni showed me how to ride,' Clara repeated stubbornly. 'Paddy didn't like the other man, b-because he made me cry. Tell Papa, Toni. Tell him there was…only you.'

There was only you.

The four words hung like a sentence in the silence of the room. After what seemed like an eternity, Sebastian turned to look at her. 'Is this…true, Miss Hadley?'

Hardly daring to breath, Antonia gazed up into the eyes of the man she loved, and saw the shock and disbelief that were mirrored in their depths. What could she say? She had never expected the truth to come out like this. 'My lord, I can explain—'

'Explain? Are you telling me that you *have* been teaching my daughter how to ride?'

'Well, yes, but—'

'And I was never *told* about this?' In deference to the child, Sebastian lowered his voice, but the caustic tone did nothing to lessen Antonia's anguish. 'Did Mr Bingham *hire* you to work for me?'

'My lord, I wish you would let me explain—'

'Pardon me, my lord,' the butler said at the door, 'but the doctor is here.'

Sebastian's eyes were stony as they rested on Antonia's face. 'Show him up.'

As the man withdrew, Sebastian's face closed down even further. 'It would seem, Miss Hadley, that I have been played for a fool. And that is too bad. Because I have never liked being part of a game where the players do not observe the rules.'

Antonia closed her eyes, aware of a wretchedness unlike any she had ever known. It was over. Sebastian *knew* that she had lied to him. And he was coldly and quietly furious.

'My lord, I *beg* you—'

'We shall talk about this again, Miss Hadley. Now is…not the time. Ah, Dr Philips, come in.' Sebastian glanced at Antonia and smiled with all the warmth of an arctic winter. 'Miss Hadley was just leaving.'

There was no mistaking the curt dismissal in his voice. Embarrassed colour flooded her face as Antonia stumbled to her feet. For the sake of the child, however, she managed a half-hearted smile. 'I have to…leave you now, Clara. The doctor is going to…look at your arm.'

'But you are coming back, aren't you, Toni?' the little girl said, her frown telling Antonia that she was aware of the tensions in the room, if not of the reasons for it. ''You will be…coming back?'

Antonia nodded, struggling to hold back the tears until she was out of the room. 'Yes, dearest. I will…be back.'

'I…love you, Toni.'

It was the one thing Antonia could not deal with. Choking back a sob, she pressed her hands to her mouth. 'I love you…too, Clara,' she whispered. Then she turned and left the room, running down the hall as the tears poured freely down her cheeks. She heard Clara call out her name, but she didn't stop. She couldn't. She flew down the stairs and out into the sunshine. She did not stop running until she reached Buntings Hill.

It was a long time after that before she stopped crying.

Chapter Eleven

The confrontation between Sebastian and his steward took place before dinner that evening.

Sebastian knew that the meeting would be a painful one. The thought of having to question one of his most trusted servants—a man who had become almost a friend—was abhorrent to him. But it had to be done. He would have the truth of the matter, and he would have it before the night was out. Hence, formally dressed for dinner, but robbed of any appetite he might have had for it, Sebastian summoned Bingham to his private office.

'You wished to see me, my lord,' the steward said, standing uncertainly in the doorway.

'Yes, Mr Bingham, I did.' Sebastian turned and made his way towards the desk, his manner purposely brisk. 'You may have heard about my daughter's accident this afternoon.'

Bingham nodded. 'Aye, my lord, I did. How fares the little girl?'

'The doctor assures me that she is…going to be fine.' There was a slight tremor to Sebastian's voice, but he quickly controlled it. 'Unfortunately, I was also made aware of some other disturbing news and I have asked you here to find out whether or not it is true.' Sebastian's eyes bored into his steward's. 'You have never let me down before, Paddy, and I have never known you to lie to me. I only hope that I can count upon your complete honesty now, to settle this matter once and for all.'

Mr Bingham nodded, but there was a pensive look in his eyes. 'What matter might that be, my lord?'

'A matter concerning Miss Antonia Hadley.' Sebastian took a deep breath. 'This afternoon, Clara informed me that Miss Hadley had been teaching her how to ride. She told me that…there was never any gentleman by the name of Tony Davlin, and that you knew about this from the start. Now I am asking you for the truth. Has Antonia Hadley been masquerading as Tony Davlin all along?'

It seemed to Sebastian that his steward actually shrank in stature, but it was the expression on his face which ultimately gave him away—and which caused Sebastian the greatest pain of all. 'So it is true,' he said stonily. 'You did lie to me.'

'My lord, if you would but allow me to—'

'I will have no excuses, Mr Bingham, only the truth. Did you or did you not hire Miss Antonia Hadley to fill the position of riding master to my daughter?'

Bingham swallowed hard. 'Yes, my lord, I did.'

'And did you, or did you not, try to pass her off as a man by referring to her as Mr Tony Davlin whenever you were in my presence?'

'No, my lord, that I did not do,' Bingham said quietly, and with dignity. 'The only time I made reference to a *Mr* Davlin, was when I first received the letter of application. I had no reason to suspect that the person who sent it was not…who they said they were, but once I learned the truth of the matter, I referred to her only as…Tony Davlin.'

Sebastian gave a scornful laugh. 'And I suppose you feel that lessens the severity of the transgression.'

'No, my lord, I do not. I avoided using any form of address because I had…no wish to lie to you outright. I felt bad enough deceiving you as it was.'

'But not so bad that you were willing to come to me and admit what you had done, eh, Paddy?'

Mr Bingham hung his head. 'No, my lord.'

Sebastian's lips twisted in a cynical smile. 'Tell me, Mr Bingham, did you have Miss Hadley's complete and willing co-operation in this little deceit?'

Damn it! That was a question Sebastian had not been intending to ask. Unfortunately, once the words were out, there was nothing he could do to withdraw them.

And so he waited, willing his steward to say anything but what he most desperately feared he would. He wanted to believe that Antonia had not understood the nature of what she was doing. That she had been… forced somehow, by circumstances beyond her control, into doing something she would not normally have done; something that had been totally out of character for her.

Anything would have been easier than knowing that she had purposely set out to deceive him.

Sadly, it was not to be the case.

'Yes, my lord, Miss Hadley…did co-operate with me,' Bingham admitted at length. 'In fact, it was…she who convinced me to give it a try. But that was only because—'

Sebastian held up his hand. 'Spare me, Mr Bingham, I have no wish to hear the reasons.' He slowly sank into his chair and struggled to come to terms with the information he just received.

So, it was true. He had been deceived; both by a man he trusted, and by a woman he had come to admire and respect. A young woman whom he had come to look upon with affection. A lady whom he had begun to hope might have been…everything he had been looking for. But in less time than it took to blink, the truth had been made clear to him.

Antonia Hadley was no better than the rest. She had lied to him without compunction, showing that she was every bit as capable of treachery as the rest of her sex. How could he believe anything that she said now? She claimed to care for his daughter, yet who was to say that it wasn't all part of the deception? Even the affection which he thought he had glimpsed in her eyes. The softening of her face when she spoke to him. Were those all lies too?

'When were you going to tell me, Paddy?' Sebastian asked in a hard, expressionless voice. 'If you were going to tell me at all.'

Mr Bingham looked down into the face of the man whom he had watched grow from a young strapling to the sophisticated man of the world he was now, and sadly shook his head. 'I wasn't going to tell you, my lord. When I informed you last week that…Mr Davlin had left your employ, I intended that to be an end of it. I saw no reason to…complicate matters by telling you the rest of the story.'

'I see.' Sebastian stared at the heavy gold paperweight on his desk and marvelled that he had been so blind. 'And what made you and Miss Hadley decide that this was an appropriate time for—' his mouth curled with distaste '—Mr Davlin to leave my employ?'

'Because we knew that it would be impossible for Miss Hadley to conduct Clara's riding lessons without being observed,' Bingham said quietly. 'And because…you had expressed a desire to see Mr Davlin upon your return. As such, we had no choice but to…make him disappear before you had opportunity of discovering his true identity.'

Sebastian nodded perfunctorily. If nothing else, he could respect his steward for being honest with him. There was affection for Miss Hadley in Bingham's voice, and Sebastian knew what it had cost him to admit to her part in the proceedings.

Unfortunately, his loyalty to her did nothing to abrogate the seriousness of what he had done to the man who had given him a living for the past twenty-five years. After all, once the trust was gone, Sebastian reflected grimly, what else was there?

'I think it would be best if you were to look for…other employment, Mr Bingham,' Sebastian said slowly. 'In recognition of the years of service you have given me, I shall pay your salary to the end of the month, and provide you with a letter of reference. But that is all. I think that, under the circumstances, it is fair.'

Bingham paled at the enormity of what had just taken place, but his voice was steady as he said, 'More than fair, I should say, my lord.'

Sebastian nodded. He did not feel vindicated by what he had done. He felt only regret and disappointment at having been betrayed in such a manner. 'That will be all, Mr Bingham.'

Knowing that the interview was over, the steward bowed and turned to leave. At the door, he hesitated. 'Will you be…speaking to Miss Hadley about this, my lord?'

Sebastian's expression gave nothing away. 'I think it only right that I do so. You have been taken to task for your actions and been made to pay a price. I see no reason why the lady should escape so lightly.'

A flicker of pain lodged in the older man's eyes, and it seemed to Sebastian that, for the first time in his life, he saw no sparkle in the deep green depths. But he could not allow that to weaken his resolve. The man had made a mistake. He deserved to suffer the consequences.

'We only did it for the sake of the child, my lord,' Mr Bingham said softly. 'It was never our intention to…cause you grief.'

Sebastian locked his hands behind his back. 'That is a shame, Mr Bingham. Because that is precisely what the two of you have done.'

There was no expression in Sebastian's voice, but the words still made Bingham flinch. 'For what it's worth, I am…deeply sorry to have disappointed you, my lord.'

There was a long, pregnant pause. Then, like frost caught in the first warm rays of the sun, Sebastian's anger melted away, leaving him physically drained, and emotionally bereft. 'So am I, Paddy. For what it's worth, so am I.'

Fifteen minutes later, Sebastian walked into the drawing room to face his guests. He had stopped in the library for a stiff drink, followed by an even stiffer one in the study. But neither had helped to ease the pain which gnawed at his insides. He had found out too much this afternoon—and none of it good.

As expected, he was besieged with questions.

'Ladies and gentlemen, thank you for your concern,' Sebastian said, finally holding up his hands for silence. 'Clara has suffered a broken arm and some bruising, but that is all. The doctor said that she was badly frightened by her ordeal, but that with rest and quiet, she should make a full recovery.'

'Thank God!' Mr Mallett said sincerely.

'Yes, indeed,' Lady Montague breathed. 'I do not think I have ever been so frightened.'

'No, nor have I,' Lady Jane said in agreement.

Sebastian took a deep breath. 'Mr Benbrooke, I owe you a debt of gratitude. Had you not been able to catch Clara as she fell, her injuries might have been a good deal worse. It takes a brave man to stand in the path of a charging horse.'

Benbrooke grinned sheepishly. 'Yes, well, I'm not sure I would do it again if I had time to think about it, but I am relieved that she is all right.'

'And, Robert,' Sebastian said, addressing the other man who had played such a large part in the afternoon's rescue, 'if you hadn't acted so quickly, I think Clara would have been half way to Yorkshire by now.' He clasped the Baronet's hand in a firm grip. 'You will never know how grateful I am.'

Sir Robert lightly brushed aside his thanks. 'Glad to be of service, Sebastian. But I think you are downplaying your own role in the proceedings. Standing in front of a charging horse, leaping for the reins and hoping not to get trampled in the process—I would say that takes a very special kind of courage indeed.'

'Oh, yes, Lord Carlyle, what you did was exceedingly heroic,' Harriet Spencer said fervently.

'But nothing less than we would have expected of him,' Lady Rosalind put in smoothly. 'Lord Carlyle is, in all ways, the most admirable of men.'

'Speaking of admirable,' Lord Montague said, 'is Miss Hadley not joining us this evening?'

A muscle jumped in Sebastian's jaw. 'No. She was…distraught over the events of the afternoon and begged leave not to attend.'

'Oh, what a shame,' Harriet said. 'I was so looking forward to talking to her.'

'Well, I am not surprised,' said Lord Montague. 'Miss Hadley did not look at all the thing when she left with you this afternoon.'

'No, it was obvious that she was extremely upset by the accident,' his wife said.

'But surely no more so than the rest of us,' Lady Rosalind spoke up. 'After all, we have all had time to come to know and…love Lady Clara over these past few days. Miss Hadley's behaviour would lead us to believe that *she* was the one who was nearly thrown from her horse.'

Everyone suddenly began to talk at once, offering opinions, and shouting down others. Aware that his head was beginning to ache, Sebastian once again appealed for silence. 'Ladies, gentlemen, please, it has been a tiring afternoon, and an emotional one. I suggest that we say no more about Clara's accident, and that we try to enjoy the evening and each other's company. After all, is that not why we are here?'

The sentiment was a genuine one, but it was not surprising that dinner was far from the jovial occasion it had been on the past two evenings. Sebastian tried to rouse himself to play the part of the genial host, but it was a poor attempt at best. Because, despite everything that had happened, and everything that she had done, Sebastian was startled to discover that he still missed Antonia Hadley. He had been looking forward to seeing her at his table tonight; to hearing the gentle sound of her voice. He liked seeing the way her eyes sparkled when she laughed, and he had wanted her to be here to share his feelings. Even now, with everything he had learned this afternoon, he still found himself thinking of her.

And for the first time in his life, Sebastian realised how wretchedly empty his life had been before Antonia Hadley had walked into it.

The mood at Buntings Hill was little better. In the privacy of her room, Antonia lay on her bed and stared up at the ceiling, too shocked to think, too numb to feel. She only knew that the afternoon, which had started out to be such a delightful interlude, had turned into a nightmare of catastrophic proportions. Not only had Clara been involved in a terrifying accident, but *she* had been exposed as a liar and a fraud—and by the very man whose good opinion she had come to value above anyone else's.

Antonia reviewed over and over what had happened that afternoon. She thought about Sebastian's selfless act of heroism, how he had thrown himself into the path of a charging horse in the hopes of bringing it to a stop, knowing full well that he could have been knocked aside, or trampled under the weight of it.

She thought about Clara, and what could have happened had the child lost her grip and fallen from the mare's back. What would have happened had her foot caught in the stirrup, or her skirt become tangled around the crutch?

Sadly, Antonia knew the answer to that. Clara would have been dragged across the field, helpless to stop the horse and unable to free herself until, finally, her screams would have ceased.

Just as Edwina's had.

Grief, primitive and deep, rose through the ashes of her mind as Antonia closed her eyes and willed the memories away. Memories of a warm summer's afternoon five years ago, when another riding accident had taken something precious from her. Something… irreplaceable.

Unfortunately, the memories would not go away. Because the events of the afternoon had brought them all back with such painful clarity that Antonia felt her past become her present once more. Less than an hour ago, she had lost Sebastian's respect and admiration. She had lost the man she loved, as surely as though he had fallen from a horse and been killed.

Just as she had lost…Edwina.

The anticipated summons to Ashdean did not arrive that night. Nor did it come the next morning as Antonia sat alone at the breakfast table, staring at her plate, all semblance of an appetite gone.

She had lain awake most of the night, envisioning how the dreaded interview would take place. She imagined Sebastian summoning her to Ashdean and accusing her of lying to secure the position of riding master. In her mind, he went on to reprimand her for not watching Clara closely enough at the picnic, and then telling her that he wanted nothing more to do with her.

And then would come the final stroke when he advised her of his intention to marry Lady Rosalind Grey.

That was undoubtedly the worst nightmare of all, Antonia reflected miserably. It was the one which had made her give up on the idea of sleep altogether, and which had forced her to rise with pale cheeks and red eyes to a cool, grey dawn.

But now, this endless waiting was even worse,

Antonia decided. Sitting in the breakfast room, listening to the ponderous ticking of the clock and waiting for the note to arrive, was like a condemned man waiting for the axe to fall.

At half past ten, she could wait no longer. She went upstairs and made ready to pay a house call.

At eleven o'clock, Antonia presented herself at the front door of Ashdean.

'Good morning, Miss Hadley,' the butler said, surprise evident in his voice as he opened the door to her. 'Is Lord Carlyle expecting you?'

Antonia coloured slightly. It was not the approved hour for paying calls, but she had to see Sebastian. She had to know what he was thinking. 'He is not, Hildegarde, but I wonder if you could tell him that I am here. It is on a matter of…some urgency.'

The butler inclined his head and stood aside. 'I shall tell him at once.'

Antonia drew a deep breath as she stood and waited in the front hall. She saw neither the priceless tapestries and paintings which graced the walls, nor the lovingly polished woodwork. She saw instead the harsh, unforgiving face of the man she loved. The man who was about to shatter her world.

In anticipation of their meeting, Antonia had donned one of her most becoming outfits. The well-cut carriage gown was flattering to her figure, while the rich emerald green drew attention to her eyes and hair. And with an elegant new bonnet fixed atop her curls, Antonia knew that she looked the picture of composure as Hildegarde escorted her to the library—even if she was not.

'Miss Hadley, my lord,' Hildegarde announced.

Sebastian was leafing through a volume plucked from

the shelf behind his desk. He did not turn around at her entrance, but merely closed the book and returned it to its place as the butler silently withdrew. 'To what do I owe the pleasure of this visit, Miss Hadley?'

Antonia took a deep breath. His manner was distant. Unconcerned, almost. Neither of which made for an auspicious beginning. 'I…came to enquire after Lady Clara,' she said in a halting voice. 'I was…very concerned when I left yesterday.'

'Thank you for your consideration. My daughter suffered a broken arm and some bruising,' Sebastian said briefly. 'She was also badly shaken. Other than that, the doctor has assured me that she will be fine.'

'I am…relieved to hear it.'

'Yes, I am sure you are.' Finally turning to face her, Sebastian offered her a cool smile. 'I trust that *you* are fully recovered from the events of yesterday afternoon as well?'

Antonia caught her bottom lip between her teeth. She had not been sure what kind of behaviour to expect from Sebastian. Anger, perhaps, or disgust. Maybe a combination of the two. But not this. Not this chilling air of polite…indifference. 'I am…quite well, my lord, thank you. But you must know that it is…because of yesterday that I have come to see you.' When he said nothing, Antonia forced herself to go on. 'Lord Carlyle, I pray that you can…find it in your heart to forgive me. I owe you a great apology. I am guilty of deceiving you, and I sincerely regret the manner in which you found out about it. I lied to you about the part I played in this, but you must believe me when I say that it was never my intention to cause you grief as a result of that deception.'

Sebastian shrugged eloquently. 'You are mistaken, Miss Hadley, you have caused me no grief at all.'

Antonia faltered. 'I…beg your pardon?'

'In reviewing the circumstances, I would say it was more…an error of omission.'

'I do not understand.'

'It is really quite simple. For you to have lied to me, you would have had to have been asked a direct question, and given a direct answer. But at no time did I ask you if you *were* working for me, if you were *interested* in working for me, or whether you would have lied about your identity in order to *secure* a job working for me. I did not ask you if you *were* Tony Davlin or if you knew of him. That question, I believe, was directed at your father. So you see, Miss Hadley, the fact that you did not volunteer any of the above information cannot, I think, be construed as lying.' Sebastian waited for a moment before delivering the final blow. 'It is, in fact, Mr Bingham who has paid the price for not telling me the truth.'

Antonia paled. 'Why? What have you done?'

'What any self-respecting employer would do in the face of dishonesty. I have turned him off.'

Antonia's breath caught in her lungs. 'But you cannot!'

'Ah, but I can, Miss Hadley. Oh, you needn't fear that. I have left him bereft. I have given him more money than he deserved, and a letter of recommendation to ease his way into a new situation. We both agreed that it was more than fair under the circumstances.'

'But none of this was Mr Bingham's fault,' Antonia cried passionately. '*I* wrote the letter pretending to be Tony Davlin. *I* was the one who met with your steward, and convinced him to let me do this. If it had been left up to Mr Bingham, I would most certainly have been turned away—'

'But you were not turned away,' Sebastian interrupted, his easy-going manner vanishing. 'And the fact that Mr Bingham was in my employ when you concocted your little subterfuge makes him totally accountable for the crime. I will not tolerate anyone lying to me, Miss Hadley. Not my family, not my friends, and certainly not my servants. Mr Bingham knew the consequences of his actions when he agreed to take you on.'

'But there were extenuating circumstances. Please, Lord Carlyle, you *must* let me explain why—'

'No. I have no wish to hear another Banbury tale, Miss Hadley. I know that you set out to deceive me, and I must say that you did a very good job of it. Had Clara not let slip your little secret, I doubt I should ever have figured it out.' Sebastian laughed, but the sound was hollow, and without mirth. 'You and Mr Bingham must have enjoyed a great laugh at my expense.'

Antonia closed her eyes, her throat aching with despair. 'My lord, you do not understand, I only did it for Clara—'

'Yes, so Mr Bingham tried to tell me,' Sebastian interrupted harshly. 'But what kind of help did you think you were giving her, Miss Hadley? What kind of…example did you think your behaviour would set? That it was all right to pretend to be someone else? That it was permissible to lie and to deceive people, if the cause was perceived to be sufficiently motivating? Is that what you hoped to teach her by your actions?'

A sick feeling of despair settled in the pit of Antonia's stomach. He was shutting her out. She began to wonder if there was anything she could say that would make him see the situation in a different light. 'No, my lord. I only hoped to…instil in Lady Clara the basic principles of good horsemanship. I wanted her to be able to feel…at ease around horses. And I felt that I could do that better than anyone else. Your daughter is not comfortable with strangers, Lord Carlyle. And though you may not know it, she had already begun to develop a fear of horses.'

'Rubbish! I saw no signs of any such fears on the day of the picnic.'

'No, because I had been working with her for some weeks beforehand,' Antonia explained. 'But the gentleman Mr Bingham interviewed before me did not recognise Clara's fear. He put her on a horse and started giving her commands so that, within minutes of being in the saddle, she was in tears.'

'Most children experience moments of…anxiety when they are first exposed to something new, Miss Hadley,' Sebastian said coldly. 'And, like most children, she would have grown out of it.'

'No, my lord, she would not. Because Clara's was not a simple case of anxiety. She was afraid of Teddy and, without careful handling, she might have held on to the fear for the rest of her life.'

'And you think you could have made a difference?' Sebastian all but sneered.

Antonia nodded. 'Yes, because Clara knew me. And she trusted me. She knew that I would not ask her to do…anything that she was not ready to do. All I wanted to do was make use of that trust—'

'To take advantage of it, you mean,' Sebastian snapped.

'No!'

'You can dress it up any way you wish, Miss Hadley, but the simple truth is, you took advantage of my daughter's feelings, and of my own absence, to lie your way into a position which you would not otherwise have secured. Can you honestly tell me that you were ignorant of the fact that I do not choose to have women working for me?'

Antonia swallowed. 'I am…and was, aware of your preferences, my lord, though I do not pretend to understand them.'

'Not understand them?' Sebastian's tone was incredulous. 'I find that very strange, Miss Hadley, since to my way of thinking, this little episode demonstrates exactly why I feel the way I do. Women lie and cheat,' he said bluntly. 'They care nothing for the feelings of a gentleman so long as they achieve what they set out to achieve, and they cannot be trusted. A regrettable fact demonstrated to me by my wife and others of her ilk, and now by you. Now do you understand why I choose not to have them in my employ?'

It was a scathing condemnation, and Antonia flinched at every cruel verbal thrust. 'My lord, I only wanted to do what I felt was best for Clara.'

'Yes. By deceiving her father. Well, I will not have it, Miss Hadley.' Sebastian stared at her with hard, passionless eyes. 'Mr Bingham has already told me that he did not intend to tell me the truth of your deception, so I shall ask the same question of you. Would *you* have told me the truth, had I not been so unfortunate as to stumble upon it?'

Antonia looked into those icy blue eyes and knew that it did not matter what she said any more. The damage was done. He believed that she had lied to him and, in doing so, she had lost his respect and good opinion. What use would anything but the truth be to her now?

She lifted her chin and met his gaze straight on. 'No, my lord, I likely would not have told you. It was my…greatest wish to teach Clara how to ride, for reasons that I have tried to explain, and for…others, which are my own and entirely private. And if the only way I could do that was by pretending to be a man, then yes, I would have continued to do so. It is not my fault that you hold the entire female race accountable for the mistakes of a few, and that you choose not to hire *any* of us as a result.'

'You are, of course, entitled to your opinion, Miss Hadley. But what would you say, if I were to accuse you of being the cause of my daughter's accident?' Still smiling, Sebastian passed a knife-edged glance over her face. 'What would you say then about your ability as a teacher?'

Shock and disbelief siphoned the blood from Antonia's cheeks. Was it possible that…Sebastian was *blaming* her for his daughter's accident? Yes, by God, he was. He was suggesting—no, he was accusing her, of being an inferior instructor.

And that was where he made his mistake. Because while Antonia was willing to accept blame for what she had done to him, she would not accept blame for an accident to his child over which she had had no control.

'How dare you?' she whispered, her face rigid with anger. 'How dare you imply that I was the cause of Clara's accident? You know nothing of me, or of my abilities. And the idea that I could be responsible as a result of negligence or…lack of training, is insulting and hurtful, and I will not accept it.'

'Then perhaps we should consider ourselves even, Miss Hadley,' Sebastian said coldly, 'for it would appear that we have both suffered over this sad affair. You are hurt and insulted by my behaviour, and I am offended and disappointed by yours. However, since you openly admit to perpetrating the deceit, wherein lies the bulk of the blame, do you think?'

Antonia struggled to contain her anger, aware that her feelings of guilt had vanished in the face of his overwhelming arrogance. 'I have offered you an apology for what I did, Lord Carlyle, but I will *not* be vilified for something I did not do. Nor will I allow you to ease your conscience by laying the blame for what happened to Clara at my feet. I am afraid you will have to find another whipping boy for that. Good afternoon, Lord Carlyle!'

Chapter Twelve

Antonia's anger over Lord Carlyle's insinuations carried her through the rest of the day and well into the next.

How dare he be so bold as to blame her for Clara's accident! How could he just…assume that she did not have the necessary qualifications to teach his child how to ride. Had he but taken a moment to ask, he would have discovered that she was every bit as qualified as any of the gentlemen who would have applied, and more than most.

Then, to add insult to injury, he had had the gall to make sweeping statements as to the integrity of women—condemning them as a whole, and holding her accountable simply because she was one—without so much as an apology or a by your leave. He had had the audacity to hold up her behaviour as an example of extremely bad judgement, while *he* had openly admitted to refusing to hire women simply because his wife had been untrustworthy.

His wife had been untrustworthy.

Antonia slowly put down the silver-handled brush, and stared thoughtfully into the glass. That had come as

a shock. She had heard whispered rumours concerning
Sebastian and his first wife, of course, but she had believed them to be just that. Now, it seemed, they were
true.

Still, it did not lessen the fact that he was an over-
bearing, opinionated man, who was little concerned with
the feelings of others, and who felt there was no way to
do things but his own, Antonia decided mumpishly.
Indeed, she began to think that her original assessment
of Sebastian Hastings was correct.

And Clara. Dear little Clara. What was to become of
her now? Would she be sent away to boarding school in
some far distant county? Brought home at holidays, but
kept out of the way until it was time to send her back?

She would if Lady Rosalind Grey was to be the new
Countess, Antonia reflected grimly. Because Lady
Rosalind—or Lady Carlyle as she would be then—
would be far too busy with her friends in London Society
to concern herself with the welfare of a little girl.

Antonia heard a door close downstairs, and assumed
that her father had left for a soirée at Lord and Lady
Markham's home. She knew that he was meeting Lady
Sheraton there, and that, if nothing else, brought her a
modicum of pleasure. At least *his* romance was turning
out well. In fact, Antonia was quite sure that her father
was in love with the beautiful Lady Sheraton, and she
could not have been happier. He needed someone to
share his life with again, and Lady Sheraton was perfect.
Indeed, Antonia did not think she could have chosen
anyone nicer.

But when she opened her door to a knock a few moments later, she was astonished to see Lady Sheraton
standing there, her gentle face alight with concern.

'Lady Sheraton!'

'Hello, Antonia. I hope I did not wake you.'

'No, I had not yet retired,' Antonia assured her. 'But...what are you doing here? I thought you were to meet Papa at Lord and Lady Markham's?'

'I was to have done, but...your father asked me if I would come and speak with you beforehand.' Lady Sheraton looked keenly into Antonia's face. 'He is very concerned about you, my dear, and he wondered if everything was all right?'

'Yes, of course everything is all right,' Antonia replied, though the tremor in her voice gave lie to the words. 'Why would you ask?'

Lady Sheraton's eyes softened. 'Come, my dear, you shall never a gambler make. Your face and your eyes betray you. Please, will you not tell me what is wrong?'

Her gentle probing eventually broke down Antonia's defences and, reluctantly, she told Lady Sheraton about Lady Clara's terrifying experience. Even more reluctantly, she told her about the bitter argument she had had with Lord Carlyle. Lady Sheraton listened but said nothing, the tightening of her lips, or a slight movement of her eyes, the only indication of her response.

'So you see, Lady Sheraton,' Antonia concluded sadly, 'not only have I lost Lord Carlyle's respect, but I fear that I have lost...everything else as well.'

'Everything else?' Lady Sheraton said, venturing a guess on the one thing Antonia had not admitted to her. 'Then you are in love with him.'

A dozen responses trembled on Antonia's lips—all of them heated denials that she could ever love such a man. But when she saw the expression on Lady Sheraton's face, and realised that her own heart would not accept it as truth, Antonia knew there was little hope of deceiving her. 'Yes, I love him,' she admitted wretchedly, 'though I cannot imagine why I was so stupid as to let myself get involved. Lady Rosalind warned me that it would come to nought.'

'Lady Rosalind?' Lady Sheraton repeated in surprise. 'Lady Rosalind Grey?'

'Yes. Do you know her?'

'I certainly know *of* her,' Lady Sheraton said in a manner which implied that the acquaintance was not a favourable one. 'A beautiful woman, without question, but as cold as the winds of winter. I have heard that she is looking for a rich husband.'

Antonia was surprised to hear that. Lady Rosalind had given no indication that she was in restricted financial circumstances. 'Well, Lord Carlyle seems to like her well enough, and most of his friends believe that they will make an excellent match. But I shudder to think of what will become of Clara if they marry.'

'She will be sent away to boarding school and left there until she is of an age to marry,' Lady Sheraton stated tonelessly. 'As I was.'

Antonia's eyes flew to the face of the elegant woman beside her. '*You* were sent away?'

'Oh, yes. Not by a stepmother, as Clara will be, but by a mother who had no time for a daughter who even from an early age, showed a surprising tendency towards independence. I was not a pretty child, Antonia,' Lady Sheraton said without embarrassment. 'I did not like having ribbons in my hair or being made to wear nice dresses. As such I was viewed as something of…an oddity. My mother used to tell me that I was possessed of a most unbecoming stare, and it was some years before I learned to temper it. Unfortunately, by then, she had given up on me altogether and sent me away.'

'How dreadful for you!'

'Perhaps. And yet, perhaps I was better off away from her,' Lady Sheraton conceded. 'But it is because of my experiences that I know what Clara will go through.'

They were silent for a moment, each lost in their own thoughts. Finally, Lady Sheraton rose. 'Well, I suppose I had best be getting back downstairs. I should not like to keep your father waiting. But do not lose heart, my dear.' She placed a comforting hand on Antonia's shoulder. 'Sebastian Hastings is many things, but a fool is not one of them. He has been courted by beautiful women since he was a lad, but he is not one to be swayed by pretty eyes and words. At least, not any more.'

'Lady Sheraton, was Lord Carlyle's first marriage…a happy one?'

Antonia knew it was an intrusive question, but she had to ask. She had to know why Sebastian held all women in such…contempt.

For a moment, it seemed that Lady Sheraton was not going to answer. Then, with a sigh, she nodded. 'I do not suppose that I am telling tales out of school, but, no, my dear, it was not. I know it is not kind to speak ill of the dead, but the first Lady Carlyle was not an admirable woman. Her wanton behaviour caused Sebastian grief on many occasions, but to his credit, he never renounced her in public. And once her health began to fail, I suppose he saw no reason to.'

'But what about Clara?' Antonia persisted. 'How could he have just…abandoned her in such a cruel and heartless manner? He barely saw her for over two years.'

'I have no answer for that, my dear,' Lady Sheraton admitted. 'But I do know that Sebastian is neither a cruel nor an insensitive man. I have seen him be generous to beggars in the street and to ragged urchins barely strong enough to stand. He is good to his servants, and he rewards loyalty where he finds it. But there is no question that he can be ruthless to those who are foolish enough to cross him.'

Thinking of poor Mr Bingham's plight, Antonia lowered her head. He had enjoyed a good living in the Earl's household for over twenty-five years. Now, because of her, he had been made to forfeit it.

'I only know, Antonia,' Lady Sheraton went on to say, 'that I believe in Sebastian's case the lessons of the past will have been well learned. This time, he will do what is best for his daughter. And for himself.'

Impulsively, Antonia rose to embrace the other woman. 'Thank you, Lady Sheraton. I did not realise how much I needed someone to talk to about this.'

'I am glad you felt you could talk to me about it, Antonia. But remember, you must trust in Sebastian's good judgement. He sees far more than you give him credit for.'

'I hope so, Lady Sheraton,' Antonia replied quietly. 'Because I cannot help but feel that…after this stupid episode with Tony Davlin, he will not wish to have anything to do with me ever again!'

Surprisingly, thoughts of a very different nature were running through Sebastian's head as he sat at his desk in the library, lost in a brown study. The events of the past few days had left him more troubled than he had been in years. First Clara's accident with all of its attendant anxieties, then having to dismiss Paddy as a result of his conduct and, finally, the unpleasant confrontation with Antonia Hadley. Lord knew, he would remember for all time the look upon her face when she had stormed out of the door.

That wasn't to say that he hadn't been angry too,

Sebastian reflected, because he had. Angry, hurt, and disappointed. But it had not taken long for the edge to wear off his anger, leaving him with feelings of regret and dismay that the entire episode had taken place. He was also more than a little curious, he admitted, as he thought about Antonia and her involvement with his daughter.

What could have compelled her to seek the position of riding master in the first place? He knew how deeply Antonia cared about Clara. That much had become clear to him over these past few days. But what could have possessed her to take a servile position in his household?

Sebastian set his glass down on the desk and rose, his brow furrowed as he stared into the blackened, empty hearth of the fireplace. Antonia was a gentleman's daughter and, as such, a young woman who had been trained to take her place in a gentleman's house. What could have driven her to seek employment? Could it be that they needed the money?

Sebastian thought about that for a moment. He had not taken a close look at the state of Buntings Hill but, now that he thought about it, he seemed to recall that the lawns and gardens had not been looking as immaculate as they once had. And while the house itself seemed in decent enough repair, there was that broken gate on the way in. Could it be that Hadley himself had encouraged his daughter to seek outside employment as a means of increasing their revenues?

No. Sebastian immediately dismissed the notion as preposterous. Peter Hadley loved his daughter. He cared about her reputation far too much to condone such uncommon behaviour. But, at the same time, he had to have known what she was about. Antonia simply couldn't have vanished for two hours every day without offering some kind of explanation as to where she had been. Surely her father would have seen the irregularity in what she was doing, and put a stop to it.

Or would he?

The thought brought Sebastian up sharp. Would Hadley have stopped his daughter from doing something she truly loved, if he had known beforehand how strongly she felt about it?

Would *he* have been able to deny Clara anything now, were she to ask him for it?

'Lord Carlyle, what are you still doing up?'

Startled by the unexpected interruption, Sebastian turned—and froze at the sight of Lady Rosalind standing in the doorway. She was wearing a long silk robe, the neck of which lay open to reveal the translucent whiteness of her skin beneath. Her glorious hair was unbound and tumbled down her back. She could not have looked more seductive had she come to him wearing nothing at all.

'I might ask you the same thing, Rosalind,' Sebastian said quietly. 'The hour is well advanced.'

Lady Rosalind slowly glided forward. 'I know, but I could not sleep. I have not been able to rid myself of the memories of Lady Clara's accident. Every time I think about it, it just...upsets me more.' She shuddered convincingly. 'It was all so very...frightening. That is why I came downstairs. I thought, perhaps, to find something to read. Reading always helps me to sleep. In fact—' Lady Rosalind glanced at the book-laden shelves '—just being here makes me feel more...rested.'

It was hard to imagine anyone looking less *rested* than Rosalind, Sebastian thought sardonically. The ruby red gown brushed lightly against her limbs, leaving him in no doubt as to the length of her legs, or the voluptuous curve of her hips and breasts. As she moved closer, her fragrance wafted around him, the scent as exotic and provocative as the woman who wore it.

'I also wished to apologise to you for my rather…emotional behaviour the other day, Sebastian,' Lady Rosalind said, meekly lowering her eyes. 'It was thoughtless of me to reproach Miss Hadley like that. I can only say that I was…overcome with grief. Certainly, if I was as close to Clara as Miss Hadley professes to be, I would have been as devastated as she.'

A thoughtful smile curved Sebastian's mouth. 'I was not aware you harboured such maternal feelings, Rosalind. In fact, I have heard it expressed on more than one occasion that you do not like children.'

'No doubt you heard it from sources who would enjoy disparaging me,' Lady Rosalind said. Her eyes flashed even as her voice betrayed no emotion other than concern. 'I am as anxious to have…children of my own as any other young woman. As you must be for a son and heir.'

Sebastian smiled, but his darkly fringed eyes narrowed like those of a jungle cat. 'And had you someone in mind to be the mother of my son and heir, Rosalind?'

Lady Rosalind edged closer so that Sebastian could almost feel the warmth emanating from her body. 'That is a decision only you can make, my lord, but I know that any woman would be honoured to be so chosen. I know that…I should be.'

Her eyes were dark and slumberous, her lips raised to his in an invitation that no man could mistake. Sebastian was not sure what she would have done next, had a scuffling sound in the hallway not alerted her to the presence of a visitor, and made her take a hasty step backwards.

'Well, I think I had best return to my room, my lord.'
With a belated—or perhaps a feigned—attempt at modesty, she pulled the neck of her gown closer together. 'It would not do for us to be found here...alone.'

Sebastian wordlessly inclined his head. He knew that if anyone were to come in and find Rosalind looking the way she did, her reputation would be in shreds—and his own future assured. In relief, he watched her turn and walk away from him, but waited until she was almost at the door before saying, 'Aren't you forgetting something, Rosalind?'

The young lady slowly turned back to regard him with a hopeful smile. 'Am I, my lord?'

'I believe you came down for...a book.'

'A book,' Lady Rosalind repeated blankly. Then, colouring, she laughed in pretty confusion. 'But, of course, how silly of me. But do you know, my lord, I suddenly find myself...rather tired after all. I think perhaps a brief conversation was all I needed. Goodnight, Lord Carlyle.'

'Goodnight, Lady Rosalind.'

The noise in the hall turned out to be nothing more than the nocturnal wanderings of Clara's spaniel, Bartholomew, but, in truth, Sebastian was grateful for the interruption. His unexpected meeting with Rosalind had been nothing if not illuminating. It had brought home a number of very important truths, not the least of which was the realisation that it was indeed time he chose a new Countess. Clara needed a mother. A stepmother, granted, but a mother nevertheless. Someone to hold her when things didn't go right. Someone who would always be there to listen at the end of a long day. Someone with whom he could share his joys and his failures. Someone who—

Abruptly, Sebastian broke off, staring into space as

though a cannon had gone off. When had he started thinking about what *he* needed in a wife rather than what Clara needed in a mother? When had be begun to impose his own desires on what was supposedly the justification for his daughter's needs?

And why the hell did the image of Antonia Hadley keep appearing in his mind—again and again and again?

The following afternoon, wishing to do anything but have time alone to think, Antonia got dressed and took a stroll into the village. She needed to purchase some fabric to trim up one of her gowns, and Lady Sheraton had informed her that the modiste in town had just received a shipment of fine Nottingham lace. But when, after paying for her purchase and turning to leave, Antonia suddenly found herself face to face with Lady Rosalind Grey, she sincerely wished that she had stayed at home.

'Why, Miss Hadley, what a surprise. I had not thought to see you again before my return to London.' Lady Rosalind's eyes lingered on the simplicity of Antonia's attire, comparing it, no doubt, to the elegance of her own, and her lips curled. 'I hope you are suitably recovered from your fit of anxiety over Lady Clara's accident.'

'I am well, thank you, Lady Rosalind,' Antonia said, deciding to ignore the sarcasm in the woman's voice and the arrogance in her manner. 'And, yes, I was relieved to hear that Lady Clara had sustained no serious injuries.'

'Poor child,' Lady Rosalind murmured. 'I told Lord Carlyle that she should be receiving more careful tutelage, and he did say that he would give it some thought.

Of course, he has so many other things on his mind right now, as I'm sure you are aware.'

Antonia met Lady Rosalind's smile with one equally cool. 'If you say Lord Carlyle has matters on his mind, Lady Rosalind, I would certainly not take leave to disagree.'

'No, and well you should not,' Lady Rosalind informed her archly. She glanced at the modiste, who was openly listening to their conversation, and snapped, 'Have you any wide lace?'

'Yes, my lady. I have some very nice—'

'Fine. I shall need two lengths of it. And a pair of those,' she said, indicating the long white silk gloves arranged on a separate table.

'Yes, my lady,' Mrs Taylor said, scurrying to fill the order.

Satisfied that the woman was suitably occupied, Lady Rosalind turned to Antonia with a triumphant smile. 'I shall be returning to London this afternoon, Miss Hadley, but I thought you might like to know that Lord Carlyle has asked me to dine with him soon after his own return to Town.'

Somehow, Antonia managed not to flinch. 'How… pleasant for you.'

'Yes, and I am sure you can imagine why. Oh, but you must try not to be too disappointed, Miss Hadley,' Lady Rosalind said sympathetically. 'I know that you had hoped to secure Lord Carlyle's interest yourself, but I did warn you that it would take more than gaining the child's affection to win the father's. Pity you did not redirect your attentions earlier. Pity for you, that is, since I shall have no such regrets when I am the Countess of Carlyle.'

The remark was spoken loud enough for everyone in

the shop to hear, and Antonia had no doubt that Lady Rosalind wished it to be so. She watched the lady instruct her maid to pay for the purchases, and then grandly make her exit, sweeping out of the shop as though she already was the Countess.

'Well, if what she says is true, I can't help but think that his lordship's second choice of a wife won't be much better than his first,' Mrs Taylor observed in a caustic tone. 'She's a right 'un and no doubt about it. But it's the little one I feel sorry for, Miss Hadley. She'll not do well out of this marriage, I fear.'

Antonia bit her lip. 'I fear that is none of our concern, Mrs Taylor. If Lord Carlyle is…in love with Lady Rosalind, no doubt the decisions they make regarding Lady Clara will be by mutual agreement, and…for the benefit of the child.'

Unfortunately, even as she said it, Antonia knew that it was little more than wishful thinking. If and when Lady Rosalind Grey became the Countess of Carlyle, there would be a number of changes taking place. And as far as Lady Clara was concerned, none of them would be for the better.

When Antonia arrived home from her unpleasant confrontation with Lady Rosalind, it was to find her father in a similar state of agitation. He was running his hands over the clutter of papers on his normally organised desk and muttering in consternation, 'Dash it all, where have I put them now?'

Antonia frowned as she removed her gloves. 'Put what, Papa?'

'My blasted spectacles. I had them a moment ago.'

Noticing the familiar bulge in her father's inside pocket, Antonia smiled and shook her head. 'Your spectacles are in your jacket, Papa. Just where they always are.'

'What?' Mr Hadley glanced down. 'Well, how did they—?'

'No doubt because you put them there. Papa, are you feeling well? You seem to be at sixes and sevens this afternoon.'

Mr Hadley withdrew the offending spectacles and blew the dust off them. 'Course I'm all right. A man gets distracted every now and then, that's all. Ah, good, there we are. Now, my dear, how are you? And how was your shopping excursion?'

Antonia laughed, and fondly kissed the top of her father's head. 'I shall tell you about it over dinner.'

'Ah. Well, I am afraid that won't be possible,' Mr Hadley said. 'I am taking Elean—Lady Sheraton out to dine this evening.'

His manner was so brusque that Antonia began to wonder whether something dreadful hadn't happened between her father and Lady Sheraton. But when she asked him if that was the case, he quickly assured her that matters were fine, and then turned his attention to the papers on his desk.

Sighing, Antonia picked up her gloves and her purchases, and slowly made her way upstairs. Love certainly did peculiar things to people. Her father's behaviour was a perfect example of that. He was as uncertain and bewildered as Antonia had ever seen him.

Was that what love was supposed to do? Antonia pondered glumly. Was this constant…wrenching of one's heart all part of it?

Because if it was, she truly began to wonder whether it was really worth all the fuss.

* * *

After her father had left for Newton Spinney, Antonia asked Mrs Grenfall to make a light supper, and informed Abbott that she would eat in the small dining room. She then set to work, pulling out two of her gowns which required repairing, and trimming up one of her old favourites with the newly acquired lace. She did not go downstairs again until Abbott called her.

But after sitting down to the table, and listlessly picking at her food for the better part of ten minutes, Antonia finally gave up and pushed the plate away. She was too upset to eat. All she could think of was Lady Rosalind's gloating face, and the coldness of her voice when she had spoken of Clara.

Dimly aware that neither needlepoint nor reading were likely to hold her interest this evening, Antonia wandered aimlessly towards the music room. She stared at the miniature of her mother on the piano, and her eyes filled with tears. 'Oh, Mama, how I wish you were here. I miss you so much. And I need your wisdom now more than ever.'

And yet, what words of wisdom could her mother have offered? Antonia thought sadly. What did her mother know of unrequited love? She had met and married the only man she had ever loved, and they had lived happily ever after until the accident which had so tragically taken her life. What words of comfort could she offer her daughter on the loss of the one man who meant everything to her?

Restlessly, Antonia sat down at the pianoforte. Sebastian and Lady Rosalind were to dine together in London. Was that for some special purpose, as that lady had hinted?

Perhaps, Antonia thought, as she absently ran her fingers over the keys. Or perhaps it was just a dinner between friends and there would be others in attendance. That was certainly a more comforting thought, she decided, as she began to play the opening notes of one of her favourite pieces.

Of course, if it was to be just the two of them, that must mean there was a purpose to the meeting. And what purpose could there be other than to offer a proposal of marriage, Antonia decided, as she brought her fingers down a little harder on the keys.

But if it was marriage they were to discuss, would Sebastian choose to make his feelings known over dinner in the formal dining room of his house in Park Lane? Or would he wait until they were sitting together in a smaller, more…intimate salon?

Antonia frowned as the tempo of the piece increased. Would he talk to her first of generalities, discussing the vagaries of the weather and other such trivial matters? Or would he come quickly to the point? He was a direct man by nature—surely he would not equivocate over such an important issue as marriage? Would he kneel at her feet and gaze at her in adoration, or would he slowly draw her to him as he uttered those wonderful, long-awaited words—?

'Good gracious, Antonia, if you bang those keys any harder we shall be forced to have Mr Gordonston in to see to them!'

Antonia blinked, and abruptly spun around to see both her father and Lady Sheraton watching her from the doorway. 'Papa!' She jumped up from the stool, her cheeks burning in mortification. 'I did not…hear you come in,'

'I doubt you would have heard an elephant come in given the way you were playing, my dear.' Her father chortled and pressed a kiss to her forehead. 'Rather a spirited rendition of the nocturne, wasn't it?'

Antonia smiled weakly. 'I was...in the mood to play.'

'And you were playing beautifully, Antonia,' Lady Sheraton said, sending Mr Hadley a reproving glance. 'Take no notice of your father, he has been like that all evening.'

To this rather surprising remark, Mr Hadley merely chuckled. 'Antonia seldom takes notice of what I say, my dear. But you will soon come to learn that my darling daughter does much as she pleases, when she pleases.'

Antonia's eyebrow rose in surprise at the term of endearment, and she glanced from one to the other with unconcealed curiosity. Her father was now totally at ease and bore no resemblance to the nervous, thoroughly distracted man he had been earlier. He smiled at Lady Sheraton with a new closeness and, aware that the lady returned the gaze fondly, Antonia drew in her breath. 'Papa, have you something to tell me?'

'Yes, my dear, I have. And I hope you are going to be as happy as I am about it.' Mr Hadley held out his hand to Lady Sheraton and drew her close. 'Eleanor has just consented to be my wife, and I—that is, we hope very much that you will give us your blessing.'

'Oh, Papa! How could I do anything else?' Antonia ran forward to embrace them both. 'I am so very happy, for both of you.'

'Thank you, Antonia,' Lady Sheraton said, her hazel eyes misting. 'I know I shall never be able to take the place of your own dear mother, but I do hope that we shall be able to develop a special relationship of our own.'

'I think we already have, Lady Sheraton. And I can

see how happy you have made my father.' Antonia glanced at him with amusement. 'I thought he was a trifle more upset this afternoon than the loss of his spectacles warranted.'

Mr Hadley chuckled. 'Well, you cannot expect a man not to be a little nervous when thoughts of matrimony enter his head. I knew that I wanted to ask Eleanor to marry me tonight, but I was rather doubtful as to what she might say.'

Lady Sheraton glanced at him coyly. 'Oh, Peter, I am surprised at you. I was afraid I had given myself away weeks ago.'

'The devil? I never saw it. I only wish I had. Perhaps then I wouldn't have been such a ninnyhammer this past week.'

As Mr Hadley went off in search of the bottle of champagne he had been keeping just for such an occasion, Antonia chatted to Lady Sheraton about the details of the wedding. It seemed that they were to be married at the end of the month, since neither Lady Sheraton nor her father saw any reason to wait, and that, if Mr Howard agreed, the ceremony would take place in the village church.

Antonia was delighted, not just because of the happiness it would bring to the two people she loved so dearly, but because there would be a hundred-and-one details to see to before it actually took place. It might only be a small wedding, but it was a wedding nevertheless, and Antonia welcomed the opportunity of helping in any way she could.

At least by being involved in one wedding, she would have precious little time to spend worrying about another.

Chapter Thirteen

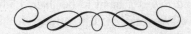

Lord and Lady Shand were as delighted with Mr Hadley's news as Antonia had been, and promptly decided to hold a celebration for their dear friend and his future wife. As such, they sent out invitations to all of their friends and to most of their neighbours.

Sebastian was one of the invited guests; though his first impulse had been to decline, he later decided that it might be more judicious to accept. He might have had a falling out with Antonia, but he had no wish for his refusal to be taken as a slight against her father and his new lady, both of whom he cared for very much.

So he dressed for the party three nights later in a state of mixed emotions. Antonia had not been far from his mind since the day of Clara's birthday, but he had not had occasion to see her since then. Now he would be forced to face her—along with the inevitable consequences which would result from that meeting.

It was hardly surprising that Sebastian availed himself of a generous glass of brandy before calling for his carriage and setting out.

In her bedroom at Buntings Hill, Antonia put the finishing touches to her toilette, while Lady Sheraton, re-

splendent in a gown of shimmering gold silk, affectionately looked on. 'Antonia, you look absolutely beautiful.
I vow, the single gentlemen in attendance this evening
will be utterly captivated by your loveliness. And I am
so very pleased at what Nicolette has done with your
hair. The style is most becoming to you.'

Antonia's smile was a trifle anxious as she stared into
the glass and raised a hand to her hair. Lady Sheraton
had kindly allowed her maid to arrange it this evening,
and even Antonia was startled by the difference it made
in her appearance. The upswept style made her look
older, and far more…sophisticated.

'Thank you, Lady Sheraton. I admit, she has done an
excellent job. And the gown is one of Papa's favourites
so I wanted to wear it tonight in honour of the occasion.'
Antonia tried to relax as she turned to face the woman
who would soon become her stepmother. 'But I have no
doubt that it is you who will draw the gentlemen's
glances tonight.'

Lady Sheraton laughed softly. 'The gentlemen are
coming to celebrate my betrothal to your father, my dear,
so it is unlikely that any of them will be looking at me
like that. But you are a dear for saying so. Now come,
we must not keep any of them waiting.'

Shand Hall was ablaze with lights by the time Mr
Hadley and his party arrived. The rooms were filled to
overflowing with invited guests, and even the officious
Lady Farrington had deigned to put in an appearance,
no doubt due to the fact that she approved of the woman
her brother-in-law had chosen to marry.

'There, did I not tell you that your father was right to
get out into Society?' Lady Farrington said to Antonia

soon after her arrival. 'Lady Sheraton would certainly have chosen someone else, had Peter not had the intelligence to make his presence known. Speaking of that, where is Lord Carlyle this evening? I had expected to hear news of a betrothal between the two of you before now.'

Antonia's cheeks flushed a brilliant red. 'Aunt, please keep your voice down. As I have told you all along, there was never anything beyond friendship between Lord Carlyle and myself.'

'Bosh! I know that look when I see it,' Lady Farrington snapped. 'Carlyle was as deeply enamoured of you, as you were of him. Ah, here he is now. I have a good mind to go and speak to him—'

Antonia blanched. 'Aunt, I *beg* you, do not—'

'Calm yourself, Antonia, I was not going to say about you. I thought merely to enquire after the health of his daughter.'

'You heard about that?'

'Of course. I hear about everything sooner or later. By the way, Antonia, you are looking…quite well this evening,' Lady Farrington observed with more charity than Antonia had ever heard in her voice. 'You should take advantage of it. Mr Hawksworth is looking for a wife, as is Mr Mortimer. They are both prosperous gentlemen who would provide you with a good name and a decent home. Of course, I would far rather see you as Lady Carlyle, but that may take considerably more effort, if, as you say, you and Carlyle are nothing more than friends. And there is Lady Bathgate standing on her own. I shall go and have a word. Remember, make yourself pleasing to the gentlemen, Antonia, and I dare say we shall soon be celebrating another marriage.'

As Lady Farrington moved away, Antonia wearily

closed her eyes. This was simply too exhausting. Having to deny any kind of feelings for Sebastian, and then watching him as he smiled and greeted others in a manner which he would never use towards her, made her feel absolutely wretched. How on earth was she supposed to get through the evening? Especially when her aunt was expecting her to mingle with other single gentlemen?

Across the room, Sebastian was thinking much the same thing. He had immediately noticed Antonia standing with her aunt at the other side of the room, but he had taken care not to meet her eye. To do so would have necessitated an acknowledgement of their acquaintance, and right now he was not at all sure that she would not have given him the cut direct.

Damn it. He could smile at anyone in the room and be assured of their response. But not Antonia. She would not smile at him. Not for all the tea in China…

'You looked…perplexed, Sebastian,' Lady Sheraton said, suddenly appearing by his side. 'Or should I say…troubled.'

A shutter dropped down over Sebastian's eyes. 'If either such expression is apparent, then I must endeavour to change it, Eleanor. For I would not wish to present anything but the most amiable of faces to you upon this most happy of occasions.' He leaned his head towards her and smiled warmly. 'Congratulations, my dear, I wish you every happiness.'

'Thank you, Sebastian. I feel very fortunate to have met a man like Peter Hadley and to have secured his love.'

'What man could not love you, for you are all that is admirable in a woman. I should tell you that I consider Hadley to be the fortunate one.'

Lady Sheraton laughed softly as she slipped her hand through his arm and drew him towards a less populated area of the room. 'Dear Sebastian. I have always wished that you might have found the happiness you craved. You did not deserve the treatment you received at Violet's hands. But come, tell me what is the cause of your despondency now, for I can see it quite clearly in your eyes.'

Sebastian grimaced as he fell into step beside her. 'I must remember to guard myself against you, Eleanor. You always were too perceptive.'

'It is easy to be perceptive when the people you love are at the centre of those perceptions. Has this something to do with Antonia?'

Sebastian stiffened. 'Why would you think that?'

'Because I know that the two of you have had… words.'

He was silent for a moment. Then he sighed. 'Words are…a kind way of putting it. Are you acquainted with the details?'

'Most of them.'

'Then you will understand why I was so angry. Miss Hadley lied to me. And you know better than most how I feel about such things.'

Lady Sheraton tilted her head to one side. 'Did Antonia tell you why she was so determined to teach Clara how to ride?'

'She mentioned something about…Clara being uncomfortable with strangers and afraid of horses.'

'And did you believe her?'

'At the time, I do not think that I paid it much heed.'

Lady Sheraton came to an abrupt halt and turned to look up into his face. 'Then talk to Antonia, Sebastian. Ask her to tell you about…Edwina.'

Sebastian frowned. 'Edwina?'

Lady Sheraton nodded. 'Her father only recently told me the story. But it is important that you know. Because if Antonia will tell you, I think you will have a much better understanding of why it was so important for her to do what she did.'

'Are you saying that I was wrong to be angry with her?'

'No, not wrong.' Lady Sheraton smiled at him kindly. 'Perhaps it could have been handled in a better way, but we do not always see those ways at the time. All I know is that whatever deceit Antonia perpetrated against you was done innocently and with your daughter's welfare at heart. And that is all I will say. The rest is up to you.'

It was a good hour and a half before Sebastian was able to speak with Antonia alone. Not only because of the crowds which constantly seemed to surround either one or both of them, but due to the fact that Antonia seemed determined to keep him at a distance. It was almost as though she was purposely surrounding herself with people. Finally, he hailed her as she made her way towards the ladies' withdrawing room. 'Miss Hadley, I would speak with you.'

Caught offguard by his unexpected appearance, Antonia faltered. 'I do not think we have anything to say to each other, Lord Carlyle.'

'Nevertheless, I would beg a moment of your time. I did not give you a fair chance to speak the other morning, and I regret that. I would like to give you that chance now.'

Antonia lifted her chin. 'What makes you think that I wish to speak to you about anything, my lord?'

'I wish you would, Miss Hadley. For the sake of Clara's happiness, if not for mine.'

It was taking an unfair advantage, and Sebastian knew it, but he wanted to hear what she had to say. Eleanor was right. He owed her that much.

'Very well. For…Clara's sake, I will speak with you,' Antonia relented.

'Thank you. Shall we take a stroll outside?'

Antonia hesitated for a moment, clearly reluctant to be alone with him. But when he pointed out that they would be within plain sight of the windows at all times, she tentatively placed her hand on his arm and allowed him to escort her onto the balcony.

It was a perfect evening and, judging by the whispers and subdued laughter emanating from the gardens, they were not the only two people enjoying it. But Sebastian had not brought her out here for a seduction. His reasons for doing what he was doing were far more important than that.

'Miss Hadley,' he began quietly, 'you told me that…you were eminently qualified to teach my daughter how to ride. You also said that you *wished* to teach her, but for reasons that were private and…entirely personal to yourself. Since I have a feeling those reasons have…a direct bearing on our situation, I would ask you…would you consider sharing those reasons with me now?'

Antonia's eyebrows flew up. 'Is this what you brought me out here to discuss?'

'Yes.'

'But…why? You have already told me what you thought of my behaviour. You have said that…there was no excuse for my lying to you and that it was my fault that Clara was injured. What makes you think that anything I might say now would alter your opinion?'

'Miss Hadley, who is…Edwina?'

If he had pulled out a pistol and held it to her head, Antonia could not have looked any more shocked. Her face went white, and she actually stumbled. 'Who told you about…Edwina?'

'No one told me about her,' Sebastian said gently. 'But someone who cares…a great deal about you, asked me to enquire after her.' When she still made no reply, Sebastian placed his hands gently upon her shoulders and turned her to face him. 'Miss Hadley, please. Who is Edwina? What has she to do with this, and why is it so hard for you to talk about her?'

Antonia backed away, needing to give herself some space. When he was so near, she lost the ability to think rationally. When he touched her, even in the most casual of gestures, she was lost altogether. 'My lord, I…fail to see what difference it will make—'

'Perhaps you will let me be the judge of that,' Sebastian interrupted softly. 'Because I do believe that it will make a difference. And so, I shall ask you again. Who is Edwina?'

A heavy silence followed his question. Antonia refused to meet his eyes and Sebastian began to wonder if she was ever going to answer him. But he would not let her escape. Not this time. And finally, as if realising that, Antonia breathed out a long, heavy sigh.

'Edwina was…my cousin,' she began slowly. 'She was two years younger than me, but we were…very close. More like…sisters, really. We used to…play together all the time.'

Sebastian listened in silence. He saw the lines of tension in her face, and knew that she was having a hard time talking about this, but he could not let her stop. He had to know it all. 'Go on, Miss Hadley.'

Antonia nodded, and forced herself to continue. 'Edwina's mother was…a skilled equestrienne. She loved…riding to hounds, and thought nothing of getting up before dawn and going out with the hunt. Papa used to say that…she rode better than most gentlemen of his acquaintance.'

'Did Edwina like to ride?'

Antonia shook her head. 'No. She was…deathly afraid of horses. She was thrown from her pony at the age of five and she never got over it. Her mother forced her back into the saddle, of course, as did her riding master, but she never conquered her fear. I used to sneak away and try to talk to her about it. I even used to let her ride my own pony, who was as docile as a kitten, but it did no good. Every time Edwina was forced back on to her own horse, she just got worse. And then, one day, her mother decided that…it was time for Edwina to join the hunt.'

Sebastian watched Antonia's face, saw the way her mouth quivered, and suddenly had a terrible sense of what was going to come. 'What happened?'

'I tried to tell my aunt that Edwina was not a good enough rider, and that she needed more time, but she would not listen. She told me that…Edwina was too soft, and that she needed discipline. She said that no child ever benefited from being mollycoddled, and that she would certainly not see a child of her own so indulged. And so, the very next week, she…took Edwina with her to one of the larger hunts, and she put her on a strange horse.'

Sebastian caught his breath. 'A foolish thing to do.'

'Yes. I heard…later, that Edwina had been terrified, which was probably why she fell behind the rest of the field, but she was obviously more afraid of what her mother would say if she did not finish, so she gamely carried on. But it was as she was leaping a hedge that it happened.' Antonia paused for a moment, and Sebastian saw the brightness of tears forming in her eyes. 'The hedge was not high, but it was thick, and something must have darted out from amongst its branches. The horse shied and…Edwina fell. Unfortunately, her foot…caught in the stirrup.' Antonia sadly shook her head. 'No one seems to know how far the horse galloped before it finally came to a stop, but in the end, it did not matter. By the time they found her, it was already…too late for Edwina.'

A bleak silence followed her disclosure. Sebastian looked down at Antonia's lowered head, and swore softly under his breath. Damn. He could only imagine how she must have felt last Sunday afternoon; having to watch Clara cling helplessly to the pony's back—and knowing that, at any minute, she might have fallen. Was it any wonder she had looked so horrified? Because in that one moment, all of the painful memories of her own cousin's death had come flooding back.

And then, she had had to suffer his anger and condemnation on top of it. She had stood in front of him and listened as he had all but blamed her for his daughter's accident. He had berated her for lying to him, and had coldly sent her away.

Was it any wonder she despised him now?

'I am…so very sorry, Miss Hadley,' Sebastian said bleakly, his voice husky with emotion. 'I had…no idea.'

As though waking from a dream, Antonia slowly raised her eyes to his. 'You could not have known. The accident was kept…very quiet.'

'What did your aunt do?'

'She moved away. To the north of England. We never

heard from her again.' Antonia looked at him with eyes that were suddenly devoid of expression. 'Would you take me back in, Lord Carlyle? I find it…rather chilly, all of a sudden.'

'Of course.' Sebastian offered her his arm. Antonia placed her hand upon his sleeve, but her touch was so light that Sebastian had to look to see if it was there. In the face of her silence, he said nothing, but he understood.

For the first time in his life, he understood—everything.

At Ashdean the next morning, Sebastian stood in his study with his hands clasped behind his back. He had lain awake most of the night, going over and over the startling conversation he had had with Antonia. And now, more than ever, he realised that her reasons for wishing to teach his daughter how to ride were of the most noble and admirable kind.

In recognising Clara's fear, Antonia had set out to prevent another accident like Edwina's from taking place. But because she had been prevented from having anything to do with Edwina by the child's mother, she had resorted to subterfuge in her dealings with him.

But Eleanor had been right. What Antonia had done, she had done only with Clara's safety in mind. She had not set out to deceive him in any malicious or personal way. She had simply thought to take care of his child. And whether Antonia had lied to him about it or not, no one could condemn her for such worthy sentiments.

It also explained why Padrick Douglas Bingham—a man whom Sebastian had known all of his life—had agreed to help her, and why he had lied because of her. Sebastian had no doubt that Paddy knew all about poor

Edwina. He had discovered over the years that there was very little his steward did not know about what went on in the county.

'Mr Bingham, my lord,' Hildegarde said quietly.

'Thank you, Hildegarde.' Taking a deep breath, Sebastian turned to see his former steward standing in the doorway. The man was dressed more formally than usual, and there was a shadow in his eyes, no doubt in anticipation of what was to come. 'Please, come in, Mr Bingham. Sit down.'

Bingham took a seat in front of the desk and waited.

'How have you been, Paddy?'

The steward started at the familiar term of address, but he gamely managed a smile. 'Well enough, thank you, my lord.'

'Good, I am glad to hear it. Have you been able to secure alternate employment?'

The smiled disappeared. 'No, sir. I have sent out a few enquiries, but—'

'Good. Because I would like you to come back.'

Bingham's mouth fell open in astonishment. 'Come…back?'

'Yes. I owe you an apology.'

Bingham's shaggy brows drew together. 'My lord, I'm not sure I understand—'

'I made a mistake, Paddy,' Sebastian said bluntly. 'I reacted to a situation based on information I had at hand, and I said things that were…unfair. And I regret that very much.'

'My lord, you didn't say anything that wasn't deserved. I shouldn't have lied to you about Miss Hadley.'

'No, but I now realise that Miss Hadley's reasons for wishing to teach Clara how to ride were totally beyond reproach, and that I was wrong to condemn you and her in the manner I did. And for that I should like to make amends. If you would consider resuming your employment here, I would be very pleased to take you back, and to give you an increase in salary.'

Bingham glanced at him in astonishment. 'An increase?'

'Yes. What do you say?'

Too bewildered to say much of anything, Bingham slowly got to his feet. 'I'd say this isn't what I was expecting to hear when I was told you wished to see me, my lord. But I won't deny that it is very much what I was hoping to.' His face broke into an honest, open smile. 'I would be pleased to come back, my lord, if you're sure that's what you want.'

'I'm sure, Paddy. I cannot think of anyone who loves Ashdean more, nor any man who could look after it better.'

Bingham's ruddy cheeks went a deeper hue. 'You do me an honour by saying so, my lord.'

'There are, however, one or two small requests I would like to make of you.'

The steward inclined his head. 'You have but to name them, my lord.'

Sebastian smiled. 'First, I would like you to ride over to Buntings Hill and ask Miss Hadley if she would be willing to see me at three o'clock this afternoon. You may tell her, if she asks, that there is some news I wish to give her which concerns both Lady Clara and herself.'

'I shall deliver the message, my lord. What else would you have me do?'

Sebastian reached for a sealed letter which lay atop his desk and handed it to the other man. 'I would like you to call upon Miss Hadley's father and give him this letter. Make sure that you deliver it personally into his hand. And I would ask you to wait for his reply.'

Mr Bingham glanced down at the folded piece of parchment, sealed with the Carlyle crest, and nodded. 'If Miss Hadley is out, shall I still deliver this letter to her father?'

'Yes. I would like him to see it either way, and I will call upon Miss Hadley regardless of his reply.'

'I shall see to both your requests at once, my lord.'

'Thank you, Paddy. Oh, and there is one last thing,' Sebastian added, studiously avoiding the steward's eyes. 'I do not think you will be surprised to learn that I hope to be announcing my betrothal in the very near future. I trust you will be available to handle the arrangements.'

At that bit of news, the easy going smile faded from Bingham's face. 'Your...betrothal, my lord?'

'Yes.'

'Ah.' There was a moment's hesitation before the steward said, 'My most sincere congratulations, my lord.'

The lack of enthusiasm in the man's voice was palpable, and Sebastian smiled. 'I thought you would have been pleased, Paddy. It means that Clara will finally have a father *and* a mother again.'

'Well, yes, I am...pleased, my lord, but I'm also a bit...surprised that it's all happened so quickly.'

'Quickly? Good Lord, Paddy, I've been accused of taking more time to make this decision than it would take to sail to America.'

'Aye, but sometimes it's better to wait and be sure, than to rush into a situation and regret it later.'

Sebastian's gaze narrowed. 'Are you suggesting that I do not know what I am doing, Mr Bingham?'

The steward sighed and shook his head. 'Not at all,

my lord. I am simply telling you what I think. But I do wish you…every happiness. And I shall see to these messages at once.'

After Bingham left, Sebastian sat down at his desk. Poor Paddy. It was obvious that, while he was pleased at having his old position back, he was less than happy about the news of the impending engagement. Obviously he had drawn his own conclusions with regard to the woman who would be the next Countess.

Sebastian couldn't say that he was surprised; word of Lady Rosalind's boasts had trickled back to his ears too. But what troubled him more was the fact that, if *he* had heard such rumours, Antonia was sure to have too. And, right now, he was far more concerned about *her* feelings than he was about anyone else's.

Antonia greeted the news of Mr Bingham's reinstatement with unaffected joy and relief. 'And he actually said that he had made a mistake?' Antonia asked as she sat with Mr Bingham in the drawing room.

'He did indeed, miss,' Bingham told her. 'Told me he'd been too hasty in making his decision, and then asked me if I would consider coming back. With a rise in salary.'

'Well, I am delighted to hear it, Mr Bingham,' Antonia said in all sincerity. 'You have no idea how guilty I have felt about this—especially since I knew that it was my fault you were turned off in the first place.'

'I'll grant you, it did surprise me, his lordship apologising. It's not typical behaviour for him at all. But then, what with his getting married again, I suppose he is feeling…differently about a lot of things.'

'Married!' Shock wedged the rest of the words in Antonia's throat. *Sebastian was to be married?*

'Aye, miss,' Bingham said quietly. 'He told me that…he would be announcing his engagement in the near future.'

'Did he say…when?' she finally choked out.

'No, miss.'

Antonia stared at the floor, numb with shock and disappointment. She wished with all her heart that she might have been able to toss out a light-hearted reply, or at least the expected words of congratulations, but nothing came to mind. Her mind went totally blank as she struggled to come to terms with the disturbing news that Sebastian was to be married.

Which was stupid, Antonia chided herself, because she had known that it was coming. So why did it strike her now, like a knife to the heart all over again? Why, after she had convinced herself that Sebastian meant nothing to her, was the news that he was to wed another tearing her apart?

'He also asked if…he could see you, miss,' Bingham gently went on to say.

Antonia gasped. 'Me?'

'Yes. Here, at…three o'clock this afternoon, if that was convenient.'

Self-preservation coming to the fore, Antonia adamantly shook her head. 'Lord Carlyle and I have nothing to say to each other, Mr Bingham. I made that…very clear to him on the occasion of our last meeting.'

'I don't know anything about that, miss. But his lordship did ask me to tell you that it was regarding a matter of some importance to both you and the Lady Clara.'

Clara? Antonia frowned. What could he possibly want to say to her about Clara? Surely he did not intend to bring up details of the accident again. She would far rather not see him at all than be treated to another display of his anger.

Granted, they had taken leave of each other in a civil enough manner at Lord and Lady Shand's, but Antonia knew that much of Sebastian's temperance that evening had been as a result of what she had told him about Edwina. She knew she had not imagined the look of shock and dismay on his face.

But beyond that, nothing had changed between them. He had not tried to talk to her as he had escorted her back inside, nor had he asked to see her again. He had simply bowed and taken his leave. And now, Mr Bingham had brought word that he was engaged to be married—and that he wished to come here this afternoon and speak to her about Clara.

She could only wonder at what could be so important that he would need to go to all that trouble.

At precisely three o'clock, Lord Carlyle's carriage drew to a halt in front of Buntings Hill. Antonia was in the morning room when he arrived, seemingly lost in the pages of her book. Truth was, she had not been able to move past the first few lines, given the state of her nerves.

She started when she heard the sound of footsteps in the hall, and felt her pulse begin to race when she realised that he was approaching. To Antonia's surprise, however, it was not Abbott who opened the door to announce her guest, but her father.

'Papa, what are you doing here?' Antonia set down her book and rose. 'I thought you were going to see Lady Sheraton.'

Mr Hadley smiled as he followed Sebastian in. 'I was, my dear, but when I learned that Lord Carlyle was to call, I thought it would be a good opportunity to ask him about his daughter's health. And I am relieved to hear that she is coming along very well.'

'Have you time to stay and take tea with us?' Antonia enquired.

'Thank you, but as I have just told Lord Carlyle, I dare not stay a moment longer. Even now I have kept my dear lady waiting, and I hardly think that is appropriate behaviour for a newly engaged gentleman.' He turned and offered his hand to the Earl. 'Thank you, Lord Carlyle, for bringing along such good news. I look forward to the pleasure of our next meeting.'

'As do I, Mr Hadley.'

There seemed to be an air of conspiracy between the two of them, but Antonia could not imagine why, so she did not let it trouble her. But she was surprised that her father seemed so willing to leave the two of them alone together.

'Please do pass along my regards to Lady Sheraton, Papa,' she said, kissing her father's cheek as he turned to leave. 'And tell her that I look forward to seeing her the day after tomorrow.'

'Yes, my dear, I shall.' Then, with a fond smile, he walked out of the room and closed the door behind him, leaving Antonia very much alone with her guest.

Sensing her discomfort, Sebastian offered her a warm smile. 'Thank you for agreeing to see me, Miss Hadley. To be honest, I was not sure that you would.'

Surprised by the gentleness of his voice, Antonia merely inclined her head. She wished that he did not look quite so handsome in his beautifully cut black jacket and buff-coloured breeches. But then, to her, he would have looked wonderful in the most simple of garments.

'Mr Bingham told me that…it had something to do with Clara.'

'And with yourself.'

'As you will, but it is the issue concerning Clara which is of interest to me. Please, will you sit down?'

Sebastian did, choosing the chair directly opposite the wing chair in which she sat. He crossed one booted ankle over the other, and looked, Antonia thought, enviably at ease. She wished she could have said the same about herself. 'I was…very pleased to hear that Mr Bingham was to have his old job back,' she began tentatively.

'And I am pleased that he wished to have it,' Sebastian told her. 'Paddy is an excellent steward. I half expected him to tell me that he had offered his services to someone else and been accepted. I was relieved when he agreed to come back.'

'He also told me that you are…shortly to return to London.'

'Yes. There are some matters which I must attend to, and which cannot be resolved here.'

'Yes, of course,' Antonia replied woodenly. 'Matters, no doubt, concerning your imminent…marriage.'

It was all she could do to get the words out. And once she had, Antonia could not look at him. She could not bear to see the happiness on his face, knowing it had been put there by another woman. Sebastian, however, merely regarded her with a look of gentle amusement.

'I see that Paddy has been busy again. I only instructed him to ask you if you would see me, and to tell you, if you asked, that it concerned Clara and yourself. The other was not supposed to be mentioned just yet.'

'But you are…planning to be married?' Antonia asked, unable to stop herself.

'I am hoping to be, yes.'

Hoping? Antonia looked at him in bewilderment. 'I do not…understand. Have you not already spoken to the lady?'

'In point of fact, I have not, Miss Hadley,' Sebastian said, suddenly leaning forward. 'Which was one of the reasons why I wished to see you today.'

Now thoroughly confused, Antonia shook her head. 'My lord, I confess myself baffled. Surely I do not need to be involved in a decision such as this?'

'On the contrary you do, because the lady in question is not the only one whose life is going to change, if and when she agrees to marry me. There is Clara's welfare to consider as well.'

Antonia quickly got to her feet. 'I should have thought that…Clara's welfare would have had even less to do with me. Surely that will now be an issue to be discussed between you and…your wife.'

Aware that she was totally oblivious to his intentions, Sebastian smiled and also rose. 'Miss Hadley, I think it only fair to tell you that Mr Bingham is not the only one who is deserving of an apology. You, also, were treated badly at my hands, and I regret that…more than I can possibly tell you.'

Antonia turned around and stared at him in astonishment. 'You regret it? My lord, I confess myself surprised. At the time, you left me in no doubt that I was…very much deserving of your censure.'

'Yes, because at the time I was not in possession of all the facts.'

Antonia took a deep breath. 'If you are referring to the incident involving…Edwina, I take leave to tell you that it can have no bearing upon the matter. It does not alter the fact that I intentionally set out to deceive you, or that I purposely involved one of your servants in my plans.'

Sebastian slowly narrowed the distance between them. 'Perhaps not. But knowing about Edwina, and knowing that she was the justification for what you did, casts an entirely new light upon the subject, Miss Hadley. You cared about your cousin. You loved her, in fact, but you were unable to help her because of the damage which had already been done. Perhaps, had you had time with her, you would have been able to break through her fears, but circumstances did not grant you that time and you lost her. And that, Miss Hadley, is what makes everything different.' Sebastian's voice softened, and a tiny smile began to flicker in his eyes. 'What you could not do for your cousin, you attempted to do for Clara. You saw the beginnings of fear in my daughter, and you knew that it had to be dealt with at once. So, in spite of the fact that you had no affection for me, you went ahead and devised a way to help her regardless.'

An unwelcome blush crept into Antonia's cheeks. 'It was not that I did not…like you—'

'Oh, come, Miss Hadley, now is not the time to play coy. I remember the way you looked at me the first time we met in the village, and it was certainly not with any degree of respect, let alone affection.'

The blush deepened in Antonia's cheeks. 'I was… wrong to be so opinionated.'

'No, you were not. Because knowing you the way I do now, I think I can safely hazard a guess as to what the source of that animosity was.'

'You can?'

'Yes. Like so many others, you thought me a cold-hearted bastard for abandoning my daughter to the depths of the country when she was only four years old.'

Antonia closed her eyes in mortification. 'H-how did you know?'

'It does not matter. Suffice it to say that I did.'

'Then…why?' Antonia asked, needing to pull the rest of the pieces together. 'Why did you bring Clara to the country and…leave her here?'

Sebastian hesitated for some time. 'Because, for a very long time, I did not know if…Clara was my child.'

The simplicity of the statement—and the significance behind it—rocked Antonia to the very depths of her soul. *Clara—someone else's child?*

Antonia felt her knees begin to tremble—and hastily sat down. 'My lord, I…hardly know what to say.'

'There is little enough to say, Miss Hadley. Fortunately, at length I discovered that my fears were groundless, but by then, so much time had passed that…I was…almost afraid to see Clara again for fear that she might hate me.'

'But what made you think that she…that she was…?'

'Another man's child?' Sebastian finished for her. At her mute nod, he sighed. He had never told anyone this before, and he wondered if he was doing the right thing now. But it was imperative that Antonia know. He would have no secrets from her.

'My wife was not a happy woman, Miss Hadley. Nor was she entirely well. She had…a number of lovers after our marriage, and she was foolish enough to write letters to them. I came upon one such letter, which I often wonder if she intended me to find, in which she told…the gentleman with whom she was involved that she had reason to suspect that she was with child. The problem was, she could not be sure whether the child was mine— or his.'

Antonia bit her lip, even as her heart wept for him. 'My lord, how dreadful.'

'For a long time, I said nothing. As it turned out, Violet was with child and as the weeks went by, she grew even more temperamental. However, as I had no wish to instigate a fight, I spent most of my time away from the house. I was at my club when the child, a daughter, was born. It was a week before I could bring myself to look at her.'

Antonia heard the anguish in his voice and yearned to reach out to him. She could not imagine what it must have been like, to have been betrayed by the woman he had married in such a terrible way.

'Not surprisingly, my relationship with Violet began to deteriorate,' Sebastian continued. 'Or perhaps I should say, continued to. I had no desire to be with her or with the child, for the simple reason that I could not be sure whose child it was. And when, eventually, Violet's health began to fail, there was nothing between us but a cold…indifference. Which was why I felt no real sorrow when she died.' He looked at her and smiled sadly. 'Are you shocked, Miss Hadley?'

'I am not shocked so much as saddened, my lord,' Antonia whispered. 'It seems like such a…terrible waste.'

'It was. But what was an even greater waste was my relationship with my daughter. A child who, through no fault of her own, had been born with a shadow hanging over her head. I brought her to the country after my wife died, and took pains to ensure that she had everything she needed. I made Paddy personally responsible for her. And then, satisfied that I had done my duty by her, I returned to London.'

Sebastian glanced at her then, half afraid that he

would see a look of loathing on her face. When he did not, he took a deep breath and told her the rest.

'I did not mention it before, Miss Hadley, but I knew the man Violet had been involved with.'

Antonia's eyes widened in shock. 'You knew him…personally?'

'Oh, yes. We had socialised together in the early days of my courtship with Violet.'

'But…what did he say?'

'Nothing, because at the time, I did not confront him with it. I was afraid that in my anger and jealousy, I would have killed him. For that reason, I thought it prudent to turn the other cheek. But one night when I been drinking rather freely at my club, I decided to call in at his house on my way home. I'd begun to realise that…what I was doing to Clara was unfair, and I knew that I could not go on wondering whether she was mine or another man's. I felt that I might learn something from speaking to him.'

'And did you?' Antonia asked breathlessly.

'Yes. I called at his house, hoping to speak to him, but to my dismay, found only his lady at home.'

Antonia all but held her breath. 'What did you do then?'

Sebastian smiled. 'I told her that I would call again. And I would have left, had she not stopped me, and called me back. We then proceeded to have a very…enlightening conversation about her husband and his—habits.' Sebastian shook his head. 'In hindsight, I can only wonder that I did not figure it out before.'

'Figure out what?'

'That the man my wife was having an affair with was physically incapable of fathering a child.'

Antonia stared at him, her heart pounding as she realised what he was saying. 'You mean, there was…no question that the child your wife was carrying…was yours!'

'So it seemed. I had no reason to suspect that anyone else had been involved with Violet at the time. My wife took several lovers during the course of our marriage, but she was wise enough to finish with one before inviting the next one in.'

'And this fellow's wife…confirmed it?' Antonia repeated. 'That her husband could not…father a child?'

'Yes. I will not go into the details,' Sebastian said, wishing to spare her the embarrassment, 'but by the time I left her that night, there was no doubt in my mind that Clara was mine. And that was when everything began to…change for me. Shortly after that, I decided that it was time to come to Ashdean and get to know my daughter.'

The explanation was not one which Antonia had been expecting to hear. But it more than served to eradicate the last of her doubts. Sebastian wasn't a cold, unfeeling man at all. He was simply a man who had been betrayed by his wife and made to carry the burden of it his entire married life.

How could anyone blame him for his conduct towards Clara? While it was true that the fault did not lay with the child, under the circumstances, Antonia could understand why he had kept her at arm's length. And yet, even with the doubt in his mind, he had made sure that she was fed and clothed and well looked after. Surely that was commendation enough.

Rising, Antonia slowly walked towards him, aware that her heart was beating much faster than it ought. 'I think, Lord Carlyle, that it is I who must beg your forgiveness. I accused you of…reprehensible conduct when

I knew nothing of the circumstances which prompted it. I did not see a man suffering, and I was wrong to think so ill of anyone without justification.'

'Thank you, Miss Hadley. Your charity means…a great deal to me. I have never told…another soul about Violet. I only did so today because I did not wish there to be…any secrets between us.'

This time, Antonia could not stop herself. She raised her hand to his face, and brushed it lightly against his cheek, feeling her heart break a little more as she did. 'I think, Lord Carlyle, that I am not the one to whom you should have unburdened your soul. That honour should have been reserved for…the lady you would marry.'

Sebastian caught his breath. He would not have believed it possible to be so moved by the simple touch of a woman's hand. But then he had not thought it possible to feel such a depth of emotion either. And that was when he realised that, for the first time in his life, he was in love. Not infatuated, as he had been with his first wife, but deeply and truly in love. The kind of love that lasted a life time.

'Miss Hadley, I came here today because I wanted to ask you a question,' Sebastian said in a low voice. 'A very important question that will have far-reaching effects on both Clara's life—and mine.'

Antonia sighed as she dropped her hand. 'I cannot imagine what that would be.'

'Can you not, my darling Antonia? Have I truly been so bad at showing you my feelings that it did not cross your mind, even once, to think that *you* might be the lady to whom I wished to propose?'

Antonia stood there, blank, amazed and very shaken. 'M-me?'

'Yes.' To her astonishment, Sebastian dropped to one

knee in front of her. 'Will you marry me, Antonia? Will you be my wife, and a mother to Clara? For I can think of no one who I would rather have beside me in the years to come, or who could love Clara more.'

He must have read the answer in her eyes, because long before Antonia had a chance to put it into words, Sebastian rose and pulled her slender body into his arms. He brought his lips down on hers, and kissed her with a passion that left them both trembling.

'Oh, my darling girl,' he whispered against her hair. 'I love you so very much. Say that you will marry me as soon as it can be arranged, for I long to have you to myself.'

'I would marry you…tomorrow if it were possible,' Antonia whispered, not sure whether to laugh or cry, 'but I think we should wait until…Papa and Lady Sheraton return from their wedding trip.'

Sebastian held her close. 'Do you wish to wait?'

Antonia shook her head and smiled tremulously. 'No.'

'Then I shall go to London for a special licence. We can be married within the week. But we will postpone our own wedding trip until after their celebration, if that is what you wish.'

'Oh, yes, Sebastian, that is exactly what I wish,' Antonia told him with shining eyes. 'And I wish that…we be married in the village church, if you have no objections.'

'I do not care where we are wed, so long as we *are* wed, beloved,' Sebastian replied huskily. His eyes devoured her with a hunger she was only just beginning to understand. 'But it suddenly occurs to me that I shall have to make a choice as to whose name I apply to the licence.'

'My lord?'

'Well, am I marrying the beautiful Antonia Hadley or the extremely competent Toni Davlin?'

Antonia suddenly threw back her head and laughed. 'Dear me, I wonder if I shall ever live that down. But, now that I think of it, perhaps it is I who should be asking you that question. Who would you prefer to marry, Sebastian? The lady or the riding master?'

'I think I have the answer to both questions,' Sebastian said, his mouth hovering above hers. 'I shall ask the riding master to become the lady, and the lady to become the Countess. Does that adequately solve the problem, my dear Miss Hadley?'

'Admirably, my lord,' Antonia murmured, happily giving herself up to the magic of his kisses. 'I do believe even the elusive Mr Davlin would approve!'

* * * * *

MILLS & BOON®

Makes any time special™

Mills & Boon publish 29 new titles every month. Select from...

Modern Romance™   **Tender Romance**™

Sensual Romance™

Medical Romance™   **Historical Romance**™

MAT2

2 FREE

books and a surprise gift!

We would like to take this opportunity to thank you for reading this Mills & Boon® book by offering you the chance to take TWO more specially selected titles from the Historical Romance™ series absolutely FREE! We're also making this offer to introduce you to the benefits of the Reader Service™—

★ FREE home delivery
★ FREE gifts and competitions
★ FREE monthly Newsletter
★ Exclusive Reader Service discounts
★ Books available before they're in the shops

Accepting these FREE books and gift places you under no obligation to buy, you may cancel at any time, even after receiving your free shipment. Simply complete your details below and return the entire page to the address below. *You don't even need a stamp!*

YES! Please send me 2 free Historical Romance books and a surprise gift. I understand that unless you hear from me, I will receive 4 superb new titles every month for just £2.99 each, postage and packing free. I am under no obligation to purchase any books and may cancel my subscription at any time. The free books and gift will be mine to keep in any case.

H0ZEA

Ms/Mrs/Miss/Mr ....Initials................................
                                                              BLOCK CAPITALS PLEASE

Surname ....

Address ....

....

....Postcode.................................

Send this whole page to:
UK: FREEPOST CN81, Croydon, CR9 3WZ
EIRE: PO Box 4546, Kilcock, County Kildare (stamp required)

Offer valid in UK and Eire only and not available to current Reader Service subscribers to this series. We reserve the right to refuse an application and applicants must be aged 18 years or over. Only one application per household. Terms and prices subject to change without notice. Offer expires 30th April 2001. As a result of this application, you may receive further offers from Harlequin Mills & Boon and other carefully selected companies. If you would prefer not to share in this opportunity please write to The Data Manager at the address above.

Mills & Boon® is a registered trademark owned by Harlequin Mills & Boon Limited.
Historical Romance™ is being used as a trademark.